The Magic of Murder

By

Susan Lynn Solomon

For Robin
As a girl my cousin was my sister.
As she did then, she continues to bring joy to my life
and life to my joy.

Prologue

When my nerves finally settled to the point where I could write what I learned of Jimmy Osborn's death, this is how I began:

March in Niagara Falls. Though the calendar declared winter had neared its end, the thermometer outside the Pine Avenue Bank of America branch read nine degrees. On this mid-March Wednesday night, a new Corvette turned into an alley north of Pine Avenue. Houses lining the alley were old structures in an older section of town. Most were abandoned, boarded-up, and would never again be occupied.

Packed snow crunched under the tires as the Corvette skidded in and out of ruts at five miles an hour.

At the far end of the alley sat a dilapidated barn, the slats of its walls so shrunken with age streetlamps along the roads on either side shone through. Halfway to the barn, the driver pulled into a garage with a sagging roof. No birds chirped their night song at this time of year, so the only sound was a click when the car door opened. Seconds later, Jimmy Osborn emerged.

Osborn wore a brown leather coat over jeans and a blue and white sweater. His brown beard was neatly trimmed. The scent of his cologne almost covered the mildew stench of the garage's soaked and rotting wood. In his gloved hand was a bottle of scotch in a brown paper bag. As his breath misted in the cold moonlight, he glanced quickly around before he trudged through snow drifts toward the rear door of a nearby house. The door was sealed by two loose one-by-six slats. Osborn shoved the bag into his coat pocket and pried the boards apart. There was a low, creaking groan when the nails gave. Then the alley was again silent.

As he began to slip between the boards, he stopped, listened. A crack of footfalls in the frozen snow came from the shadows to his left.

"That you?" he asked. There was no need to whisper. He'd chosen this place because it was deserted.

A figure an inch or two shorter than Osborn edged along the broken fence of the house next door. The figure wore a black ski jacket zipped over a black hooded sweatshirt. In the shadow cast by the hood, the figure seemed to have no face. If somebody had peeked through a window, this figure might look like a wraith—a dark spirit.

Osborn moved close, and peered into the hood. This wasn't the person he expected to meet. "What the hell...?" he said.

The figure raised a Glock .45, and hissed words heard only by the howling wind.

Osborn's breath escaped as a gasp when a shot caught him in the chest with such force it slammed him to the ground.

The pistol held in both hands, the figure stepped toward its prostrate victim and stood over him.

A dark stain spread on the snow under Osborn. He tried to raise his head. "Why?" His life tiptoeing away, he had no strength to say more.

A second shot split Osborn's heart. Now the figure's face relaxed and the fire dimmed in its eyes. With casual ease, the Glock pumped six more rounds into Osborn's chest.

On its knees, the hooded figure dug into Osborn's coat pocket, pulled out the liquor bottle and heaved it at the garage. The figure then slipped a hand deep into the pocket, and came out with the Corvette's keys clutched in its fist.

Minutes later the car backed from the garage, retraced its tire-tracks to Pine Avenue, and drove twenty blocks to Flannery's Bar. It was there Jimmy Osborn had started his night, bragging about the special liaison he had planned. It was there the Corvette was found the next morning.

Details of Jimmy Osborn's murder didn't appear in the *Niagara Gazette* the next day. They weren't in the following editions, either. It was more than a week before I learned why he died. When I did, I felt as though I'd been struck in the chest by the bullet that took my friend Jimmy down.

As might be suspected, I've taken a few liberties in describing what happened. Though the basic facts are precisely as the killer subsequently related them to Detective Roger Frey, I've dramatized them a bit. I won't apologize for that. It's what I do.

I'm Emlyn Goode, a writer—short stories mostly, with a few essays thrown in and an occasional poem when the muse elbows me in that direction. Emlyn is an old family name. The Goode part...as I learned several months before Jimmy died, the moniker doesn't describe every leaf on my family tree.

So, a fallen leaf is what got me embroiled in the murder. And since a new friend, Rebecca Nurse, pulled me out of the hole into which I dug myself, I should begin by explaining why and how she and I met, and how I learned of the special...uh, talent running in my genes.

Chapter One
Rebecca

Late on an evening the December before Jimmy Osborn was killed, I sat hunched over my computer in a corner of the living room of my Niagara Falls home. I had the thermostat turned down to a chilly sixty-two degrees. The room was lit by a single low-wattage bulb, which caused shadows to crawl across the walls. I desired that atmosphere. It matched the story I was working on. Wrapped in a heavy sweater, I let my imagination wander though a dark landscape in which my heroine, beaten and beset by a man she'd been sold to, escapes into the mist of a New England swamp. I typed: *Hands blistered from oars twisting with each stroke, she rows her small boat beneath bent tree limbs. In the dark, glaring at her are the eyes of snakes, and—*

Hmmm. What other creatures, slithering along the bank, cackling in lairs and behind trees would frighten Sarah (Sarah was my heroine's name)? I made a note to research that and then turned my attention back to the computer screen.

After what she feels are hours of rowing, Sarah comes upon a small island where she—

Stuck again. What would a woman alone on an island in a northern swamp do? What would she eat? How would she wreak vengeance on the fiend who'd maltreated her? Alone. In the winter. On an island in the—

Of course! Sarah would be a witch.

Quickly, I scrolled up the pages and deleted my story's title. In its place I typed, *The Swamp Witch.* Then I stripped the heavy coat from Sarah's frail body, and replaced it with the thin rags my villain made her wear. I turned the thermostat up to seventy-three degrees. My story would take place in the spring. Sarah would plant a garden filled with vegetables.

Herbs, spices—she'd know how to mix them together while whispering an incantation. From her pot—a cast iron cauldron—her spell would rise, float across the damp ground, and—

But what herbs would have to be mixed together? What words would shoot her spell like arrows into the heart of her tormentor? For my story to ring true, I had to know these things. More than that, I had to touch them, smell them.

I swiveled in my chair to face the bookcases lining the wall next to my sofa. Hundreds of volumes, some reference works, some novels, were piled haphazardly on the shelves. None of them was a witchcraft instruction manual. At least, I didn't think I'd ever bought such a book.

I stretched, rolled my neck to loosen muscles that were tight after hours of typing, and rose to inspect what was printed on the spines of my books. I was right: none of them would help.

I sighed, returned to my computer, and logged onto the internet. These days the knowledge of the world is stored at one website or another. Still, an hour of surfing produced little but advertisements by women with Eastern European names, who would read tarot cards or my palm for twenty dollars. Just when I was ready to give up and assign my heroine a less complicated role, my finger cramped on the mouse. The involuntary tic caused me to click on the site of a shop advertising it had what I needed in stock. It was fifty miles south of my home, an hour by car. Still, if fate suggested I travel there, who was I to argue?

I turned off my computer. Tomorrow I would make an excursion to an arcane bookstore down an alley off a side street in Ellicottville.

***

The shop was everything *Google* promised it would be: *The Black Cat* in filigree gold letters on the window, double doors with weathered brown and black paint, and the head of a bat for a doorknob. As soon as I stepped through the door, my nose twitched from the sweet smell of incense. A glance to right showed me rows of shelves crammed with books titled *Hebalism for Life*, *Wicca for the Lone Practitioner*, and the like. On the wall to the left was a framed poster from the vintage film, *Bell, Book and Candle*. Next to the poster, I saw a row of jars labeled Frankincense, Sandalwood, Orris Root. Others had names I recognized: Clove, Cumin Seed, Cinnamon—I had those at home. In front of the shelves, glass display cases held glittering trinkets.

I pulled back my hair so it wouldn't fall across my eyes when I bent to examine a jeweled spider. Not that I like spiders—at least not the live kind. But this was a pretty collar pin. I pictured myself wearing it when I went on a date, if I ever did again.

"That's a nice piece," the woman behind the counter said.

I nodded.

"Not too expensive." She pulled the spider from the case, rubbed it on her sleeve, and laid it front of me on a velvet cloth.

While I examined the price tag, a cat, as round as a snowman's head and just as white, paraded past. Before disappearing behind a bookcase, it stopped, turned its face, and stared at me. I stared back. The cat's irises were pink, and so light they almost weren't there. I'd never before seen an albino cat. After a minute, it snorted and raised its tail. It swayed its rear end and strutted off.

"Elvira likes you," the woman said.

I glanced over to where the cat had been, then back at the woman. She was taller than I—about five feet ten or so—and her salt and pepper hair dropped to her waist in tight curls. She wore a long cotton vest over a ribbed turtleneck sweater. Smiling at her, I asked how she could tell.

"Most people who come in here," she said, "Elvira sniffs at them once then doesn't give them a second look." She leaned past me to peer at the row of bookcases.

When I followed her eyes, I saw a white head peek around a corner. The pink eyes seemed to be focused on my chest. More, I felt as though the cat was able to see through my clothes, past my flesh, and into my soul. Goosebumps popped up on my arms. I shivered, and shifted my attention back to the woman.

"I...uh, I came in to find a book about...um..."

My face felt warm. Why was I embarrassed to tell the woman I wanted to read about witchcraft? That's what "The Black Cat" was about. Why else would I have come to her shop? It's not as though it were illegal.

The woman nodded at the cat, as if it had spoken to her. "You might be right," she said.

"Excuse me?"

"Sorry. I was thinking out loud. I do that, sometimes." Her smile didn't at all look apologetic. "What's your name?" she asked, staring at me in the same way the cat had.

As if I'd been caught doing something I shouldn't, my face again got hot. "Does it matter?"

I took a step toward the door and pulled my car keys from my purse. Coming to this shop had been a bad idea. Maybe writing *The Swamp Witch* was a bad idea. I decided to delete it from my computer as soon as I got home.

The woman reached across the counter and touched my arm—a gentle touch, yet it held me in place. "No, it doesn't matter," she said. "It's just that sometimes a name gives me an idea of the best book to recommend." She looked at the cat, as if seeking its approval.

The woman, the cat: the relationship was positively weird. I don't know why I didn't leave right then. The only reason I can think of is that the two of them froze me with their eyes. Well, that's how I felt, and it left me unable to move. "Uh, Emlyn," I said, sounding as though I were not at all certain that's who I was. "My name's Emlyn."

She nodded.

I forced a smile. "Emlyn Goode—I'm a writer. Maybe you've heard of me?" I rushed on, "I'm researching a story. About—" This was getting way out-of-hand. I actually whispered, "—a witch."

She didn't seem to hear. She glanced down at the cat that now squatted beside me and rubbed its head against my leg. "Goode?" the woman said. "Emlyn…"

I stiffened, resisting an impulse to brush at the white hairs I was certain had clung to my black wool slacks.

The shopkeeper peered down an aisle between two bookcases. After a minute, she stuck out her hand. "I'm Rebecca Nurse."

She leaned back against the wall, head tilted as if she expected me to recognize the name.

I pulled up the sleeve of my jacket, checked my watch. "Oh, my, it's so late," I said. "Sorry to have taken your time. I'll have to come back another—"

"Wait, don't leave just yet," Ms. Nurse said. "I believe I have what you're looking for."

She took my arm. Followed by the cat, she led me down a narrow aisle. At the end, in the very back of the shop, she brushed aside sprigs of dried herbs hung from the hammered tin ceiling. She ran her hand across several volumes on the highest shelf. When she touched the spine of one lying flat on top of the bookcase, she said, "Ah, yes," and rose to her toes to take it down.

Not thick, the book appeared to be rather old. Hidden behind the sprigs of herbs, I thought it might have been forgotten by everyone but the shopkeeper. With both hands, she held out the book.

The dust jacket was so faded I could hardly make out the title. I opened the book to the first page. *Salem 1692—The Witch Trials* was printed in thick block letters.

Her head cocked, with the slightest smile on her full lips, Rebecca Nurse said. "This is the very thing you need, I think."

Leaning against my leg, Elvira looked up at me and rubbed a paw across her eyes. It seemed as though the cat also couldn't believe I'd be interested in that book. I nearly laughed at the thought—if I wasn't careful, I might wind up talking to this animal the way the shopkeeper did.

I tried to hand the book back. "I don't think so. I'm looking for—"

"Take it," Ms. Nurse said. "You'll find something in there you need to know." With a flip of her long graying hair, she turned from me and headed to another counter at the front of the shop.

"Thank you, but I really don't want this," I said, trying again to hand her the book when I caught up. "What I want is—"

"Yes, I understand," she said. As if she'd been waiting for me and had them ready, she lifted a pair of soft-covered books from beneath the counter. "These have the information you came in for." She laid them side-by-side.

On a shelf behind her was a row of knives with runes etched into their blades. Next to those was a glass jar filled with clear liquid in which something that looked like a dead bat floated.

I cringed, forced my eyes from the jar, and focused on the covers of the books: *Magical Herbalism*, and *Earth Power: Techniques of Natural Magic*. Both were by somebody named Scott Cunningham. This was better. I reached in my purse for my wallet. "I'll take these."

She pulled a plain brown shopping bag from beneath the counter and dropped the books into it. On top of those she placed her business card and a handful of advertisements

13

for local restaurants and the Ellicottville Jazz Festival. Because I was warily watching the bat float in the jar, and wondering what on earth someone might use it for, it wasn't until I arrived home that I realized the book about the Salem witches was also in the bag.

Rebecca Nurse had made a mistake, I decided. I gathered up her card so I could call and tell her I had her book. When I turned the card over, I saw a note written in a sprawled script. *Elvira wants you to have this,* it said.

***

I live in the roomy two-story cottage my father bought when he married Mom. That is, the house was a cottage until Dad, a carpenter by trade, knocked out walls, expanded the kitchen, and added a room or two. The ground floor living room in which I do my work, and most everything else, is one of those add-ons. It has French doors which open on the field out back that runs to a line of beech, maple, and birch trees. Beyond the trees is the Niagara River. My living room is a marvelous place from which to watch the seasons change and is a comfortable place to read. I've arranged the room so my favorite chair, plush and oversized, sits next to my book cases and faces the field. A week after my trip to Ellicottville, I was settled in my chair with the book about herbalism on my lap along with a yellow pad on which I'd made several bulleted notes. The other two volumes were stacked on the lamp table beside me. I reread what I'd written:

- *Sarah needs protection against the evil chasing her.*
- *An amulet. White cotton, 7" square, tied by red silk thread.*
- *Basil, dill, fennel, rosemary, tarragon.*

14

I knew those herbs, had each of them in my spice cabinet. *Wonder what would happen if I try out this mixture,* I thought, and laughed at the idea.

As evening approached, a stiff wind, harbinger of a lake-effect snowfall, rustled the tree branches in my yard and the azalea bushes on either side of the terrace. I switched on the light, made another note on the pad, then settled back to watch the sun disappear behind the trees.

I must have dozed off, because when I opened my eyes it was dark outside. Wind-blown snow pelted the French doors. I rose from my chair to close the mini-blinds. As I did, I heard something scratch the glass. It couldn't be the azaleas—I'd cut them back months ago. I shoved the blinds aside and looked out. With the snow rushing past it was a whiteout. As a result, I almost missed what caused the scraping. Then the fat white cat opened its pink eyes.

Startled, I jumped back. An albino cat was staring at me.

"Elvira?" I said, knowing it couldn't be. Elvira lived in The Black Cat. In Ellicottville. Fifty miles from Niagara Falls.

The cat mewed, shivered, and scratched the glass again. I thought about dropping the blind and returning to my comfortable wingback chair. But that was only for the second it took to be overcome by guilt. I pulled the door open. Blowing snow stung my face.

Her tail raised, the cat swaggered into my house. She stopped by my legs, sniffed, and looked up at me though one eye.

The slats of the blind rattled as I slammed the door. When I turned, I saw the cat curled up on my chair.

"Hey, get off there!" I shouted. "You're drenched."

The cat glanced at me, and yawned. Then she put her head down and began to snore. I mean it, the cat actually snored! Friends who have cats tell me theirs also snore. With deference to those friends, their animals don't snore.

They make a whistling sound. Elvira, on the other hand— I stand by my statement.

I wasn't a cat person. In fact, I had no desire to share my home with any four-legged critter. Feline, canine, didn't matter. I didn't want to share it with a two-legged one, either. Since my ex walked out on me, I'd lived alone. I preferred life that way, so I certainly didn't want this creature to get comfortable in my house.

Screwed into a corner of my living room wall is an old railroad station clock I'd picked up at a yard sale. The clock's hands formed a right angle. Nine o'clock. It was too late to call Rebecca Nurse, and tell her to drive up to the Falls and retrieve her pet. I laid her business card on the kitchen counter next to my coffee pot. I would make the call in the morning.

Chapter Two
Elvira

When I came downstairs the next morning, I peeked around the partition separating my living room from the front hall. The cat had rearranged the pillows on my chair to make a nest. With a groan, I settled on a stool at the kitchen counter, my first morning cup of coffee at my elbow. Glaring in the direction of the cat—the comfortable wingback chair she had claimed as her own was where I preferred to begin my days—I dialed the phone. It rang five or six times.

"Seems Rebecca Nurse doesn't want you, either," I muttered to the white lump of fur.

Elvira opened her eyes, blinked twice, and turned to face the French doors. That damn cat was ignoring me.

The phone rang another three times. Annoyed at the cat, even more annoyed because it appeared the only way I'd get rid of this pest was to drive her back to Ellicottville, I was about to slam down the receiver.

At last, "Black Cat," Rebecca Nurse said. She sounded half-asleep.

"Not black cat, white cat," I rasped, my throat burning from the mouthful of hot coffee I'd gulped.

"Huh?"

"You heard me. Your cat followed me home."

"Oh, I wondered if she'd done that."

"Now you know. Come get her."

"Can't," the Nurse woman said. "She isn't mine."

This time *I* said, "Huh?"

"Elvira comes and goes as she pleases," the sleepy voice said. "She settled in with me a year or so ago, but I knew she wouldn't stay. She was just waiting here for the person she's supposed to be with. You finally came."

17

"She's supposed to be with me?" I said. "What are you talking about?" I almost asked, *What are you smoking?* But insulting the woman wouldn't get the cat out of my house.

I reached into the refrigerator for milk to put out the fire now burning my stomach. Then I looked over at my favorite chair. Elvira turned her head to me, and yawned.

"You haven't read *The Witch Trials* yet, have you?" Rebecca Nurse said. "Read it and you'll understand why Elvira gave it to you."

"I don't intend to do any such thing," I said. "It has nothing to do with the story I'm writing."

"Oh, but it does. That's why Elvira wants you to have the book."

Before I could object—which is a polite way of indicating what I was about to say—she hung up.

While I sat, fuming, on the hard wooden stool, a voice broke into the music on my radio.

"Hope you're all safely tucked in at home," the disc jockey said. "The National Weather Service in Buffalo just issued a severe winter storm alert for all of Western New York. We're getting hit by the worst blizzard in years. Gonna go now to Tracy Storch who's braving the weather in the WLOV traffic helicopter."

"Thanks, Dan," a bright feminine voice called from amid beating blades. "We're over the intersection of the 190 and the 290. The road's slick, traffic's at a crawl. Out by the Delaware exit it looks like a van's slid off the road."

"Be careful out there, Stacy," the DJ broke in. "So folks, there you have it. If you don't have to go out, stay home."

The voice was replaced by an instrumental version of *Winter Wonderland.*

The recorded sleigh bells heightened my annoyance. No way would I be able to drive the cat back to Ellicottville where she belonged. Muttering, I grabbed *Magical Herbalism* and my pad from the lamp table. Parked at my desk, I flipped the back cover of the book, and ran a finger down the index.

The cat lifted her head, opened her mouth, and then snapped it shut. It was as if she were telling me I could look all I wanted, this book didn't list a combination of herbs and spices that would get her out of my house. Or even off my chair.

I scowled at her and turned on my computer. In a few seconds, *The Swamp Witch* appeared on the screen. I glanced down at the notes on my pad, started to type:

Sarah sprinkles ground mistletoe in the plot she's carefully prepared. Pointing to the north, east, south, and west, she calls on the gods of the four elements to bless her efforts with renewed life.

On her knees now, she works the mistletoe into the soil with bare hands. "Gotta feel the earth, let it feel me, too," she reminds herself as she leans back on her bare heels, and brushes unbound hair the color of autumn wheat from her face. She won't make the mistake she's made before. This time she will follow the old ways from earth to pot—

After five minutes, I deleted what I'd written. It wasn't right. I couldn't concentrate. Though the cat hadn't done anything, hadn't even moved, the fact she was curled up on my chair was a major distraction. This was impossible!

I rolled my desk chair back, went to the French doors, and pulled the mini-blind aside. Large snowflakes blew across the field and clung to the branches of the birch tree to the left of my terrace. Crystals settled on the window. I wrapped my robe tightly around me and opened the door. A blast of wind made me shiver.

My voice quivering from the cold, I announced, "Oh, what a beautiful day. A perfect morning to be outside. Look at that squirrel scamper across the lawn."

I peeked over my shoulder. Elvira hadn't moved.

"It's nice out," I said. "Get out there and play!"

Her expression said, *Who are you kidding*? Most cats can't make that kind of face. I swear this one did.

"Give me a break, Elvira. Go haunt someone else. I need to work."

At last she moved, but not toward the open door. She stood on the chair, circled twice, and settled against the armrest with her head on the books I'd left on the lamp table.

Frustrated, I slammed the door. Still shivering, moving as quickly as I could in my half-frozen state, I yanked the books from under the cat's head. The one on top was *Salem 1692—The Witch Trials.* It was as if the cat insisted I read it.

I threw my hands up in exasperation. Why ever had I gone to The Black Cat? And once I'd seen Rebecca Nurse conversing with an albino cat, why hadn't I immediately run from the shop? That's what a normal person would have done. Not me, though. I'm a writer, which by definition means I'm slightly off kilter. Besides, my mind had been wrapped around the story I wanted to write. I had no idea what brought that story to mind, it just bounced into my head because I couldn't figure out how to save my heroine. Now I had a cat in my house and a book I didn't want to read in my hand. To quote the comic-strip character, Charlie Brown, Augh!

I dropped my eyes to the chair. Elvira grinned at me. I know cats can't smile—their lips don't have the proper muscles. But it sure looked as though she grinned.

While I hovered over her with the book raised to swat her off my chair, I wondered how much worse this situation could get. That's when the sky went totally dark. The wind howled, the windows rattled, and the lights went out.

Before my trip to The Black Cat I'd been trying to create an atmosphere in my living room, a sense of place to fit my story. Now I had it. As people say, be careful what you wish for, especially when you're writing about witchcraft.

***

Where I live, a blackout caused by evil weather patterns was nothing new. As a result, over the years I'd amassed a collection of candles: tea lights, tapers, scented ones in jars. When I needed to find a moment of total relaxation, I would fill my bathroom with them, turn off the florescent light, and read until my skin looked like a prune. If candles surrounding my bathtub worked, surely my ill-humor could be assuaged by a living room lit like an old-fashioned Christmas tree.

Glittering candles on the window ledge and every table, I stretched out on the sofa with my legs covered by the afghan my grandmother knitted during a snowstorm almost a century before. The novel I was in the middle of reading was on the coffee table next to me. The blackout handed me a perfect excuse to spend a lazy day away from my computer and my half-written story. The idea of doing nothing, not even bothering to dress, brought a smile. I reached for the novel.

Elvira shifted on the wingback chair. Her head on her paws, she shot me a pink-eyed glare. *Read about Salem, dammit! You've got time now,* she seemed to say.

"You're an oversized pest," I told her. "I ought to tape you in a box and ship you back to The Black Cat."

That outburst reminded me of Rebecca Nurse, and what she'd said: I'd find something I needed to know in the book about the Salem witch trials.

My stubborn streak kicked in. "Not gonna do it," I muttered.

Lower lip out in a pout, I closed my eyes, and took a deep breath. When I opened them again, the cat was on the floor next to me, staring up.

"Stop it," I said. "You're not gonna change my mind."

Elvira didn't move. Her eyes didn't waver.

I pulled the afghan up to my chest, as if it were armor. It didn't help. Those pink eyes penetrated my resistance, took control of my intention. I put down my novel, and reached for the Salem witches.

Now that the cat had accomplished with her eyes what Rebecca Nurse hadn't been able to do with words, she returned to the wingback chair.

Settled again under the cover on the sofa, I opened the book.

The first page contained a chronology. As I skimmed down the lines, I saw movement from the corner of my eyes. The cat was sitting up, alert.

"What now?"

She leaned toward me.

"Go to sleep," I said, and turned my attention to the book. That's when I saw it:

July 19, 1692: Susannah Martin, Elizabeth Howe, Sarah Wildes, Rebecca Nurse, and Sarah Goode are hanged on Gallows Hill.

Rebecca Nurse. Sarah Goode. Gallows Hill. *Hanged!*

I sprang from the sofa in stocking feet to stamp out the flame of the candle that, in my shock, I'd knocked to the floor. Panting, I stared down at the black spot on my carpet.

Elvira jumped from the wingback chair, circled my legs, and rubbed her back on my flannel pajamas.

"Look what you've done!" I growled.

She licked her face, and looked up at me, as if to say, *Don't blame me. I wasn't there when they got hanged.*

I shivered now from both the cold, annoyance, and from something else I couldn't name. I went to the kitchen to brew a mug of tea. Minutes later, I returned. With the mug clutched to my breast, I retrieved the book and plopped onto the sofa. Elvira leaped up and snuggled between me and the cushions. Cold house, chilled by what I'd just read, a warm cat lying beside me: without realizing I was doing it, I scratched the cat's neck. Her response was a contented purr.

With the book resting on my lap, I raised my mug and blew at the steam. "Satisfied now?" I said.

The cat rubbed her head on my arm.

"Yeah, I'm going to read it."

She mewed.

I rested the mug on the coffee table. The afghan pulled nearly up to my chin, I opened the book.

Through the rest of the morning and most of the afternoon, I devoured the text as if it were food and I was starving. It told that, though accusations of witchcraft in Salem had begun years before, the witch-scare reached a crescendo in January 1692, when a group of young girls began to behave as if they were high on LSD. Which they were. Sort of. I'd read somewhere it was ergot poisoning—something in the wheat they harvested back then. It didn't dawn on the girls to say they'd been bewitched until a country physician named Griggs suggested it. In short order, suspicion ran wild, and a farm woman asked a slave named Tituba, to bake a 'witch cake'—a concoction guaranteed to lift any spell cast by Devil worshippers. Then, as if late at night people heard Macbeth's three witch sisters cackling around their cauldron, the madness spread. Pressured by the townsfolk, at the end of February one of the girls identified Tituba as the source of the spell. Then they said it was Sarah Goode. No one thought to catch his breath, step back, and logically consider what was going on—not after Judge Cotton Mather insisted the Court of Oyer and Terminer had to conduct the trials so quickly, the accused might have been hauled in the front door, condemned, and dragged out the back door to Gallows Hill in less than an hour. That's what happened to the Goode woman, who in July took what was once called a 'short-drop'—dangling from a tree branch until she choked to death. Fearful she might be the next to be accused, Sarah's daughter, the child of her first marriage to Daniel Poole, fled Salem. The girl's name was Emlyn.

Emlyn. Sarah Goode. The book spoke about my family! My great, great, great, great—I gave up trying to count back generations—grandmother had been hanged as a witch. No wonder my parents never spoke about our family.

When I closed the book, perspiration was dripping down my neck. I'd been so lost in the trials, convictions, and executions, I hadn't realized the power had been turned on. My house was now overly warm. Or perhaps it was my brain that had gone hot.

Stiff from lying in one place so long, I rolled over on the sofa and lifted the afghan. Something about it caught my eye. I held up the knitted cover, and closely examined it for the first time. The designs my grandmother had sewn looked like runes I'd seen in the book about magical herbalism. Those were symbols a witch might draw. What the hell was going on here?

I got up and stumbled to the telephone.

This time Ms. Nurse answered after two rings. "Have you finished reading it?" she said.

"Why'd you give me that book?" I demanded.

"Wasn't me," she said. "It was Elvira."

"Yeah, right."

She didn't respond.

The phone tucked under my chin, with my hands on my hips, I said, "Why would a cat want me to have it?"

I heard her take a deep breath. "*Your* ancestor wasn't the only one killed by those crazy people."

"Yeah, I saw," I said. "Someone named Rebecca Nurse was hanged the same day as Sarah Goode."

"It wasn't her I meant."

"Who, then?"

"Elvira's ancestors have been around as long as ours."

I couldn't help myself—the words got out before I could stop them. "How do you know that?"

Without a moment's hesitation, she said, "Elvira told me."

My eyes rolled back, I slowly shook my head.

"She wants you to avenge what was done to her family."

"Me?" *The lady's nuts,* I thought.

"It's in the genes, you see," she said.

"What is?"

Instead of rushing on, Rebecca Nurse said very slowly, "Of all the people hanged in Salem for being witches, only one really was."

This was too much. I slammed down the receiver.

***

I tossed the book into the trash, which was where it belonged. It was dark now—winter nights fall early in Niagara Falls. My stomach grumbled. Except for a couple of mugs of coffee and tea, I hadn't put anything in it all day. I pulled a box of corn flakes from the kitchen cabinet, and settled down at my dinette table with *Magical Herbalism* open in front of me. Though I knew it's impossible for herbs and incantations to alter the workings of the universe, I was now fascinated by the prospect of it. Credit my family history and a writer's imagination for that.

It's in the genes, the Nurse woman had told me.

Ridiculous! I snorted at the idea. Still, I kept reading.

Elvira strolled over and sat at my feet. When I glanced down, she seemed to say, *Aren't you going to do anything about it?*

"About what?" I said to her. "That happened more than three hundred years ago. People got caught up in mass hysteria, what can I do about—?"

I stopped in mid-sentence. I was talking to a cat. Worse, she was talking to me. I felt as though I'd lost my mind. I shoved the cereal bowl and book aside, and sat, head cupped in my hands. I must have stayed that way for an hour or so. I might have remained like that all night if my phone hadn't rung. It was my mother, calling from Florida to check up on me.

"I just heard the weather forecast for up there," she said. "Are you all right?"

"It's snowing, Ma," I said. "This is Niagara Falls. It snows here. Have you forgotten already?" Ten years before, my mother had traded the frozen north for the beaches of Naples.

"Don't bite my head off," Mom said. "I worry about you."

"There's nothing to worry about. I'm fine."

She was quiet for a minute before she said, "You don't sound fine. What's the matter?"

"Nothing's wrong!" I said too quickly, which, in the parlance of mothers and daughters, told her something was.

"Tell me," she insisted.

I've never been able to resist that tone in my mother's voice, so I told her all of it. The Black Cat, Elvira, the book, and what Rebecca Nurse told me about our family tree. When I finished, I heard her breathing hard.

I sighed. "How ridiculous can anyone be, Ma?"

I heard her light a cigarette and inhale the smoke.

"Ma?" My stomach began to do a slow twist. I was afraid of what she was about to tell me.

***

I had started out to write a short story about a woman using witchcraft to wreak vengeance on a man who mistreated her. I knew where the vengeance part came from—I wanted vengeance on the man I'd married and divorced three years later. It doesn't matter that I call what I write fiction, there's always a smattering of truth behind the storyline. The idea of smacking him with a spell popped into my head when I read the book about herbalism. Apparently, Rebecca was right about this thing being genetic.

I've kept the books she sold me and bought a few others from her on the subject. More than a few, actually. Over the next three months she became a friend and helped me understand my family. She helped me with a bit more too—it seems that causing my ex-husband to go bankrupt was more than I could manage alone. With the two of us, though, chanting together over the right herbs—

We'd just begun to work on what Elvira asked me to do—*Ancestry.com* led us to some descendants of Cotton Mather—when fate spun its head and stuck its tongue out at me. By which I mean my genetic bent was dragged into the middle of the Osborn murder.

Chapter Three
Detective Frey

March brought a worse storm than the one we were hit with in December. It seems that's how we celebrate St. Patrick's Day around here. When it ended after four days, a reserve unit from the Niagara Falls Air Base declared war on the snow. With military precision, the reservists piled the stuff into dump trucks and carted it to Lake Ontario, Lake Erie, and the Canal. They might have hauled it to the top of the mountains if their trucks' tires could get enough traction. Since they couldn't, it appeared as though they shoved what was left to the shoulder of River Road and into my driveway. When I gazed through the kitchen window at gray heaps so high my mailbox was buried, I was certain the dunes would still be there in July. They weren't, of course. In two days the streets had been plowed and salted, and cars crawled past. Thanks to my neighbor, Roger Frey, even my driveway had been cleared. In Western New York we know how to deal with the white stuff.

My preferred way of dealing with it is to turn up the thermostat and remain inside, comfy and warm. At least until the sun pokes through the clouds. This is why, still in my robe and flannel pajamas with thermal socks pulled up to my knees, I was snuggled on the sofa under my grandmother's grey wool afghan. I still wondered about the runes Grandma had sewn into the afghan. Maybe one day Rebecca Nurse would find a book to help me interpret them.

From a corner of what had become *her* wingback chair, the hefty albino cat—Elvira detested it when I referred to her as fat—glared at me. She seemed annoyed I was wasting the morning on a made for TV movie.

"What?" I said to her.

She rolled her eyes—well, that's what it looked like to me.

"Give me a break, will you?" I said. "I was up half the night writing."

She snorted.

"What do you mean I didn't write anything that mattered?"

She tilted her head.

I shifted on the sofa and bent toward her. "I'm not bullshitting you!" My voice went up an octave. "You were there. You saw what I was—"

At the very moment I realized the cat had again drawn me into an argument, I heard a knock on my front door. My face hot—from anger at Elvira or embarrassment at letting her get the better of the argument?—I jumped from the sofa and yanked the door open.

"What?" I demanded with a sharp edge to my voice.

On my door stoop stood a black quilted jacket, green rubber boots laced over baggy jeans, a flannel scarf wound around the little I could see of a face, and a knit cap pulled so low on a head the figure looked like a cartoon character with no ears. The man on the stoop might have been a predator who intended to break into my home, ravish my body, and make off with my treasures. Okay, I've already admitted I have an active imagination. There are no treasures in my home, and my body—well, let's just say it's been a long time since anyone would risk jail for ravishing me. Besides, I knew who this was. Earlier, while I poured my coffee, through the window I'd watched my neighbor ride his snowplow like it was the mechanical bull at Flannery's Bar.

On the frigid side of the storm door, Roger Frey swiveled his head from side-to-side, as if searching for who I hollered at.

At times, I've stood before a mirror, arguing with myself, and seen what I look like when I blush. My neck gets as red as my hair, then the color dashes uphill past my face to my forehead. So, I knew what Roger saw when he looked at me.

"Sorry," I mumbled to what I could see of his face. "Cranky. I was up half the night."

His voice muted by the scarf covering his mouth, he said, "No need to apologize." He knew the hours I kept when the muse plopped down next to me.

The glass door misted when he leaned close to peer past my shoulder.

I looked behind me. Elvira had followed me to the door. She stared at us, head slightly tilted. The pale pink of her eyes darkened as if she'd decided something.

Roger nodded at her. "At least you're not alone anymore."

"Me or the cat?" I said.

"Both, I suppose." When Roger pulled down the scarf, his grin showed the small gap between his front teeth.

"I prefer being alone," I said. "If *you* want company, feel free to take the cat."

My friend and neighbor had been alone since his wife took off for a warmer place three years ago.

Elvira sniffed once. Then she turned abruptly, wiggled her large derriere at me, and curled up on the floor at my feet.

Roger laughed out loud.

As if loosened by the laughter that exploded from deep inside him, a sheet of snow skidded off the roof. He must have heard the rumble, because he took a quick step backwards. He wasn't fast enough, though. While half the snow thudded to the ground, the rest flattened his wool cap and spilled down his face. His hazel eyes rounded in surprise.

Now *I* laughed. With snow all over his body, it looked as though Frosty the Snowman was on my stoop. I opened

30

the storm door and brushed the snow from his cheek. "Come in here," I said. "Let me dry you off."

He stamped his feet on the mat to rid himself of most of the snow.

As I stepped aside to make room for him to pass, I stumbled over the cat.

Roger moved faster than he had to avoid the snow drift from my roof. His arm shot out. "Careful!" he said, and grabbed me around the waist just as I began to flop like a rag doll to floor.

The man is certainly strong. In a single motion, he lifted me from my feet then set me down. His arms still surrounded me.

"You okay?"

I nodded, but couldn't speak, not even to say yes. I'm sure it was because I was a little bit in shock.

At last he released me, and bent to stroke the cat. "That wasn't nice, Elvira," he said. "You could've hurt Emlyn."

I also leaned down to stroke her. "This beast probably intended to do it."

When I glanced at Roger, his face was precariously close to mine. The look in his eyes told me he might not mind being nearer still.

"Uh, yeah," I mumbled, and pulled back to put a safe distance between us. "She probably did it on purpose..." My words drifted into a crimson haze.

His cheeks also a bit red—I told myself this was probably from the near-zero temperature outside—he straightened up, and unwound his scarf. His chin and upper lip were dark. The morning stubble enhanced rather than detracted from his chiseled cheekbones and slightly cleft chin. This was a handsome man by anybody's reckoning. More than that, he was kind. He looked after his neighbors, and made sure we were safe. I'd often wondered why Judy, his ex-wife, would leave such a man.

"I, uh, stopped by to, um..." he said.

31

I looked down. I had nothing on but my pajamas and robe, and the robe had fallen loose when I nearly fell. Trying not to be obvious about it, I tied my robe closed.

Roger took a deep breath. "Yes, uh, the UPS guy brought this."

He pulled off his gloves, unzipped his jacket, and took a cardboard box from a large inside pocket. Holding it out, he said, "It came yesterday afternoon. All the snow, the UPS guy couldn't get to your door, so he left it with me."

The box was about nine inches wide, a foot long, and maybe two inches thick. I turned it over in my hands, examined the label. The return address said the package came from Naples, Florida.

"It's from my mother," I said.

"What is it?" Roger asked.

I shrugged. "I'd have to open the box to find out."

"So, open it."

Glancing sideways at him, I smiled. "Later."

"Come on," he said, and reached for the package. "I hauled it all the way over here. Plowed out your driveway while I was at it. You gotta show me what's in there."

"All the way over, huh?" I laughed. "You live next door."

"Yeah, well." He took off his jacket, and draped it over the back of a kitchen chair. His black hooded sweatshirt barely made it to his hips. "I had to wade through three feet of snow to get here. That's gotta be worth something."

I laid the package on the kitchen counter. "How about some coffee?"

I yanked the wet knit cap from his head, and tossed it into the sink. Snow clinging to the fibers sprinkled onto his dark brown hair, and melted into the gray that had begun to invade his temples. While I brushed the wet beads from his curls, I said, "A gentleman takes off his hat when he comes inside."

He picked the box up and handed it to me. "Don't try to change the subject. I know you, Emlyn Goode. You're dying to look inside."

I was. But it was just so much fun to tease him. A girl's got to do that now and then, just to stay in practice. I turned my back, and refilled my mug then poured coffee into a second mug.

He pushed the box in front of me.

"You're a big snoop, you know that?" I said.

He let out the laugh that never failed to disarm me. "Of course I am. I'm a cop. Snooping is what I do."

"Yup, and I'm your good buddy. Like in novels, it's the sidekick's job to give the cop a hard time. That's in my job description." I pointed at the package. "And see, it's written right here."

Another deep, resonant laugh burst from him. "You're definitely a piece of work," he said.

Elvira seemed to grow impatient with my stalling. She leaped onto the counter and pawed at the package. How the devil did she manage to move her large body so lithely?

"Okay, okay," I said. "I can't fight both of you."

I took the box to my dinette table, and sat, glancing around.

"What now?" Roger asked.

"I need something to slice the tape with."

He tilted sideways in his chair and pulled a Swiss army knife from his pants pocket. As he flicked open the smaller blade, he said, "I was a boy scout, I'm always prepared."

Settled on Roger's lap, the cat smacked his hand with her paw. Then she glared at me. *C'mon, knock off the flirting and get to it,* she seemed to say—well, that's what her growl sounded like.

I slit the tape and raised the cardboard flaps. Inside was what appeared to be a very old book. Without removing it from the box, I carefully lifted the leather cover. The words on the first page were faded. Still I was able to make some of them out.

"What is it?" Roger asked.

"Seems to be someone's diary." I suspect I sounded puzzled. Why would my mother send me something like this?

Between the next two pages was an envelope addressed to me. Inside was a note. *I've been holding onto this,* Mom wrote, *hoping the line that's led from Sarah Goode would end with me. Apparently it hasn't, so I'm sending you this. Please, Emlyn, try to make better use of this than some of our ancestors have.*

Elvira sniffed the book and purred.

Quickly, I refolded the letter.

Roger leaned over, peered into my eyes. "What is it?" he said.

"It's...um, it's..." I stammered as I searched for a lie he might believe. I didn't want to tell him my mother had sent me Sarah Goode's *Book of Shadows*. A guy like Roger—his life was built on the belief every mystery could be logically explained, and magic is nothing but sleight-of-hand. He'd remarked about that the night we saw David Copperfield perform at the Seneca Niagara Casino. The fastest way to end our friendship was to tell him I'm the latest in a 350-year line of witches. If I said that, he would stare at me as though I'd winked at him from a third eye in the center of my forehead. Then he'd leave and not come back. Oh, he'd be polite about it—Roger's always polite. But our friendship would be over. I mean, if it ever got out Detective Roger Frey of the Niagara Falls Police Department had a witch for a friend, he'd die of embarrassment. Or maybe he'd have to resign his position or even move to Rochester or something. If he did, who would plow my driveway then knock on my door to share my morning coffee and help me with the Sunday crossword puzzle?

What? I already said I have a vivid imagination.

34

As if Sarah Goode's book was catnip, Elvira dropped her head on it, mewed, and rubbed her paw across her face. Roger shoved her aside, and leaned over to see, I supposed, what caused my concern.

Before he could remove the book from the box, I closed the flaps.

"It's, uh...um, just an old family diary," I said. It wasn't much of a lie. A Book of Shadows *is* a diary of a sort. Witches record their herbal mixtures in it, and the words they chant to work their magic. My friend, Rebecca Nurse, had explained that when she showed me hers.

"Gotta be something more than a diary to startle you like this," Roger said.

I glanced at the coffee pot and raised my mug. "Yours must be cold by now. I'll get you some more."

"Emlyn?"

It's tough having a cop for a friend, especially a perceptive one. Only the truth would satisfy him.

"Uh, well...there's, uh, something I ought to tell you." I crossed my fingers. I hoped when I told him about my family and what was in my genes, his reaction wouldn't match what I'd imagined.

His elbows on the table, his head in his hands, he locked his eyes on mine. "You can tell me anything. You know that, don't you?"

I took a deep breath—

A fan of the pugilistic art might say I was saved by the bell. In this instance, a bell didn't save me from having to confess my heritage. That was accomplished by the song Roger's cell phone played.

He reached around to his quilted jacket, pulled the phone from the pocket, and looked at the digital display. Holding up a finger to indicate our conversation wasn't over, he said, "Work. Gotta take this." Then he said into the phone, "Frey here, Chief. What's up?"

He listened for a minute. As I watched, his face went as pale as the snow outside my door. "Gotta go," he murmured as he shoved the phone back into his pocket.

"What is it?" I asked, more than a little worried. My friend wasn't easily rattled.

He shook his head. His hazel eyes hard, he grabbed his jacket and wool cap. With no explanation, he bolted through my front door, and ran through the snow to his car.

I didn't hear from Roger for a few days, didn't learn what happened until I read in the *Niagara Gazette* his partner had been shot in an alley off Nineteenth Street. Eight bullets in the chest declared someone was more than pissed at Jim Osborn.

Chapter Four
Jimmy's Funeral

Squad cars with flashing lights halted eastbound traffic on Saunders Settlement Road. In the middle of the slow procession, made up, it seemed, of the entire Niagara Falls Police Force, Roger steered his black Chevy Trailblazer into Sacred Heart Cemetery. He looked smart in his navy blue dress uniform with service medals pinned to his chest. Though the thermometer still hovered well below freezing, he wore no overcoat. I suspected he was still in shock from news of his partner's death, and didn't feel the cold.

I shifted in the passenger seat and gazed around. Roger hadn't asked me to accompany him to the funeral. I insisted on being there. I knew Jimmy Osborn and his wife, Margaret, too. Marge and I grew up together, went to school together. The Osborns had been more than kind to me when my ex decided it would be exciting to have a fling with his boss's secretary while we were still married. They invited me to barbecues, their daughter's wedding. Marge tried to set me up with her cousin. When, three years ago, Roger's wife finally had enough of life as a policeman's spouse, Jimmy decided Roger and I might make a good couple. "Couple of what?" I'd asked when he suggested it. Now, next to Roger in his car, I smiled at the recollection. My smile immediately turned downward, and I brushed tears from my cheeks. Jimmy would no longer be part of the Osborn matchmaking tag-team.

I glanced to my left. Roger's eyes were locked on the cortege ahead. It was as if he saw before him each of the twelve years he and Jimmy had been partners and best friends—both in the military reserves and on the Force. This was hard for Roger, I knew, probably the hardest thing he'd ever faced; harder than the year he spent in Iraq with his reserve unit, and harder even than when he found the note from Judy telling him she'd gone to live with her parents in Arizona. Marge told me he cried the day she left. He had driven to the Osborns' house, and he and Jimmy got drunk in their backyard. Those guys were like brothers, I realized not for the first time. I suppose that's how close you get with someone to whom you trust your life.

Again, I glanced at Roger. His eyes weren't moist from the loss of a brother. Jaw set, his eyes were as hard and as cold as the headstones we drove past. His skin was taught across his face. Not just angry, he was seething.

God help whoever killed Jimmy Osborn, I thought, though I didn't want God to offer any help. I was also angry.

***

At the gravesite, Marge Osborn sat stiffly on a wooden folding chair. Under a black beret, her auburn hair was stringy, appearing as though it hadn't been washed in days. Her makeup was sparse. Her blue eyes were red and swollen. This wasn't at all like Marge. In high school she'd been a fashion-plate—hair, nails, makeup, clothes always perfect. She wouldn't leave the house unless the guys in school would swoon at the sight of her. The way she looked sitting before her husband's casket didn't surprise me, though. If the man I loved had been killed, my hair and makeup were the last things I'd think about.

Marge clasped her daughter's hand. A miniature version of her mother, Jennifer's eyes were also red, and her makeup didn't quite cover a dark ring under her left eye. Jennifer's husband, Sean Ryan, sat next to her. He appeared to have such a firm grip of her arm, I was sure she would find bruises when she got undressed. While the minister offered prayers and words of condolence, Chief of Detectives Harry Woodward stood behind the widow, his hand resting on her shoulder. Woody, his men called him.

There was no disrespect in the informality. The Chief would die for his men—Roger told me he once nearly had in Iraq. As a result, if Woody said run out for coffee, his men would try to break the world record for the hundred yard dash. Chief Woodward's wife, Amy, dressed entirely in black as if she, too, were in mourning, stood just to his right and behind him with her head bowed.

Roger and I were off to the side of the flag-draped coffin. In front of us, an honor guard stood at rigid attention.

As I said, it was a bitterly cold morning—cold enough that instead of a dress, I put on a black alpaca sweater over gray wool pants. Though the clouds had parted and the sun shone bright overhead, the chill sneaked between the threads of my overcoat. Roger must have felt me shiver.

Wrapping an arm around me, he whispered, "You didn't have to come."

"Even if Jimmy weren't my friend," I said, "I wouldn't have let you go through this alone."

He squeezed my shoulder then looked away.

Amy Woodward nodded at me. Her face was nearly as pale as the winter streets, and her neck-length black hair was, as always, perfectly coiffed. An accomplished hostess, the few times I'd accompanied Roger to one of her gatherings—this was during the time the Osborns thought they might be able to set us up—I found her to be gracious though not overly warm. In fact, it struck me her hospitality was almost businesslike. That's why it surprised me when she walked over.

I saw her eyes were red, and I thought, *She isn't made of stone.* For a moment I wondered whether an underground river of passion ran through her. I decided I'd find out and then use her as a character in a story. Or, if I never found out, I'd invent a passionate stream for her. As I've said, I'm a writer. It's what I do.

Amy leaned close to me, almost against my shoulder. "I hate funerals," she said, "and this one...this one..."

A heart *did* beat in her chest.

I made a mental note then touched her wrist. "I feel so bad for Marge. She adored Jimmy and he did everything for her. I don't know how she'll manage without him."

Amy unsnapped her purse, pulled out a tissue, and blew her nose. "Losing a man you've given you heart to, promised your life to..." Anything else she might have said got lost in a sob.

For a second I wondered whether the strain in her voice spoke of a fear she might one day learn *her* husband had been killed in the line of duty. That thought fled when her tears brought on my own. Gone was any thought of constructing a character for a story: her words had dredged up the way I felt when my unfortunate marriage fell apart. Sniffing, I said, "Thank goodness you have such a steadfast husband."

She tilted her head toward him. "Yes, thank goodness for that. I suppose."

There was coldness in the way she said it, and her tone jarred against where we where and why we were here.

A little startled by the weather change in Amy Woodward, I gazed past her. What I saw at the end of the row of graves caused me to gasp. A man in a dark gray overcoat and gray slacks, with a gray cap pulled low on his head, crouched near one of the mausoleums. Was that Kevin Reinhart, my ex? I took a small step in his direction, and rubbed my eyes. It sure looked like him. He appeared to be trying hard to blend into the gray stones.

Roger leaned down to me—he's over six feet tall, and I'm just five-seven, more or less. "Something wrong?" he asked.

"It's—" I raised my hand to point. When I looked again, I saw only the gray stones of the mausoleum. Shaking my head, I said, "I thought I saw—no, it's nothing."

The graveside service was mercifully short. After fifteen minutes, the minister looked up from his prayer book. "Rest in the arms of our Lord and Savior, James Osborn," he said. "You were a good man. Your wife and daughter will miss you. You were a good police officer. Niagara Falls will miss you."

When the minister snapped his book closed, a piper dressed in green, red, and blue plaid with black leggings under his kilt, stepped from behind a nearby tree. His bagpipe moaned.

I looked up at Roger. He was mouthing, "Amazing grace, how great thou are, God saved a wretch like me—"

Two cops broke rank from the honor guard, and lifted the American flag from Jimmy's coffin. With deliberate movements, they folded the flag into a triangle and tucked in the ends. A hand on top, the other on the bottom, one of the cops knelt and offered the flag to Margaret Osborn.

She stared blankly at him, then at her daughter, then at the folded flag. She seemed hesitant to take it. I thought I understood why: if she accepted the gift, every day it would remind her she was a widow. Marge proved me right when she gazed again at the flag, shook her head, and pulled her hands back.

Amazing Grace droned on.

The cop who knelt with the flag in his hands, turned his head to Chief Woodward. They both seemed uncertain about what to do.

Roger took a step forward, as if he intended to settle the matter by accepting the flag.

"You can't," I whispered to him.

At last, as the bagpiper's final notes floated across the cemetery, Marge's son-in-law reached over and took it.

Harry Woodward let out what could only be a relieved breath.

Marge dropped her head.

The service was over. One by one, those present filed past Marge and her daughter, stooping to whisper a few words then move on. In front of me, Amy Woodward silently patted the window's shoulder. When it was my turn, I kissed Marge's cheek. Though words are my life, my career, at that moment I couldn't utter a single one.

When I stepped away, Roger bent down. "I'll get the bastard who did this," he said. "I'll even the score. I swear on Jimmy's grave, I will."

Marge didn't blink. Her face remained expressionless.

Chief Woodward, still standing behind the widow, heard what was said. He frowned, and leveled his gray eyes at Roger.

With his hand on the back of Marge's chair, Roger returned Woody's stare. Tension ran along a taught rope between those two long-time colleagues. Losing someone you care deeply for can do strange things like that. I tugged at Roger's jacket, held the hem to urge him to leave with me. Finally, the two men broke eye contact.

"I'll stop by later, and sit with you a while," I said to Marge.

She gave a slight nod.

After one more tug at Rogers's jacket, he and I left the funeral gathering and walked in silence past a row of stones dedicated to generations who'd lived and died in this corner of Western New York. Now and then I recognized the name of someone I'd known: a friend of my parents or my grandparents.

At my father's grave, I stopped and brushed snow from his headstone. Roger waited patiently while I knelt, and whispered, "I miss you, Daddy. I wish you were here to tell me what to do with Sarah Goode's book."

Again I brushed at the snow, then at my tears.

Five minutes later we were at Roger's car. He opened the door for me. As I slid in, I noticed the anger still burning in his eyes.

"What are you thinking?" I asked.

He peered over the roof of his Trailblazer, back in the direction from which we'd come. "Nothing."

"Roger?"

His hand dropped to his waist where he usually wore his holster.

A bit nervous, I said, "You're not gonna go vigilante on us?"

His eyes hooded, he muttered, "I'm gonna do exactly what I told Marge I would."

He slammed my door, marched around the car, and climbed in. I sat with my eyes straight ahead, afraid to look at him, afraid to speak. I was afraid if I asked what he meant, I'd wind up an accessory-before-the-fact to another murder. Lost in my concern, I didn't notice someone approach the idling Trailblazer, didn't realize a man stopped beside us until I heard tapping on the driver's-side window. The *tap-tap* sounded like pounding. I jumped.

Roger glanced over, and laid his rather large hand on my arm.

"Please tell me you're not going after revenge," I said.

He gave me a tight smile. "Have you ever known me to go off the reservation?"

His careful phrasing didn't reassure me.

The tapping came again.

Before I could call him on his tacit lie, Roger rolled down his window. Only then did I see who was out there.

Chief Woodward was about as tall a man as I've ever known—better than six and half feet from toes to head. In contrast, his hair was cut extremely short. Resting an elbow on the roof of Roger's SUV, he pulled off his hat, and leaned down. Even in that position, he had a stiff military bearing reminiscent of the marine colonel he had once been. His eyes flicked in my direction, then focused on Roger. In an easy, conversational tone, he said, "A word, Detective?"

As he opened the door, Roger said, "Sorry, Emlyn. Give me a minute."

The two men strolled a few yards away. The Chief rested his hand on Roger's shoulder and said something. Roger pulled back, shook his head. Woody's expression grew stern. From the movement of his lips, I could tell his words were clipped.

Roger stiffened, began to turn away. The Chief held him in place and said a few more words. Roger gave a sharp nod and returned to the car. Harry Woodward moved slowly in the other direction.

"Damn," Roger muttered when he opened the door and climbed back in.

"What did he tell you?"

My friend sat as still as a tombstone for a minute. Normally he won't talk to me about his work, so the fact he finally answered spoke volumes: the Chief had upset him. In the slow words of a man struggling to control his temper, Roger said, "He doesn't want me working Jimmy's murder."

I bent over to watch Chief Woodward's retreating back through Roger's window. "Why?"

"Said I'm too close to it."

I thought for a minute. Woody was right. My friend was very good at his job. Sooner or later he'd learn who killed his partner. As angry as he was, he would pass up an arrest, and another killing would hang over the Falls Police Force. At last, I said, "You've got to listen to him. He knows what—"

With a raised hand, Roger cut me off. In a monotone, he said, "I'd better get you home."

***

Roger seemed to relax a bit while we drove. He chatted about the time an army buddy called from Pennsylvania, and told him a couple of bears had wandered into his town. Roger and Jimmy packed their rifles, and drove down—'ready for bear' was the way Roger phrased it. It turned out there wasn't a single ursine creature near that town, so they'd rustled up a couple of kegs, camped out for a week, and bought a pelt at a Seneca Reservation shop on the way home. Back in the Falls, they displayed the pelt and spun yarns about how they'd tracked the bear to its forest lair. The pelt now hung on a wall in Roger's den.

During his story I smiled in all the appropriate places. But my smile didn't go further than my lips. I knew my friend. Stubborn might be the best description of him. Combine stubbornness with the grief I knew simmered inside him…well, his apparent calm didn't fool me.

When we pulled into my driveway, I invited him in. I hoped if I kept him talking it would get him past the worst.

"Can't." He tugged at his uniform collar. "Gotta go home, change, and head to the station."

"I thought Woody doesn't want you on the case," I said.

"He doesn't. What he wants is me where he can make sure I'll behave myself."

Roger gave me a rueful smile. His ears were red. Card players would call that a "tell." I knew about "tells"—for years I'd put them in my stories. Roger's ears would not have been red if he intended to comply with his boss's order.

***

Elvira was curled up by the door when I came in. She opened one eye and lifted her head about an inch to acknowledge my presence.

"Sorry to disturb your nap," I said.

She blinked then yawned. When I walked past and opened the hall closet to hang up my coat, she smacked my leg with her paw.

"What now?" I leaned through the kitchen door. "You've got food, you've got milk. Leave me alone, I need to think."

She tilted her head.

I sighed. "All right, I'll tell you," I said, and led her into the living room. After tossing my coat across the arm of the wingback chair that had become the cat's property, I plopped down on the sofa.

She sat at my feet, spine stiff, pink eyes alert.

"It's Roger," I said. "I'm worried about him. He's taking Jim Osborn's death extremely hard."

Elvira's eyes narrowed.

"Oh, that's right. You don't know. Jimmy is…was Roger's partner."

As if she were processing the information, Elvira sat motionless for a moment. Then she dropped her head and mewed.

"Yeah, I care about Roger. A lot." I took a deep breath. It was the first time I'd admitted that.

A low purr came from Elvira's throat.

"I don't *know* what to do about it."

She tilted her head again. This time it was as if she asked whether I meant what to do about my feelings for Roger, or how to keep him from seeking justice with the barrel of a gun.

"I don't know that, either," I moaned.

The cat grunted.

I groaned. "I suppose you're right—they *are* the same thing." I fell back, and hugged a flowered pillow to my chest. "That just makes everything worse."

She leaped onto the sofa. Keeping her eyes on me, she settled against my leg.

"So, got any ideas?" I asked.

She swung her head until she faced my desk.

"Don't be ridiculous. Writing a story won't help him. Won't help me, either."

Elvira jumped to the floor. Her tail high, her large rear end swaying, she strutted across the living room. When she reached my desk, she scampered onto the chair, and peered at the computer screen.

I laughed. "You're going to write if I won't?" I said. "Go on, let me see you turn the computer on and type something." I caught my breath. For a minute I was not at all certain she wouldn't do it.

Her paws tapped. Thank goodness the computer didn't turn on. The way I felt at the moment, if it had I would have run screaming from my house. The cat was doing something, though. I rose from the sofa, and went to look.

Under her paw was Sarah Goode's *Book of Shadows*. Elvira was trying to open the cover.

"Why didn't I think of that?"

She twisted her neck and stared at me.

"Give me a break, will ya?" I said. "I'm new to this witch stuff."

I pushed her from the chair, sat down, and began to turn pages. On the eighth page, in an old fashioned script that had faded to a faint orange, I found something which might help.

Banishing, it said. I read what was written beneath:

Use rosemary branches, two feet long. Weave them into a circle. Tie the ends with green cotton thread. Tie to it more rosemary until the wreath is full, then seal the bottom with a red ribbon. Pluck from the field rue, mugwort, and hyssop. Tuck nine into the wreath. Hang it on the front door...

"This will work," I said, already trying to figure out how I'd explain to Roger why I nailed an herbal wreath to his door. As I said before, my friend doesn't believe in magic, and I truly doubted he would tolerate my practicing it on him. Still, if I were careful he might never find out.

I could get my hands on most everything in Sarah Goode's recipe. But mugwort? While I sat, wondering what mugwort was and where I might find some, Elvira tapped my hand.

"What?" I said, bothered by the interruption.

She pushed my hand from the book and tried to turn to the prior page. At least, I think that's what she wanted to do. To humor her, I leafed back one page. In large, bold print, Sarah had written, *TO CHASE THE DEVIL.*

Hmm, I thought, *this might be better.*

Elvira hissed.

"Yeah, what?" I said to her. "It's kind of like he's got the Devil in him."

I swear, the cat shook her head.

"Okay, what then?" I flipped a few pages forward.

After a minute, Elvira let out what sounded like a sigh.

"This is it?" I examined the page.

Written there was, *Rub cumin seed on the doorway every week while all others sleep to bring peace to the house and all within.*

"I can do this," I said to the cat. "Set my alarm for five in the morning, bundle up, and tiptoe to Roger's house—"

Elvira slid from the desk to my lap.

My finger on the page, I looked down at her. "This won't stop him from gunning for Jimmy's killer, will it?"

She craned her neck so far back, her irises seemed to roll into her skull.

"Need something stronger, huh?"

She blinked.

"I thought so. Better call Rebecca. She'll know what to do."

I don't know how she did it, but the cat shrugged.

Chapter Five
Do it Yourself

I leaned against the kitchen counter, and punched seven numbers into the phone.

As if she were waiting for my call, after the first ring I heard, "Black Cat. This is Rebecca."

"What in heaven's name is mugwort?" I said. "I looked in Webster's dictionary. It's not there."

She hesitated a moment, to digest what I'd blurted out, I suspected, before she said, "Hello to you, too, Emlyn."

"Yeah, yeah, hello and all that. Now tell me about mugwort."

Her tone grew concerned. "What are you fooling around with?"

I felt my face go warm. "Uh, nothing," I said. "I just need to know what it is."

"Slow down. I feel as though I've walked into the middle of a conversation. Start from the beginning."

"Okay." I took a breath. "I've told you about my neighbor."

She listened while I explained what happened, and what I feared Roger intended to do.

"How can I help?" she asked when I finally panted to a stop.

"I need a spell or maybe an amulet that'll keep him from doing it. But if it's an amulet, I'll have to bury it in his backyard so he won't find out I'm working a spell on him—"

I heard a long laugh. "What you need is air. Inhale deeply. You're about to hyperventilate."

I held the phone in front of my face and shouted, "You don't understand. I have to do something now!"

Rebecca was laughing so hard at this point, it sounded as though *she* couldn't breathe. At last she settled down

49

enough to get a few words out. "First thing you have to do," she said, "is stop drinking whatever potion you've concocted. I've told you, haphazardly mixing herbs isn't something to fool around with."

I inhaled through my nose and out through my mouth a couple of times—a relaxation technique I'd learned in the yoga class I took after Kevin and I broke up.

"Okay, now," she said. "Tell me what you did."

"Nothing. Well, nothing but read a few pages in Sarah Goode's book."

"Sarah's...? What book?"

I told her.

"Where'd you get that?"

"My mother sent it to me."

She didn't respond for more than a minute. When she spoke again, it was at a slow, measured pace. "Listen to me carefully, Emlyn. I've read what Sarah Goode was up to. The first Rebecca Nurse wrote about it in a diary that's been passed down through my family. From what I can tell, she was casting some very advanced spells with her herbs. You're not near ready to try anything you find in her *Book of Shadows*."

"But you can. Or maybe together, we could—"

"I don't know enough, either."

"We were able to slice the legs out from under Kevin," I insisted.

"Your ex is a fool. It didn't take more than a nudge to push him over the edge."

"But, I've got to do something. Roger's about to walk into a field of quicksand." If I sounded as though I were begging, it's because I was.

After another moment of silence, Rebecca said, "You're really into this guy."

I twirled a lock of red hair around my finger. "Well, maybe. A little."

"You poor thing." She clicked her tongue. "Love is what got your ancestor hanged."

Love? I thought. Nothing I'd read about the Salem witch hunt said anything to suggest such a predicate. It didn't matter. At the moment I was too desperate to wonder about my ancestor's arcane history. "I've got to *do* something," I repeated.

"The best thing is to stay out of it," Rebecca advised.

"I can't."

She sighed. "No, I suppose not."

"So?"

"You could try to work on the case with your boyfriend. With you along, he won't dare kill anybody."

I unwound my hair from my finger, but a few strands got stuck. "Ouch!" I cried as I yanked my hand loose.

"What did you do now?"

"Nothing. And he's not my boyfriend!" I don't know what Rebecca thought, but to my ears I sounded like a petulant child.

"Uh-huh." She laughed again. "He doesn't know it yet, is that it? I can give you a simple spell to fix that."

Outside my kitchen window, a car horn blared. When I looked, I saw I saw a yellow Volkswagen slide into a snow drift to avoid a BMW racing around the curve in the road. Feeling as though I were as much a wreck as what I just witnessed, my worry about Roger turned to annoyance. "This isn't helping!" I shouted into the phone.

"Okay, how about this: the only way to keep him out of trouble is to solve the crime before he does. Once the killer's in jail, it'll be too late for Roger to go after him."

"Easy for *you* to say. I'm not a detective. Where do I begin?"

"Why, at the beginning, of course. Every story has a beginning. You're a writer, you know that."

"Okay wise guy, where's the beginning? Go on, tell me that."

"You're Sarah Goode's heir, you'll figure it out," Rebecca said then added, "But, Emlyn, while you go about it, don't mess around with anything you find in her book. At least, not until I see it and we figure out how to keep you from blowing up your entire neighborhood."

"Thanks a whole bunch," I said.

"Always happy to help a friend." She hung up.

I held the phone away and muttered, "Some friend. Go ahead, leave me hanging with no idea of what to do."

I tried to slam the phone down, missed, picked it up with two hands, and grumbled into the receiver, "Just wait till you need help with something, Rebecca Nurse. 'Sure', I'll say. Then I'll pack a bag and go away for the weekend. That's what I'll do."

When I tried again to hang up, I smacked my pouting lip with the receiver—but only hard enough to feed my annoyance.

Finally rid of the phone, I dropped onto a stool by the counter.

Elvira poked her head through the kitchen door. As if she were uncertain whether it was safe to come in, she peered around.

I turned on her. "And you, fur ball—you're no help, either."

She backed out of the kitchen.

I sat hunched over the counter, flicking the point of the pencil I kept near the notepad I write my shopping lists on.

As if she were in the room, I heard Rebecca say, *Don't sit there sulking. Start at the beginning.*

I lifted my head. *She's right,* I thought. *I'm Sarah Goode's heir. I can figure this out.*

Elvira tiptoed in.

I smiled down at her. "It's okay, cat. I'm over my snit."

She sat at my feet, as if waiting for me to share my plan.

"Rebecca said I should start at the beginning," I told her. "Where else can the beginning be but at Jim Osborn's home?"

She nodded.

"I'm glad you agree," I said.

She turned her back on me, and sauntered to my wingback chair. I guess cats don't like sarcasm.

I didn't have time to worry about sensitive feline feelings. From the refrigerator, I pulled the casserole I'd baked a few days before when I got stuck for the next scene in *The Swamp Witch* (changing my focus to cooking sometimes helps me get past a bout of writer's block). I uncovered the baking dish. The ziti and cheese with chicken, mushrooms, and broccoli would serve my purpose. After a funeral, people expend so much energy in mourning they don't prepare proper meals. This casserole would disguise my real reason for stopping by.

***

Most of the houses on the Pine Avenue side of downtown Niagara Falls were two-story wood-frame homes built before the Second World War. The Osborns' was newer—a brick ranch set on a well cared-for plot of land. In the spring and summer, the driveway and the front of the house would be lined with tulips, sunflowers, black-eyed Susans. When Jimmy was off duty, while Marge sunned herself on a lawn chair, he would be on his knees gardening. That is, when he didn't go off to hoist a few at Flannery's, the neighborhood bar the Falls cops frequented. On this late winter afternoon, the perennials hadn't yet begun to poke through the frozen soil, and, as if it, too, was in mourning, the leafless willow on the front lawn drooped under the weight of snow.

Parked at the curb in front of the house was the green '67 Chevy Malibu Sean Ryan had restored.

I pulled into the driveway behind a silver Pontiac. Of indeterminate age, the car had a dented rear fender and a tied-down trunk. The trim around all the doors was rusted. This was the vehicle Jimmy drove the fifteen blocks to the police station each day. Next to the Pontiac was a sporty new Corvette.

Not the kind of car a cop owns, I thought as I lifted the casserole from the seat beside me.

The Osborns' daughter answered the door when I rang the bell. I handed her the casserole and said, "Jenny, I'm so sorry about your father."

She offered me her right cheek to kiss. Though she turned away, I again saw the dark ring under her left eye. At another time I would have said something about the bruise. This day, though, my mind was locked firmly on what brought me here.

"Is your mom up for company?" I asked.

Silently, Jennifer stepped aside to let me in.

Other than the bedrooms and kitchen, the house consisted of a single large room—what decorators call an open design. The living room set was in a semicircle around a low glass coffee table. These furnishings were oriented with the couch placed in front of the oriel window. Farthest from the front door was a formal dining area: a glass table, six chairs upholstered in a light fabric, and a heavy china cabinet. In contrast to Marge's appearance at the funeral, the house was perfectly neat.

I leaned in to look around the wall at the entry. Marge was stretched out on the couch. Her shoulder-length auburn hair was pulled back into a tight pony tail, and she'd changed from her funeral dress into a floral housecoat that almost hid an expanded waistline.

What kind of friend have I been, I thought, *not to have noticed how she's let herself go?*

Jennifer held the casserole to her chest. As I've mentioned, she was a younger version of her mother: same color hair, same delicate features. But she was several inches shorter (in that, she took after her father). At twenty-two, gravity had already pulled her upper body down around her waist and thighs.

"Mom's resting," Jen said, but didn't move. Though she'd had her adenoids removed along with her tonsils when she was six, she still spoke with a decidedly nasal undertone.

"Is it all right if I see her?" I asked.

Jennifer glanced over her shoulder before she said, "Sure. I'll...uh, put this in the kitchen."

I'd expected to see a house full of people, chattering away in the hope they'd take Marge's mind off her loss for a short while. Instead, it seemed as though Jennifer was afraid to let anyone in. And if no one else was here, who owned the Corvette?

Once in the living room, I dragged an armchair next to my friend. As I reached for her hand, I said, "I won't stay long. I just want to find out if there's anything I can do for you."

Marge sniffed and shifted her body to gaze through the window. "I can't believe he—" She shook her head then glanced around the living room, as if searching for her husband. "No, I can't believe..."

Over the years, Marge had become quite taciturn. That was, I supposed, her mechanism for coping with the fear always present in the mind of a cop's wife. Jennifer tended to be the same. I used to think she'd learned this behavior from her mother. Before the week ended, I would find out this wasn't the case.

I pulled Marge's hand onto my lap. "Do you know what happened?"

She slid her hand from mine and took a tissue from the box on the end table. "That's what's so crazy. Jimmy just went out to have a drink with the guys." She didn't wipe her eyes. "It was after dinner. He said he'd be back in an hour. Three hours later..." She folded the tissue, and stuffed it in her sleeve. "I've always been scared something like this would happen. Every day of our lives it made me crazy." Leaning on an elbow, she turned to me. "Don't ever marry a cop, Emmy. Promise me you won't."

My thoughts flashed to Roger, but only for a moment. I quickly buried the idea beneath the rubble of my past. After my time with Kevin, I had no intention of marrying anyone else. As they say, once blistered you shy away from the stove.

"Do they think it might have had something to do with a case he was working on?" I asked.

Marge slid up against the cushions of the couch, and shrugged her shoulders. "I asked Woody, but he said he can't talk about an open investigation."

Jennifer came into the room, followed by her husband, Sean. They were proof of the adage that opposites are like magnets. Where she was short, he was over six feet tall. Where she approached hefty, he was as thin as the maypole my dad erected in our backyard. Moving in unison, they pulled chairs up on either side of me. Then, with a quick glance at his wife, Sean lifted his chair, and moved next to her.

Jennifer moaned, "Who would do this to us? It doesn't make any sense." She began to cry.

Sean dabbed her cheek with a tissue. She winced. I presumed this was because of the sudden loss of a father she both admired and adored. I understood her emotion: Jimmy's death made no sense to me either.

We sat in silence for several moments, looking around for something to say. On the fireplace mantel was a display of framed photographs: one of Marge, one of Jennifer in her high school graduation gown, Jennifer and Sean's wedding picture, a cute one of Marge and baby Jennifer playing with the puppy they'd had back then. This was a homey room. Still, that day it felt vast and empty. My eyes came to rest on the end table. There were more photographs of Marge and Jennifer and Sean.

While I sat there, I felt as though a bug was crawling up the back of my neck. When I reached around to scratch it, I realized it was an itch of suspicion. Something wasn't right. Reaching for what troubled me, my mind settled on the Corvette in the driveway. Sean was a reporter for the *Buffalo News*. It couldn't be his car. Marge hadn't had a job since her daughter was born. A myriad questions flooded my brain. How could she and Jimmy afford an expensive sports car on a detective's salary? Was Jimmy involved in some criminal activity that had gotten out of hand? Could Sean have been involved in it? Did Jennifer learn what her father and Sean were up to? Was the bruise beneath her eye a warning to remain silent?

When I asked about the car, Jennifer said for years her father had dreamed of owning a red Corvette. Marge added they'd saved every penny they could until they had enough for him to buy it. He'd taken delivery two weeks ago. With a dolorous laugh, she said, "It feels so stupid, spending that kind of money and he's not here—" She glanced at her daughter. Her eyes filled with tears, she pulled the tissue from her sleeve.

Sean squeezed Marge's hand. "At least," he said, "Jim had the pleasure of driving it a couple of times before uh…at least he had that pleasure." He looked in the direction of the driveway, as if he could see the red car through the wall.

Marge's eyes snapped in my direction. If she were sending me a message, it got lost in the mail. Looking again out the window, she said, "Woody also asked about the Corvette. Like he thought Jimmy was on the take or something. Christ, we haven't gone anywhere on vacation in five years. I haven't bought new clothes in almost that long."

Her protest sounded too vehement. *What about the expensive wedding you gave your daughter?* I thought. I didn't say it, though. Instead, I remarked, "You wore a lovely coat to the funeral. What kind of fur is it?"

Marge's eyebrows went up. Her expression seemed to ask if I also accused her husband of stealing.

Jennifer glanced from her mother to me. "It *is* beautiful, Mom," she said, and turned to Sean. "Fake fur. Hard to tell, isn't it? I could use a coat like that."

He frowned.

"Moroni's," Marge said. "You know, the furrier on Main Street? Stephen Moroni gave it to Jimmy as thanks for catching his brother-in-law selling coats out of his trunk."

The explanation made total sense. The explanation of the new car also made sense. All at once, I felt like the world's biggest fool for suspecting an old friend. I'd also known Jimmy since high school. He was as straight as any arrow William Tell ever shot. As for Sean's involvement in something dirty—well, Jimmy never would have let his daughter marry someone who wasn't as honest as he. *Stupid, Emlyn, suspecting this family,* I thought. *Stupid, stupid!*

We talked a while longer, recalling times we'd spent together; recalling how Jimmy, silk tie undone, tuxedo jacket off, face flushed and words slurred from too much scotch, had pulled me to the floor to dance a reel at his daughter's wedding. That was three years ago. Now he was gone.

Leaving his wife and mother-in-law in the living room, Sean walked me to the door. When he opened it for me, he said, "Marge told me Kevin stopped by about two weeks ago. She said he looked awful. Do you know what he wanted?"

I turned back to Sean. Did he think my ex was mixed up in Jimmy's death? "How would I know?" I said. "I haven't spoken to him since God knows when. Didn't he tell Marge what he was after?"

"Said he was looking for Jim, is all."

My eyes narrowed. "Do you think Kevin has something to do with Jimmy's death?"

Sean shrugged, turned away, and closed the door.

As I left the house where Margaret Osborn now lived alone, a widow, I felt like an idiot. I wanted to kick myself in the rear for the way I'd behaved. *I deserve a good kick for thinking I'm a detective,* I thought. Well, I was done sleuthing. The next time I saw Roger, I'd mention my ex had looked for Jimmy. Other than that, I'd have to trust Harry Woodward to discover the killer. I could only pray Roger wouldn't get in his way.

Unfortunately, things didn't work like that.

Chapter Six
Hello, it's Me

As the name suggests, River Road winds along the bank of the Niagara River. The old link between Niagara Falls and Buffalo, the road consists of one sparsely lit lane in each direction. Past the marina, the boat yard, and a few small industrial sites, a smattering of private residences are set back in stands of trees. One of those residences is mine.

As I rounded a curve on River Road, my headlights lit a four-by-four parked behind the snow heaped near my driveway. Smeared with road salt, the pickup looked abandoned, ghostly. Late on a winter night, nobody parks on a dark winding road. Not if they expect to find their vehicle in one piece when they return. Examining the pickup as I drew near, I again felt a tingle at the nape of my neck. This time I had no need to think about the cause: fear was the spider crawling up my spine. My imagination constructing the image of a shadowy mass murderer who skulked in my backyard, my first instinct was to race into Roger's driveway, jump from my car, and pound on his door. I would have done just that if a single light burned in his house.

He's probably out trying to track down whoever killed Jimmy, I thought.

I cursed him for disobeying his boss when I needed him here to keep Jack the Ripper from making me his next victim. Yeah, Jack was long dead. So what? Maybe his ghost hid in the snow. Muttering every invective I could think of, I parked as close to my garage as I could get, and ran the fifteen yards from my car to the front door. I left the headlights on.

What? Everyone knows murderers won't strike when lights are on. It's an unwritten rule—sort of like wearing a necklace of garlic to ward off vampires.

Okay, this was my vivid imagination gone haywire. But after all, if witches and magic spells actually exist, it's entirely logical to believe vampires and killers lurk behind the trees in my yard—

God, sometimes imagination is a royal pain!

My key held out in front of me like a Bowie knife with which I might slash at anything that dared to cross my path, I slammed through my front door. The racket I made would have wakened the dead or maybe chased off a few zombies.

Elvira's reaction was to flop over the arm of my wingback chair and glare at me with an expression that said, *Hey, how about a little quiet! Can't you see I'm sleeping in here?*

"Couldn't you at least pretend to be an attack dog?" I said.

She yawned. I was boring her.

With my hands on my hips, I glared at the oversized animal that had made a comfortable nest in my home and my life. Just when I opened my mouth to shoot a scathing remark in her direction, I heard knocking on the French doors. The killer *was* in my backyard. He wanted me to let him in.

The thought, *Ohmigod, I really am being stalked,* blew though my mind like a winter gale. Terrified, I froze.

Elvira cowered in the chair, her eyes wide. If I weren't trembling, I would have enjoyed the sight—the big coward.

There was another knock, so hard this time a pane of glass rattled.

My eyes rapidly flicked from the door to Elvira.

A high-pitched screech came from the cat. It was as if she screamed, *Board up the house! Dump all the books from the bookcases and build a barricade in front of the door!*

Garnering a very foolish courage, I took a step forward (a killer on the loose, someone pounding on my door late at night, and not immediately phoning the police smacks of foolishness). Over my shoulder, I whispered, "Be quiet while I see who's there." My only explanation for doing this is that my boggled brain figured someone who intended to kill me wouldn't knock and asked if I would let him inside to do it.

Elvira didn't look at all certain about my logic. Her eyes flicked as if she were ready to scramble under my desk.

I tiptoed across the room. I don't know why I did. It wasn't as if I were going to surprise whoever lurked out there. As I hesitantly reached to pull the mini-blind aside, I glanced back at the wingback chair. My fraidy cat was nowhere to be seen.

I turned again to the French doors, leaned over.

There was another knock.

I dropped the blind, jumped back. My voice trembling, I said, "Go away!"

"C'mon, Emlyn," a man hissed from outside. "Open the damn door!"

I let out the breath I hadn't realized I was holding. I recognized the voice—or at least the syntax. It was Kevin. I hadn't heard from him in four, six years; hadn't seen him in longer. Now he was in my backyard in the middle of the night?

I yanked the blind aside. With his face pasted against the window, my former husband looked like my worst nightmare come to life.

"What are you doing out there?" I said.

"Dammit, let me in!" He shook his fist—definitely not a gesture that would elicit my compliance.

I positioned my face close to the cold windowpanes. With my lips nearly on the glass, I said, "What do you want?"

"Will you *never* stop talking?" he said.

"Fine," I said, "I'll stop right now."

I dropped the mini-blind, and checked the lock on the door.

Elvira crawled from under the skirt of the wingback chair. *Good, you've come to your senses,* she seemed to say.

"Emlyn!" Kevin yelled. Then, as if he realized bullying me wouldn't work, in a softer tone, he said, "Please."

What is it about a man begging that melts a woman's heart, even if she's spent the last seven years cursing the day he was born? I rolled my eyes and swung the door open.

Now at my feet, looking up, Elvira glared a question at me. *What is* wrong *with you!*

I shrugged.

She turned her back and walked off with a snort suggesting a catty remark about things humans never learn.

Kevin's round face looked as though it hadn't been shaved in days. Beneath the stubble, his skin was almost as gray as his cap. His gray overcoat was dusty and where the dust hadn't stuck, the coat was stained. His shoes appeared to be so drenched he might have slogged through the snow for a week.

I stood in the doorway, my arms wrapped around my chest. I tried hard not to sound as though I gloated when I said, "You look terrible. The bimbo's not taking good care of you?"

He pushed past me. "She moved out," he said, and slouched down on my sofa.

I didn't mind his wet shoes leaving footprints on my carpet, or his damp coat staining the flowered cushions of my sofa. Those could be easily cleaned. But the way he looked, so desperate—I felt as though I'd been given a late Christmas gift, tied up in red ribbons.

"Oh, she left you?" I was barely able to hide my smile.

"You don't have to look so happy about it."

"You're right," I said, and forced a frown. "I'm sooo sorry to hear that, Kevin. What happened? She finally figured out you're a bucket of slime?"

He peered at the French doors, as if he were afraid he'd been followed. "The money ran out, and so did she."

To hide what had grown into a wide grin, I turned toward the kitchen and looked at the telephone. I wanted to call Rebecca, tell her what a good job we'd done on my ex. I wanted him hear I was the cause of his distress. Ah, that would have been such sweet revenge. I was stopped, though, by another thought. Turning to him, I said, "You don't expect me to take you back, do you?"

His moist brown eyes seemed to ask if I might. But instead, he shook his head. "I know it's too late for us." Again he glanced at the French doors. "What I need is a place to…uh, stay for a while."

I followed his eyes. "You mean you need a place to hide out? Are you in some kind of trouble?"

Tears spilled from his eyes. "Yeah. Big time. I really screwed up, Emlyn. But it was just so…easy." He straightened up, wrapped his coat tight around his chest, and shivered.

Without taking my eyes from him, I backed past the coffee table and settled primly on the wingback chair. "What was easy, Kevin?" I leaned forward, hands clasped between my knees. "What did you get yourself into?"

He ignored me. As if speaking to himself, he said, "Yeah, so easy. Should've set me up for life—" He looked up at me through red eyes. "You gotta help me. Let me stay a while? A week, maybe two at the most."

"Not a chance," I said.

"Then how about some money? You've done well for yourself, your books and all. I just need enough dough to get away from here…" His voice trailed off. He must have seen my eyes grow cold.

"You can't come barging into my home, and—"

"Please, Emlyn. They're after me."

"Who is?"

He shot another nervous glance at the French doors. "They got Jim Osborn—I'm sure it was them."

I sat up, instantly alert. Jimmy *had* been investigating some criminal activity and that's what got him killed. This could be the answer to my prayer. Kevin would tell me, I'd call Chief Woodward, and Roger wouldn't know who it was until it was too late to do anything but curse at the caged killers.

My lips pinched and my eyes narrowed, I said, "Who shot Jimmy?"

"Must've been them. Had to be. No one else would've had a reason." Once more it was as if he talked to himself, trying to reason something out.

"Tell me!"

Startled by my shout, he shrank back against the arm of the sofa. He opened his mouth. Nothing came out.

"Kevin!"

At last he seemed about to answer. But he stopped abruptly, his eyes like full moons, when we heard knocking on my front door.

"Emlyn, you still awake?" Roger called. "You left your headlights on. I turned them off for you."

I bounced from my chair. "Stay there," I said to Kevin.

"That's you neighbor…the cop?"

"Yes, and he's gonna want to hear this."

"Don't let him in!" Kevin cried.

"Whatever trouble you've gotten into, Roger can help," I said as I rushed past the kitchen to the door. *But first*, I thought, *I'll make Roger swear he'll call Chief Woodward, and not go after the killers himself.*

My friend smiled at me when I opened the door. In his dark overcoat, suit and red and blue power tie, his brown curls neatly combed, and especially with the gray at his temples, he cast the image of a successful business executive. "Can I get you to put up a pot of coffee?" he said.

I was so taken by this view of him, for a moment I forgot about Kevin. I let my eyes roam from Roger's head to his feet. "Look at you, all dressed up."

"If I've gotta sit behind a desk all day, I might as well make use of my good suit." He glanced back toward his house. "Gonna invite me in?"

I pushed the storm door open. "Of course I am. And there's someone I want you to—"

I stopped when I felt a draft from behind.

Roger must have felt it, too, because he leaned to look past me. "You've left the French doors open."

I pivoted on my heels. Kevin was gone.

Chapter Seven
Back in the Hunt

My kitchen is white. Cabinets, canisters, floor tiles, refrigerator, stove, all white. Even my microwave and coffee pot are white. I'm nothing if not consistent. To satisfy Mom, who had a penchant for cooking but didn't want to be shut away from us, my father broke down some walls and enlarged the kitchen. After that, Mom's workspace was separated from the living room and front hall only by a counter. When Dad died and Mom moved to Florida, I resurfaced the counter with white Formica.

Roger sat patiently at my dinette table, while, hands shaking, I struggled to scoop coffee into the filter on top of the pot. Bless him for his patience. He hadn't missed my eyes go wide when I saw the open French doors, so he knew I had something to tell him. More, because I knew how upset he was over his partner's murder, he might have suspected my reaction had something to do with that. As I've said, Roger Frey is a good detective: he sees things, and the relationship between those things, others don't. He's able to do this *because* he's patient. Patience, he's often told me, is the most important skill a good cop must learn.

I carried the pot and two mugs to the table. As soon as I sat, I began to blurt out what Kevin told me.

"Whoa, slow down, Trigger," Roger said. "I just got here, remember? Start from the beginning so I can catch up.

"That was Kevin's pickup outside. He knows who killed Jimmy," I began, only to be stopped by his raised hand.

"Who did it?" He slid to the edge of his seat. It was as if he intended to run from my house as soon as he knew who to chase after.

"I don't know. Kevin left before he told me."

Again I was stopped by a raised hand. His cell phone pulled from his jacket pocket, Roger moved quickly from the kitchen, and yanked open my front door. "Truck's gone," he said while punching numbers into his phone. Leaning out the door, he spoke so softly I couldn't hear what he said.

Now he was back in the kitchen. With a sigh, he slid onto the chair opposite me. "Okay, maybe we'd better do this a different way," he said.

"What different way? You've got to stop that slimy bastard before he disappears!"

Frustrated, I forgot I held a mug of hot coffee. So, when I gestured toward the door, the amber liquid slopped over the brim and burned my hand. I yelped.

Roger jumped from the table and pulled a bar of butter from the refrigerator. While he rubbed it on the burned spot, he said, "Calm down. I just called the precinct, told them what Kevin said. They're sending a unit to look for his pickup."

He put down the butter and took my hand. "Now, pretend you're a witness and I'm a detective asking you questions."

Because a police bulletin had gone out to find my ex, I was finally able to relax. In fact, I was relaxed enough to enjoy the way Roger fussed over my burn. I smiled at him. "You *are* a detective, so this isn't make-believe."

"Good. Now you've got it. Okay, one question at a time: you were out tonight—"

Before he could finish, I jumped back in. "I went to visit Marge Osborn—brought her a casserole. It's nice to do things like that. She shouldn't have to worry about dinner so soon after—"

Barely able to hold back the deep laugh I liked so much, Roger again raised his hand. The gesture stopped me as I was about to confess to having made a fool of myself by all but accusing Jimmy of being a dirty cop.

"What did you talk about?" he asked.

My face must have turned as red as the burn on my hand when I recalled what wasn't one of my finest moments. I could only hope Margaret Osborn wouldn't stop talking to me.

"Oh, this and that," I hedged. "It has nothing to do with what Kevin told me." Nothing would be gained by admitting my stupidity.

Clearly, Roger noted I held something back. When he tried to press me, I winced.

He frowned. "Okay, we'll come back to that. So, then you came home"

I nodded.

"What time did you get here?"

"About nine-thirty, I guess." I usually have a fair idea of what time it is. But, I felt so guilty about accusing an old friend, I'd lost track of time.

"Can you be a bit more precise?" he asked.

I twisted my wrist to consult my watch, as if it might provide the answer. "Uh, let me see. I left Marge's house shortly after nine and drove around a bit. So, I guess it could have been ten or later by the time I got home."

"Good," Roger said. He sounded pleased to have gotten me into the rhythm. "And when you arrived, you thought someone might be waiting for you?"

I sipped at my coffee. "I saw his four-by-four when I came around the bend—just past the gas station."

"A stranger might have been waiting outside your house, and you opened the door when he knocked?" Roger's face took on the same expression as the cat had when she all but told me I was crazy to do that.

As if to say *I told you so*, Elvira sauntered in from the living room, parked her butt next to Roger's chair, and stared up at me. I expected any moment she would stick out her tongue.

"He wasn't a stranger," I said.

Roger's face grew stern. "But, did you know it was Kevin before you opened the door?"

"I, uh…" I peered through the pass-through from the kitchen to the French doors.

"Well?" He leaned closer.

"I…saw his face outside the door," I said, and stared at Elvira, daring her to call me a liar. She might have done just that had she been able to speak. As it was, she let out a low hiss, which had the same effect.

"You looked through the door, did you?" Roger said.

Caught (hoisted on my own petard, my mother would have said), I tightened my lips and nodded.

Roger lifted my chin, and looked into my eyes. "You pulled open the blind and looked close enough for a stranger to see you and break in?"

"But…it was Kevin," I said.

Elvira lifted a paw, and smacked Roger's ankle. It looked as though she wanted him to say letting my ex in was worse than if it had been a stranger. If the stupid cat had been a female dog—well, I'm glad I stopped before I called her that.

"Hmmm," Roger said.

Was his reaction jealousy? I didn't have time to consider what his jealousy might imply. There was another knock on my front door.

"Central Station, come right in," I called as I rose from the table.

When I opened the door, I saw Harry Woodward on my stoop. Hatless on the cold night, his long face was drawn, and he had dark rings under his eyes. A workaholic, the man seemed extremely tired. Pressures of his job, lack of sleep? I was sure he'd have looked the same way when he was colonel, and lost one of his marines in Iraq.

"Good evening, Emlyn." He brushed past me. "Mind if I come in?"

"Not at all," I said to his back. "Make yourself at home."

As he entered the kitchen, in his stiffest tone, Woody demanded, "Detective Frey, I thought we agreed you wouldn't work the Osborn case."

Roger crossed his legs and replied evenly, "What makes you think I intend to work the case? My shift ended. I stopped to have coffee with my friend."

"Please, Detective, give me credit for knowing my team. You spent the day nosing around to learn what we've got, and the next thing I know you call in an APB."

A small smile crossed Roger's lips. "I didn't know this had anything to do with Jimmy until I got here and Emlyn told me her ex broke in. Tell the Chief what Reinhart told you."

Woody turned to me with his lips pinched. It was as if he asked whether Roger's alibi was too much of a sieve to hold water.

I looked him squarely in the eyes. In a curt tone, I said, "That's right. I was frightened by a man in my yard. When I let him in, he said—"

"You opened the door to someone who scared you?" Chief Woodward said.

I gulped. I'm a poor liar, always have been. As a result, I usually don't even try to do it. But, this wasn't a lie. Why was my face growing warm?

As if he were assessing my truthfulness, Chief Woodward's eyes rested on me for a minute. At last, he said, "All right, then, do you mind if I ask you a few questions?"

He settled between Roger and me at the dinette table and pulled a pad from his coat pocket. It was clear he would interview me whether or not I minded.

Over the next half hour I told him in detail what happened when I drove up to my house—leaving out the part where initially I was certain Jack the Ripper or maybe a vampire was waiting in lurk for me. Each time I paused, Woody looked up from his pad and asked another question. By the time we were done, I felt as though I'd been run over by the four-by-four I'd seen outside.

When he rose from the table, the Chief turned to Roger. "Are you staying?" he asked.

His eyes fixed on his boss's face, my friend answered, "I am."

Woody tried to pinion him with a stare. "You're staying with a friend, then, not with a witness. Am I being clear?"

"Yes, sir," Roger said.

I waited for him to jump to attention and give his boss a sarcastic salute. That's what I would have done. Thank goodness Roger had more sense than I.

"As long as you understand my letting you sit in on this interview wasn't an invitation to get into the Osborn case," Woody said as he walked out the door.

I carried my mug to the sink and began to wash the coffee pot.

"He's a good cop," Roger said when we heard the Chief's car drive off.

I turned from the sink with a dishtowel and the wet pot in my hands. "Are you going to listen to him?" I said rather harshly.

He smiled at me.

"Are you going to, Roger? If not, I can call Woody back."

He sipped coffee that by now must have been cold. "You know I can't. Forget Jimmy was my best friend, he was my partner. I can't walk away from this."

I stood, thinking. "Okay, then," I said after a minute. "If you're going after his killer, I'm gonna help."

"Don't be ridiculous," he said, "You're a—"

"A what? A woman?" I snapped at him. How dare he!

"You know that's not what I mean. But…yeah, you're a woman who I don't want to see get hurt. You heard what your husband said—"

"He's not my husband. Not anymore. Not for a long time."

As if to say he wasn't playing, Roger gave me a pinched smile. "Good. Glad to hear it. Still, you heard what Reinhart said. These are dangerous people I'm going after. Best guess is, it has something to do with drugs—that's what Woody thinks."

"What do you think?" I asked.

"He's right."

As if it were an Indy car, suspicion raced back into my mind. I told Roger about the Corvette in the Osborns' driveway; reminded him of the expensive wedding, and Marge's new fur coat. I set the coffee pot down, and carefully folded the towel. "You…you don't think Jimmy was involved in drug trafficking?" I asked, not at all certain I wanted an answer.

Roger rubbed his chin. "I'm not sure…maybe. But see, that's why I've got to keep you out of this. Drug pushers, they don't play by any rules."

"I can take care of myself," I insisted.

"Yeah, I can tell. Just look how you trembled at the thought someone was stalking you. Get involved in this, stalking will be the least of your worries."

I slid onto the chair across from him. "I was frightened because I didn't know what was out there. Now I know. I can handle this."

"How?" he asked. "You don't even own a gun."

Sarah Goode's *Book of Shadows* rose in my mind. With a glance at Elvira, I said, "I've got something better." I crossed my fingers and hoped it really was. As I said before, I'm new to this witchcraft thing.

Roger looked at me through narrowed eyes. "What are you talking about?"

I tightened my jaw.

"Stay out of this, Emlyn," he said. "You hear me?"

I looked again at Elvira. Whether or not cats have the facial muscles to do it, I know she was smiling.

Chapter Eight
Divination

Roger didn't intend to obey his boss's direct order, but he expected me to obey *him*? Not a chance!

As soon as he left, I double-locked my door, fastened the chain, and ran to my computer desk. I had placed Sarah Goode's *Book of Shadows* in the top drawer.

Elvira only remained in the kitchen long enough to lap some milk from her bowl. Then she chased after me. On her haunches by my desk chair, she raised her face as if to say, *Come on already—what are you waiting for?*

I laughed at her eagerness and leaned over to wipe away her milk mustache. Don't ask how I saw it on her white fur—we'd been together long enough for me to know she had one.

"Sloppy, sloppy," I said, as if she were a child. "I really need to teach you table manners."

She licked her lips.

"That's better."

Satisfied I'd done my duty as a parent…uh, or whatever I was to her, I opened the drawer. My stomach fluttering with enough butterflies to fill a field with a colorful cloud, I placed Sarah's book in front of me. I switched on my desk lamp so I'd be able to read the faded script. Careful not to crack the brittle pages, I turned sheet after sheet. About a quarter of the way in, I found something.

Elvira's mewing told me it might be important.

I scanned the page, then the next. What I read was as much a diary entry as an instruction manual. Sarah's heart seemed to be laid open on the vellum. *18 May, in the year of our Lord, 1692*, it said:

> *Minister Burrows has fled this Salem town, accused by girls he taught of stealing their affection*

through witchcraft. Their love was not stolen by George. It is mine that was, and no craft was needed to secure it for himself. Will I ever again walk with him through Salem's fields? I fear not.

Last night while all slept, I stole away into the barn, bringing with me three tapers of beeswax. In the candle flames, I sought to find where this precious minister of my heart lays his gentle head this night, and knowing where he is, perchance fly to join him. Alone in the dark I placed my candles in the sterling holders my mother sent as a gift when I wed Dan Poole. Around them I sprinkled leaves of rosemary, thyme, and bay laurel—one offering for each candle. Then I turned to the north, east, south, and west, praying to the earth, air, fire, and water. As I did, I said this prayer:

Winds of the north rushing and mighty, bring me the sight of my love. Winds of the east, chased by the sun, show me my heart. Winds of the south, aglow with warmth, carry my sight to where he lays his head. Winds of the west, gentle and tender, show me the journey I must take to be with him.

Alas, my rite did not end well. While indeed I saw dear George in a small room, too soon the candles sputtered and sparks flew skyward. Such a flight of sparks is an evil omen. I fear where I will end.

The passage was difficult to read: *S*'s looked like *F*'s; *Y*'s were placed where *I*'s should be; *E*'s were planted needlessly at the end of some words and missing from others. After I struggled through the old fashioned and faded handwriting to the last word of Sarah Goode's entry, I leaned back and rubbed my eyes.

"Seems our friend Rebecca might have been right," I said to Elvira. "It was love that brought my grandmother's, grandmother's, grandmother to Gallows Hill."

When I glanced down, I half expected the cat to congratulate me for correctly interpreting the true cause of Sarah's demise. She didn't. Her twisted lips told me to stop wasting time on such drivel. There was work I had to do.

"Oh, that thing with the candles," I said. "Right. Light three candles and I'll see who shot Jimmy." I nearly tripped over Elvira in my rush to leave my desk.

As she jumped away, her expression said, *Now you've got it!*

My unheated basement, with its dirt floor and cinderblock walls, was colder than frigid. No way to avoid going down there, I wrapped my sweater tight around me and flipped the light switch. A single bare bulb came to life. The raw wood steps creaked as I descended. The ritual materials Rebecca Nurse had told me to purchase were stored down here in a locked closet. *If she were here now, Sarah would hold her ceremony in the basement,* I thought as I scooted, quickly as I could, across the cement floor. After all, winter or summer, Sarah had worked her magic in a drafty old barn. I didn't know whether the barn to which Sarah retreated had been drafty or old, but that's the way I imagined it.

Feeling the cold from my ankles to my nose, I mumbled to Elvira, "The original Goode had far more stamina than I."

The cat wasn't at my feet. She hadn't followed me down to the cold cellar. I turned back to the stairs. She stared at me from the doorway with her back arched and her hair raised, shivering.

"Big sissy," I called up to her. Apparently, Sarah also had more stamina than a well-padded albino cat.

Alone, then, I unlocked the closet. From the top shelf, I took candles and the double-bladed ceremonial knife with which I would bless my herbs. I couldn't use a stainless steel knife from my kitchen. I prepared meals with those. Rebecca had told me the spell would be spoiled if my ritual knife were used for anything else.

The supplies I'd need in hand, I returned to the kitchen. Rebecca hadn't told me not to use the herbs I cook with, so I took dried rosemary, thyme, and a couple of bay leaves from my spice cabinet, and crushed them in a stone mortar.

Again in my living room, I set down on the coffee table everything Sarah said I would need. I was ready for my first solo flight, so to speak.

With Elvira parked at my feet, I arranged three candlesticks in a triangle, placed the yellow tapers in them, and sprinkled a generous mixture of the herbs. I stepped back to examine my preparations. Everything was as Sarah Goode had described. I turned off the electric lights. Why does it seem as though magic only works in the dark?

The box of kitchen matches held over my head, I struck one with a flourish.

Sparks flew.

Panicked, I threw the lit match into an ashtray and patted my hair, certain I'd set myself on fire. This clearly wouldn't be as easy as Sarah's book made it sound.

Satisfied I hadn't lit me instead of the candles, I tried again. This time I got the match lit without mishap. I cupped the match in my palms, and touched it to each of the candlewicks. Once the flames grew strong, I turned slowly, and repeated the words Sarah had written. Of course, I changed the business about her love, to a request for information about who killed Jim Osborn.

My prayer completed, as if I were a medium who'd invoked a spirit, I raised my hands above the candles and waited.

Nothing happened. No image magically formed in the room or even in my mind.

78

I stared at the candles. "Come on, show me something," I whispered.

Still no image formed. No second sight. Not even a first sight.

"What's going on here?" I asked the cat.

She snorted and walked away. If she could speak, I'm certain Elvira would have muttered, *Amateur,* as she disappeared into the kitchen.

With my head hung in defeat, I followed her. "If you're so smart," I said, "tell me what I did wrong."

She raised her head from her bowl and licked the milk from her face.

"Just like Kevin," I said. "Full of criticism, but no ideas for how I can do it right."

She rolled her eyes. I didn't know cats could do that.

***

The sun streaked through the window blinds in my bedroom the next morning. Rays of light crawled along the carpeted floor, up the walls, and onto my closed eyelids. Even more annoying, fur was in my mouth, and tickled my nose. I rolled over. The fur followed me. It was again on my nose and in my mouth.

Bleeech!

I rubbed my eyes and opened them.

Two very pale pink eyes stared down at me.

"Go away, cat," I mumbled, and rolled over.

The sunlight pried my eyes open.

"What time is it?" I asked, as if a cat could answer.

She did—though it was only a long *meowww*.

"I don't want to get up," I said. "I don't have to. Got nowhere to go today."

She licked my face leaving slime on my cheek. Yuck!

I glanced at the clock. It was almost eleven. I never sleep past nine. Still weary, again I rubbed my eyes. What time had I gone to bed last night? I got home from Marge's just before ten, and Kevin knocked on the French doors. Then Roger knocked on my front door, then Chief Woodward. By the time they left, it was past midnight. What had I done after that?

I sprang up, all at once remembering the ceremony I'd tried to perform. Had I left the candles burning?

I tumbled from my bed and stumbled down the stairs with Elvira close behind.

The ashes from last night were still on the coffee table in the living room. As I gazed at the candlesticks and the stubs of the tapers, a queer feeling rose from my stomach—a feeling there was something I should remember, but couldn't quite grasp.

Oh, well, I thought, *it'll come to me eventually.*

My slippers flopping, I cleaned the mess, and braved the cold basement to put my tools away (I had decided if I called these things tools, I wouldn't let slip what I was up to).

My house back in good order, I put up a pot of coffee and reached for the telephone.

"What trouble did you get into this time?" Rebecca said as soon as she heard my voice.

"None," I said too quickly. Feeling my face flush, I added, "Well, other than nearly lighting my hair like a candlewick."

After a long sigh, she said, "Tell me."

This time she didn't scold me for trying a spell which was beyond my experience. When I said I couldn't figure out what I had done wrong, she asked a question that caught me by surprise.

"What were the flames doing?" she said.

"On the candles?" I asked, unsure if she meant on those or on my hair.

It sounded as though she drank something while I spoke. I wondered if she might have poured a shot of whisky to settle her nerves—she couldn't have found me easy to deal with. I didn't have to wonder long.

"Ouch," Rebecca said. "Sorry, my coffee's hot."

Reminded my mug was empty, I tucked the phone under my chin, and poured some more. Finally I began to feel as though I were awake. The elixir of life steaming in my mug, I parked on a stool by the kitchen counter. "What did you ask?" I said.

"The candles. What were the flames doing?"

Again her question stopped me. My coffee mug was near my lips. I put it down. Early in my marriage, I would light candles on my table when I wanted to have a romantic dinner and signal to Kevin I wanted something else afterward. I'd never thought to notice the way the flames moved.

After I struggled for a minute or two to pull the image from where it hid among weeds in my short-term memory, I said, "Circles. I think the flames moved in circles."

There was silence on Rebecca's end of the line.

"Are you still there?" I asked. Had I said something I shouldn't?

I heard her take a breath. "Be careful, Emlyn," she said at last.

I didn't like the stretched-out words and the low timbre of her voice. Her tone frightened me more than her words. "What do you…? Why?"

"During a divination ritual, flames only move in circles if someone's blocking you."

I caught my breath. "Another witch?" I stammered.

I glanced toward the étagère in my dining room. I kept liquor in the cabinet below the glass doors. A shot of Irish whisky in my coffee might calm my nerves that now buzzed like an electric current had shot through them. I'm brave enough with things I can touch and hear. But this magic stuff—oh, it was okay when I tossed a spell at Kevin. The SOB deserved it after what he'd done to me.

81

The relatives of Cotton Mather also deserved it—the Bible says sins of the father travel through the generations. But the idea of someone at a distance fixing a curse on me was more than I could handle on just a cup of black coffee. I gulped down what I'd put in my mug, and poured myself a third cup.

"It's not necessarily a witch," Rebecca said. "It might just be someone with a secret to keep. If that person knows you're getting close—"

She didn't need to finish the sentence. I gulped my coffee to the dregs.

"Get a grip," Rebecca said when I gasped. "Remember, a cop lives next door to you, so you don't have to worry much about anything physical."

Why didn't that make me feel better?

My voice rasping from coffee burning my throat, I asked, "What did you mean when you said I'm getting close?"

I'd poured the last of my milk into Elvira's bowl. While I thought about dropping to my knees and lapping up enough to put out the fire in my throat, I almost missed Rebecca's answer.

"I think you might be," she said. "The clairvoyance spell you tried—what happened afterwards?"

With a covetous glance at the cat's milk, I said, "Not a damn thing. I stared at those stupid candles for the longest time, and..."

"What?"

"Uh..." I couldn't remember.

"Think hard," she urged.

"I'm trying," I said. Well, it was more like a whine. "The next thing I knew, I was in bed this morning with that dumb cat licking my face."

"Not so dumb. Elvira was bringing you out of it."

82

"Out of what?" This need to beg for every answer had become maddening. Now I knew how Roger must feel when he questioned a suspect.

"The trance," Rebecca said. "Emlyn, your spell was more successful than you think."

I still didn't get it. "How could the spell have worked if not a damn thing happened."

"Are you sure?"

"Yes, I'm—" The memory I couldn't grasp earlier crawled into reach. "I...I had a dream.

"Uh-huh. That's the way these things work."

When I hesitated, Rebecca laughed. "Did you think it would be like a hologram playing in your living room?"

Embarrassed, I said, "Uh, yeah...kinda."

Again she laughed.

"Don't make fun of me!"

She took a breath, and I heard her take another sip of whatever she was drinking. "Okay," she said at last. "Tell me what you dreamt."

A cloud passed across the morning sun, and my kitchen dimmed. The white appliances and countertop looked almost ghostlike.

I fought to bring back the details. "I was in a small room," I said. "I think it was a den of some kind because there was a TV against the wall. The TV was on—an old episode of *The Closer*. Someone was in the room, back turned to me. Whoever it was put a pistol into the wall—wait. No, not in the wall, in a safe hidden behind a painting."

"What did the person look like?" Rebecca asked.

"I don't know. Whoever it was wore a cowl—you know, like monks wear? The hood was up over his head—"

"Or her head?"

"I said I couldn't tell. And then the person turned to me and gasped, like he suddenly realized I was there."

"Who was it?" she practically hollered.

I narrowed my eyes, as if that would help me see past a white haze. "I don't know," I sighed. "He was just about to pull the hood off and talk to me when Elvira woke me up."

My head now ached as badly as if I'd awakened after sucking a whisky bottle dry. I needed some aspirin, desperately. Maybe half a bottle of them.

When I could focus again, I heard Rebecca say, "If the person you saw reacted that way, he knows who you are, and—"

"He couldn't," I interrupted. "I told you, it was just a dream."

"I know." She again sounded concerned. "Sometimes these spells work like that—two people's dreams getting merged. It's like you were having a conversation."

I gasped—this time not because I swallowed hot coffee.

"You could be in trouble," Rebecca said. "I think it's time you tell Detective Frey what you've been up to."

Tell Roger? That was the last thing I wanted to do. No, it was the next to last thing. First I wanted to bolt all the doors and windows in my house, and jump back into bed with the covers over my head.

"Please, Emlyn," Rebecca said. "Tell Detective Frey."

I glanced down in time to see Elvira's big rear end wiggle as she crawled under the skirt of my wingback chair. She didn't want to be around when I told Roger what I'd done.

"You big coward," I muttered after her.

Chapter Nine
How to Tell Roger

The dark cloud passed. As if a light switch had been thrown, the room was again bright. I stretched the phone cord across the kitchen and leaned over the sink to look through the window. Roger was in his driveway, scraping frost off the windshield of his car.

"Damn," I muttered.

"He's outside, isn't he?" Rebecca said.

I backed away from the window. "Uh, no. I, uh…it's the mailman."

"Right," she said. "And he's bringing you another old book?"

She waited, I supposed, for me to fess up. When I didn't, her voice grew stern. "Go! Tell him. I don't have so many friends that I can afford to lose one."

I felt as though I were a ten-year-old who'd been scolded by her mother.

"Do it now!" Rebecca said, and hung up.

I stared at the phone for a minute. I really didn't want do this.

Maybe Rebecca's wrong about the killer knowing who I am, I told myself.

But if she's right, you're in big trouble, a voice in my head answered.

I dropped the phone, and knocked on the window.

Roger opened his car door. He tossed his briefcase onto the seat.

I knocked again, harder this time.

He turned his face in my direction.

I slid the window up. The bright sun was a liar. A sudden blast of arctic air cut through my robe. I poked my hand outside, waved, and held up my index finger.

He smiled and nodded. Then he leaned against the hood of his black Trailblazer to wait for me.

I threw a heavy coat over my pajamas, pulled on my galoshes, and hurried out the door. While I slogged through the snow and around the stumps of trees between our houses, I rehearsed what I would say.

I had this vision, I would tell him.

Vision? He'd say—he had a habit of repeating my words. It was the way he encouraged me to finish telling him something I didn't want to. This was one of those somethings.

I uh…think I saw who killed Jim Osborn.

Did you now? He would try hard to suppress a smile—a father humoring his child. I'd see that in his eyes.

By then I would have no choice but to rush on. *And the person in the vision might have recognized me.*

Recognized you? Oh, he would be having a grand time now, laughing out loud. Hardly able to get the words out, through his guffaws, he would say, *And how did you have this vision?*

My imagined dialogue having reached this point, my pace slowed. I knew my face was red, and it wasn't from the cold. *It, um…well…it happened after I performed a divination ritual in my living room.*

His eyes would open wide.

I'm a witch, you see, I would whisper so no one else could hear—not that anyone else was around. *It's in my genes.*

Now he'd be rolling in the snow, holding his stomach.

I felt my blood begin to boil. How dare he ridicule me! Rebecca was wrong. Telling Detective Frey about my new-found skill was a bad idea. A very bad idea.

By the time I got to his driveway, I was ready to smack him.

Fortunately, at that very moment a stiff gust of wind howled down River Road. As if it had been sent by Sarah

Goode to save me from behaving like an out-of-control maniac, the gust caught me full in the chest, and tried to shove me back. My shoulders lowered as I pushed against the wind, I slid from the snow onto his driveway. I fought to keep my balance, but couldn't. I skidded on black ice. My feet went out from under me. I was about to land gracelessly on my derriere when two strong hands grabbed me around the waist and hauled me upright.

For what felt like half an hour, though it was no more than a few seconds, I was locked in my neighbor's embrace. I looked into his eyes. What I saw in them—well, it was one of those moments in which I might have broken my vow to remain forever celibate.

"You could've taken a nasty fall," Roger said. He still held me.

Embarrassed by my teenage romantic fantasy, I wriggled from his arms. "I...I could have," I said.

"Glad I could help." He glanced at his car. It was as if he were also embarrassed by what might become a moment of passion and wanted to make a quick getaway.

When he looked at me again, his smile went from his lips to his eyes. Hazel eyes, flecked with gold. I hadn't noticed those flecks before. Lost in a grin that showed the gap between his front teeth, I forgot why I'd come out of my house.

He touched my wrist—such a gentle touch—and said, "You want to tell me something?"

It took a minute for me to regain my bearings, and recall why I was standing in his driveway on a frigid morning. When I did, I inched away from him, and struggled to find the right words. It would have been so very easy to say I wanted to thank him for staying last night while Harry Woodward interrogated me. I couldn't do it. As I've said, I'm a bad liar. Most times when I try, my eyes won't stay steady. I get flushed and wind up stammering. I didn't want Roger to see me behave that way. I had to tell him the truth. At least part of it.

I took his arm to steady myself. "I'm a little worried," I said. "I had this dream last night. My mind must have been replaying something I'd seen, but didn't know I'd seen. You know?"

His face now serious, he nodded.

"In my dream, I saw who did it."

"Did what?"

"Killed Jimmy."

"Uh-huh." The ignition key in his hand, he reached for the car door. "I'll stop by later, and you can tell me all about your dream. Right now I've got to get to the precinct." He pointed to the briefcase lying on the passenger seat. "Been up most of the night, going through old files. Thought maybe I'd find something about Jimmy."

I grabbed the lapel of his camelhair overcoat. "It was more than a dream, Roger." My voice quivering, I barely got the words out.

He stopped and turned back to me, realizing, I supposed, how upset I was. With his legs set firmly on the ground, he reminded me of a catcher who was ready to receive whatever I tossed at him. "Okay, Emlyn," he said, "what's going on?"

This was bad and about to get worse. All at once, what I didn't want to tell him tumbled from my mouth. "That book I got—the one my mother sent me?—it isn't a diary. Except, well, it is, sort of. Sarah Goode wrote about her life and some things she did and how she did them, and last night I tried one, and—"

"Whoa, whoa, take a breath," he said. "What has you so riled? Can't just be a dream."

Overwhelmed by fear the killer I'd seen would soon come after me, and more afraid of that than of Roger's reaction, I blurted, "Sarah was a witch. My family tree blooms witches. I'm one, though I'm still just learning—"

88

He looked as though he couldn't decide whether or not to laugh. "You think you're a—?" He took a deep breath. "Okay, Emlyn, what's really going on?"

I knew he wouldn't believe me. Why had I listened to Rebecca? Why? Because I was frightened half to death, is why. "It's true, Roger. I wish it weren't, but—" Tears bubbled in my eyes, overflowed, and rolled down my cheeks. Only the salt in them kept my eyelashes from becoming frozen red spikes.

He took the brown leather glove off his right hand. With his thumb, he rubbed my tears away. "It's your imagination," he said. "Are you writing a story about witches?"

"I am, but that's not why." Now I was crying full-out from fear and frustration.

"You'd better come inside," he said.

With his hand on my elbow, he glanced up and down River Road, as if to determine whether any of our neighbors might be watching me lose my mind.

I backed away from him. "Why? Out here, inside, you still won't believe me!"

He took both my shoulders, leaned down, and peered into my eyes. "Doesn't matter if I do or don't, *you* believe you saw something."

His words and the creases of concern on his face made me feel a bit better. Not much, but better than I was. His hand again on my elbow, I let him lead me to his door.

Roger Frey's house was a one-story ranch. The front door opened onto a living room that bent right to form a dining area. All the furnishings were Swedish modern. His chairs, tables, the arms of his sofa were all built of blond wood. It was astonishingly neat for a house in which a single man dwelt. Spartan, with everything in its place. No pizza boxes on his coffee table. The pleats in the drapes were straight and sharp. No dust bunnies roamed the carpet.

He obviously saw my eyes sweep around the room. "Woody won't let me work the case, so I hadda do something." He shrugged. "Once I finished with those files, I cleaned."

I pictured this bear of a man in an apron, wielding a feather duster in the middle of the night. The image elicited my first smile of the day.

His kitchen was to the left of the door. He led me in, and pointed to a chair by the table. He placed his chair in front of me and turned it backwards. Straddling the seat, he took my hands.

"Now, quietly," he said, "tell me what this is about."

Between sniffing and blowing my nose in the tissues he brought, I explained how I found the divination spell in Sarah Goode's *Book of Shadows*. I left out the part where Elvira seemed to show me where it was. A cat leading me through a Wicca rite?—Roger would have tossed me through the nearest window. I told him how nothing had happened while I stared at the three candle-flames. I told him what I dreamed, and what Rebecca said the circling flames meant. When I finished, I sat still, looking down at my lap.

Roger's brows went down in a *V* of suspicion. "Who's this Rebecca?" he asked.

"Rebecca Nurse. She's my friend. She runs The Black Cat in Ellicottville." As if it would explain her, I described the shop: the smell of incense, the jars of herbs I'd never heard of, the rows of bookshelves packed with how-to volumes on witchcraft. Of course, I didn't tell him about the revenge she'd helped me take on Kevin.

When I at last fell silent, I waited for Roger to disparage Rebecca, call her a charlatan who was just after my money.

He didn't do that. But he did say, "C'mon, Emlyn, you know this voodoo stuff is just a bunch of hoodoo." He laughed at his joke.

I started to protest. But when he squeezed my hand, I forgot what I wanted to say.

"I don't believe in such stuff," he said. Before I had a chance to get up, and, mortified, run from his house, he added, "What I do believe is that the mind is a complex machine even shrinks don't understand."

I sighed.

"No," he went on. "You didn't crawl into the killer's brain. What happened is you saw something which didn't register at the time, and it's taken awhile for the pieces to fall into place. You were het-up from reading about your ancestor—yes, and from fooling around with what she wrote in her diary—so you had a nightmare."

"It wasn't! It was real," I insisted. "Whoever it is, knows I know."

He stroked my hand. "I didn't say I don't believe that part. Like I said, the mind works in strange ways. Being a cop, I see it all the time. You may have seen something, or heard something. In a store or walking along the street. Happens often. And though it's unlikely, it's at least possible whoever it is saw you take note of his mistake. It wouldn't have taken much—just the flicker of your eyelids could have told the killer he'd been spotted. Guilt makes people alert to such things."

I nodded so hard it felt as though I strained a muscle in my neck. "So what do I do?" Afraid again, I picked at my coat sleeve.

"Go home, lock your doors. Don't let anyone in this time—not even your ex. Even if he gets on his knees to beg, don't let him in. Then, think. Try to remember what you saw or heard, where you might have been."

He stood. I stood, and followed him outside.

As I clomped through ankle-deep snow to my house, I heard him say, "I'll check on you when I get off my shift."

I'd almost gotten to my driveway when I saw it: my front window was broken. Then I smelled smoke.

"Roger!" I screamed.

He was halfway onto the seat of his car. While I ran toward him, I saw him freeze for a moment then bang his head when he jumped back out.

"What's wrong?" he said.

All I could do was whimper and point.

"Stay here!" he commanded, and took off for my house on the run.

I don't know how he did it, but he seemed to glide on top of the snow. Must be his size fourteen feet work like snowshoes.

The entire ten minutes he was gone, my knuckles were white on the handle of his car door. When he emerged from my house, he had Elvira bundled in his coat, and he held what looked to be part of a wine bottle. Sharp points of glass poked up where the neck had broken off. Wisps of smoke wafted from what was left of the bottle.

He glanced over his shoulder at my broken window. "Good thing we came out when we did." He showed me what he held. "It's called a Molotov cocktail."

I was shaking so hard I felt my teeth rattle. "You see now? You see?" I howled. "I was right. Whoever killed Jimmy wants to shut me up!"

Before I knew it happened, he had me wrapped in his arms. This time I didn't pull away.

"Hush," he crooned. "Hush, it'll be okay."

"It won't!" I bawled. "My home...what am I gonna do?" I grabbed the cat from him, snuggled her against my chest. "Elvira might have been killed."

Even as I said it, I realized how strange that sounded. For the past three months I'd wanted the cat out of my house. Now she'd been in danger, and I feared for her the way a mother would fear for her child. Why did I? I would have to figure it out later.

As if she already knew the answer, Elvira rubbed her head on my chest and mewed. I think she understood she was now, and would always be, my family.

Roger held me away, and looked between us, first at me, then at the cat. His smile warmed me.

When he at last released me, he said, "You'll stay at my place today."

I shook my head.

"Listen to me. Whoever made this firebomb didn't do a very good job—probably didn't use enough accelerant, so it fizzled out before it caused much damage. But he might try again, and this time do it right."

"What if we're being watched?" I said. "He might already have another—what did you call it?—a Molotov cocktail?"

Roger again examined our street. "No one's watching."

I swung my head in the direction of the winding road set beyond the sea of white. I scanned the trees lining the other side of the road. Even though the branches were bare of leaves, someone could still hide among those trees.

"Please, do this for me," he said. "I'll worry less if I know you're safe in my house."

When I at last nodded, he guided me back inside.

***

Once I was settled under a blanket on Roger's couch, with Elvira curled up next to me and the television tuned to a classic movie channel, he said, "There's food in the fridge. Take whatever you want. I'll be home around seven, and we can call out for dinner."

Did he think this was a date? After someone had tried to burn me alive, could he possibly believe I might get hungry?

I lifted the cover, looked down at my pink and red plaid flannel pajamas. Swinging my legs to the floor, I said, "I have no clothes on. I have to go home and—"

"There'll be time for that." His face lit with what I would describe in my stories as a leering grin, he added, "Right now, you look fine to me."

What a strong face he had. How much he cared about me showed in the way his jaw muscles twitched. Forgetting for a brief moment the danger I was in, I laughed. I couldn't help it.

"That's better," he said.

I pointed at what was left of the bottle someone had filled with oil or gasoline or something, and tossed through my window. "What are you gonna do with that?" I asked. My mind flashed to what would have happened had the bomb worked and I was in my house. I shivered.

He snatched the bottle from the table. "Glad you reminded me," he said. "I wanna find out if there are any fingerprints on this. Also want to have forensics find out what kind of accelerant the guy used, what kind of wick. Learn that, we can check and maybe find out who bought the stuff."

"You won't learn anything from the bottle." If I were writing a story about what was happening, my villain would surely be careful not to leave such obvious evidence behind.

"Never can tell," Roger said. "In my experience, people under stress make all kinds of mistakes. If they didn't, I'd be out of work."

He was trying to lighten my mood, I knew. I forced a smile for him. "Then I hope you find something. I'd sure like to be able to get dressed sometime this year."

"Why? You look kind of nice this way."

I felt myself blush. Seemed as though I'd done that quite a lot lately. Standing in the center of his living room, I pointed to his front door. "Go!" I said.

He laughed. Before he opened the door, he turned back. Still smiling, he said, "Watch out for her, Elvira."

As if to say, *Of course I will,* the cat mewed.

Chapter Ten
In Need of Snapdragon

I lay on Roger's couch, dozing on and off through one movie, then a second. To this day, I have no idea what they were. Each time I woke, the couch seemed to be shaking. That happened a few times before I realized it wasn't the couch, it was me.

I curled into a fetal position with the blanket up to my eyes. "I'm just cold," I murmured to Elvira.

The snort she made said she didn't believe me.

I don't mind frightening characters I invent past the point of endurance—such tension is why my stories sell. In real life, I don't do scared very well. Maybe I put my fictional friends in harrowing situations, because I get to feel brave when they pull themselves together and come back fighting. The author of my characters' exploits has none of their courage. Though I put up a brave and independent front, the truth is I don't even do minor frights well. When Kevin decided he'd rather have a ditzy blond secretary than me, I grew so frightened about the unknown future—not to mention the failure my friends would see me as—I took to my bed and sobbed for days. The kind of peril a killer might yet put me in was far worse. I shivered at the thought of such danger while I lay bundled up on Roger's couch all afternoon: a bullet in the back when I parked in a lot behind a restaurant. Poison gas filling my room, or a pillow held over my face while I slept.

Gonna armor-plate my house, I decided, *bolt the doors, never come out again. Never sleep again.*

At some point—it might have been around four o'clock because the opening credits of a third movie had begun to scroll on the TV screen—Elvira apparently got fed up with my inertia. She jumped from the couch, grabbed the edge of the blanket with her teeth, and began to back away. What was with her? I thought only dogs do such things.

"Hey, stop it, cat!" I hollered.

She sat on her haunches, and gave me a pink-eyed glare.

"I don't want to get up," I said.

She blinked.

"Don't tell me I have to do something. It wasn't you that could've been killed."

Her tongue flashed across her cat-lips.

I heaved a sigh. "All right, you also could have. But what do you want me to do about it?"

She leaped onto my chest, and stared down at me.

"Uh-uh. Roger said we have to stay put," I told her. "Do you have a death-wish?"

She ran her tongue across *my* lips.

"I'm not gonna," I said. "The last spell you talked me into trying put us in this mess."

She screwed her head under my chin.

"And what if the next one doesn't work any better?" I said.

Now she twisted her head on my mouth.

I sat up, spitting out white fur.

"You're gonna get us killed," I groaned as I rose from my comfortable nest. "You know that, don't you?"

I swear it, Elvira shrugged.

Again in my boots and coat, with the large white pain-the-ass wrapped in my arms, I left the safety of Roger's home.

***

I unlocked my front door, turned the knob. As the door opened, I stood frozen on the threshold. Yes, the temperature still dipped down near single digits. That wasn't why. Were those footsteps I heard in my house?

I bent my neck so I could see Elvira. "Someone's in there," I whispered.

She squirmed free of my arms, landed squarely on all fours, and nudged the door open with her head. Before I could blink, she shot inside.

"Elvira!" I yelled.

I didn't stop to think I might have alerted someone who now hid in a closet, ready to pounce. Only fate, which brought me out of Roger's house in time to smell smoke, had saved my cat from a fiery end. If whoever tried to sauté me was inside, he might catch her. Slit her throat. Maybe flush her down the toilet.

This wasn't a rational thought, I admit. When fear crawls into your brain, it swells until there's no room for rationality.

I flung the door wide open, and rushed in.

"Elvira!"

When I rounded the corner to the living room, I saw her perched on my desk chair. She was trying to open the top drawer.

"What are you doing?" I shouted.

Her neck elongated as she peered at me. Her eyes seemed to ask, *What if Sarah's book had been burned up?*

I plopped down on the floor, laughing. I couldn't help myself and couldn't stop. Fear is step one on the road to blind panic, hysteria is step two. Bent over, holding my stomach, I thought, *I have to remember this reaction so I can write about it.*

As I said, I wasn't being rational.

Elvira jumped from the chair and snuggled on my lap. She wanted to comfort me—I could think of no other explanation. For ten, fifteen minutes, I sat, legs curled under me, stroking her fur. Then she squiggled away. When she reached my wingback chair, she looked back at me. *Enough of this nonsense, we've got work to do*, she seemed to say.

She was right. Though, as I looked around at what had been done to my house, I knew her idea of work wasn't the same as mine. First, my window had to be repaired or I'd never warm up.

One nice thing about having spent my life in a small city is I knew so many people on a first name basis. I'd grown up with most of them. I pulled the *Yellow Pages* from a kitchen cabinet, and punched a number into the phone.

"Hey, Fred, it's been a while," I said when he answered.

Fred Silbert is a glazier. I'd gone to high school with him. Though I'd turned him down when he asked me to our senior prom, we remained friends over the years.

"Hey, yourself," he responded. "Haven't seen you in a few months, what're you up to?"

I wasn't about to tell him. The down-side of where I live is how quickly rumors spread. If word got around I claimed to be a witch, even a novice one—I didn't want to think about the jokes I'd have to put up with.

"Been writing, mostly," I said. "You know how lost I get when I'm in the middle of a story."

"Yeah, I've seen you disappear inside your head. By the way, I just finished reading your last book of short stories. And, hey, I'm still waiting for you to autograph it for me like you promised."

Had I promised? With all I'd been through in the past three months, such small things had fled my memory.

"I need a big favor, Freddy," I said, drawing out the words in my most seductive tone.

"Anything for you, doll."

"My front window just got broken," I told him. "Some kids heaved a rock through it."

I heard him *tsk*. "Damn delinquents," he said. "Don't know what's gotten into 'em these days."

With a laugh which wasn't one—my mind was still too rattled to really laugh—I said, "Are they any different than we were?"

His laugh was real. "Got me there."

Did I ever. Our senior class voted Fred most likely to wind up in the Attica prison. If I'm to be quite truthful, most folks figured I'd wind up there, too (I didn't learn until much later they don't send women to Attica).

"So, my window?" I asked.

"Tomorrow morning too late?"

"Not if you won't mind hauling my frozen body to the mortuary. It's so cold in my house, I'm turning blue. Really, Freddy, it's colder than the butcher's freezer. Remember the day we got locked in Goldschmidt's freezer?"

He was quiet a minute, remembering, I supposed, the time we swiped a pair of jeans from Brubaker's Clothing, and took off on the run with old man Brubaker after us. We sneaked in the back of the butcher shop and hid in the freezer. We were almost frozen sides of beef when Mr. Goldschmidt found us there.

"Hey, bring the book," I said, "I'll sign it. I'll even write something nice about you."

"Yeah, yeah, yeah, heard that before." His words gave way to another laugh. "Be there in fifteen minutes. Have dinner with me after?"

Good old Fred, he never gave up.

"Another time," I said. "I still have to clean the mess those kids left me with."

***

When the window had been repaired, I vacuumed broken glass from the carpet and from the chairs near the window. When I reached the corner, I nearly broke into tears. My beautiful Lalique sculpture—the ballet dancer I'd bought to commemorate my first royalty check—had been knocked from the table I kept it on. The figurine's legs were now stumps. Her toes were still attached to the china pedestal. Of everything that day, this affected me most. You see, the tiny statue symbolized how far I'd come, how much I'd accomplished, since Kevin left me. My eyes overflowing, I carried the ballerina to the kitchen, and gently placed her in the wastebasket. Then, still in my rubber boots and coat, on my knees I scrubbed at the burned spots in the carpet.

Elvira sat up on my wingback chair, watching. With constant mews, she seemed to tell me, *Enough already. You're wasting time. Gotta work a spell that'll keep us both safe.*

When I couldn't ignore her any longer, I said, "Well, if you'd help me instead sitting there, maybe I'd get this done."

She screwed up her face. *What am I, a maid?* she seemed to say.

By six-thirty, I was too exhausted for any more cleaning. The physical work had taken the edge off my fear, though it hadn't completely calmed it. I stood in the center of my living room and surveyed the damage. A large hole was in the center of my carpet, and no amount of scrubbing had erased the black burn marks running like cat paws across the line where the small fire spread. Even if I could get the marks out, I knew nothing would erase them from my memory. The carpet would have to be replaced. One of the walls showed a spatter of whatever liquid had been in the wine bottle. A couple of coats of paint would take care of that.

The bottle Roger carried from my house... A recollection of what the bottle looked like rattled like a loose marble in my skull. I stopped stock still, my hand on my mouth. What was left of the label on the bottle—something about it was familiar. Where had I seen the label before? No matter how hard I tried, I couldn't recall. Still, I had to tell Roger. The label might be a clue.

I opened my front door and poked my head out. The sun had only periodically peaked though gray clouds all day. Now, like me, the sun had grown tired from all its work, and decided to go home for a nap. In other words, it was pitch dark. Neither the moon nor any stars hung overhead. I leaned to look for the Trailblazer in the driveway next door. Roger hadn't returned yet.

"Damn, where are you?" I muttered. Alone on a black night, I imagined Jimmy's faceless killer waiting in the dark for another chance to silence me. The spider of fear again crawled on my spine.

Something rubbed against my leg. I had reached step three: blind panic. *Ohmigod! He's in my house. He's got me!* I held the storm door open. I was ready to dash into the street in my pajamas and boots and run as fast as I could to the precinct where Roger worked. Yes, the precinct was a good ten miles away, but fear would be a tailwind.

As I bent with one arm forward and one arm back, as if I were a runner in starting blocks, my eyes turned down. Elvira had wound her body around my leg.

Shaking with relief, I said to her, "Okay, you win. Anything has to be better than the way I feel."

I slid the chain over the double-latched door, and settled at my desk with Sarah Goode's book. "There must be something in here to help get me through tonight," I said as I opened the cover.

It didn't take long to find my ancient relative's thoughts on the matter.

11 May, in the year of our Lord, 1692.
I have received a message. George Burroughs was arrested last week in Maine. In a dream I saw him there. It was where he fled after those wretched children swore against him an oath they saw him

cavort with the Evil One's servants. He did not dance with the Devil, but with me. Yet, in fear for their souls, they call his ministrations witchcraft. Nay, it is not, but only plants combined he offered those children. It was I who taught him to use those plants. And were it wrong, would the good God have given us these plants to heal our spirits? I believe not, but I daren't say a word in my dear George's defense lest those children next accuse me. What horrid times these be, when all strike out against what they cannot understand and call it evil. Yet, never within recollection has it been otherwise. And though I know it is not Satan's work I do, I live with a deep fear. Wagging tongues may yet place me in the jailer's keep.

Ah, this fear. When I walk in Salem town, I do so at night lest the bailiff stop and question me, and in questioning learn of my skill with plants. Courage do I need to face these troubled days, and so I will carry a stalk of mullein whence I go..."

I glanced up from the book.

"Mullein?" I asked Elvira. "What in heaven's name is mullein?"

She didn't answer. I suspect the cat was as stumped as I.

I went to the bookshelves. *Merriam Webster's College Dictionary* leaned against my copy of *Roget's Thesaurus*. This time I found an answer in the heavy volume.

"A wooly-leaved Eurasian herb of the snapdragon family," I read aloud, "including some that are naturalized in North America."

I turned to Elvira. "Where am I gonna get snapdragon at this time of year?"

She glanced toward the telephone.

"You're right," I said. "Rebecca would know."

As I reached for the phone, I heard a sharp rap on my door. I jumped back. Oh, how I jumped. I tripped over one of the stools by the kitchen counter. When I landed on my rear and kicked the stool, it skittered then toppled to the tile floor. The clatter might have been heard as far away as Ellicottville.

"Emlyn! Are you all right?" Roger shouted from outside.

What was *he* frightened about? It was I who just broke multiple bones. "I'm okay," I groaned, "though I might be crippled for life."

"C'mon, let me in!" He still sounded concerned.

I pulled myself up and limped to the door. "All right, all right, I'm coming."

Roger was on my stoop, a pizza box from Michael's Restaurant in his hands. By way of greeting, he scolded, "I thought you agreed to stay at my place."

"Uh-uh. You said I'd stay there, I didn't." He was here at last. I was able to pretend I hadn't been afraid.

With his face creased in an expression that could have been nothing short of frustration, he shoved the box at me. "How am I gonna protect you if you won't listen?"

I turned my back. "I had to clean up."

"You could've waited till morning. I would've helped."

"Didn't need help."

He shook his head. "You're hopeless, you know that?"

"Come into the kitchen," I said. "I'll get us something to drink."

He went into the living room instead, setting the stool back on its legs as he passed it. "How did you fix the window?" he asked.

"I called Fred Silbert."

He stormed into my kitchen, and stood, hands on his hips, glaring at me. "Didn't I tell you not to let anyone in?"

"It was just Fred," I said.

He took me by my shoulders. "Until we catch the guy, you can't trust anyone. You hear me?"

It was hard to be annoyed with a man who worried this much about me. I suppressed a smile, and brushed past him, carrying the pizza to the living room. When I placed it on the coffee table, I said, "Make yourself comfortable. Turn on the TV. There must be a ballgame of some kind on. I'll get plates and be right back."

The next thing I heard was a multitude of voices cheering from my living room. *Someone must have done something good,* I thought.

"The Sabres scored!" he called to me. Or maybe he said it to the television.

When I returned to the living room, I saw Roger on the sofa, his shoes off, his legs stretched out on the coffee table. Elvira was curled up next to him, her mouth turned up in contentment. I circled the table, and settled next to him with my hand on his chest and my head on my hand.

He leaned over, stroked my cheek, and kissed my forehead.

A soft purr floated up from the sofa. It didn't come from the cat.

This is sort of nice, I thought. *I could get used to this.*

And maybe get used to where it might lead?

Chapter Eleven
Sarah's Book of Shadows

After some minutes of prolonged kisses and thoughts about perhaps continuing this upstairs, I pushed away from Roger, and shook my head. "I can't do this," I said. I wanted to go on kissing him. More than kiss him. I couldn't. Damn Kevin for leaving me in this twixt-and-tween state!

Roger understood my struggle. "It's okay," he whispered, and kissed me once more.

I moved to my oversized chair with a slice of pizza and a glass of beer. He again rested his feet on the table.

I have no idea who won the hockey game. The stress of the day caught up with me. With my legs pulled up and my eyes drooping, I nodded off. The next thing I knew, it was morning. I awoke to soft snores instead of to my alarm clock. Roger was stretched out on the sofa under my afghan, with Elvira still curled up next to him.

It took me two tries to sit up. One reason was because my muscles were stiff from sleeping in a chair. The other reason I struggled: I was covered by the rose-colored quilt from my bed. Either I had walked in my sleep, taken the cover and, deciding the chair was a comfortable spot to finish the night, returned downstairs. Or more likely, Roger, bless him, had fetched the quilt so I wouldn't be cold.

At last able to untangle myself, I slogged to the kitchen to put up coffee. Then I stumbled upstairs to the bathroom to brush my teeth—I didn't want to greet my hero with morning breath.

Ten minutes later I was back downstairs, ready to straighten out the living room. When I reached for the pizza box, I froze. On the table, next to Roger's empty beer bottles, was Sarah Goode's book.

My hand went to my mouth. What had I been thinking? Clearly I hadn't been. If I had, I wouldn't have left the book on my desk where he could find it. Damn! It was one thing to tell Roger of my heritage. Detectives demand evidence and I'd given him only words. He'd marked those off to my being scared silly. I had an out. Now he had seen the evidence, and because of his total disbelief in the power of magic, he must have concluded the Goodes, from first to last, were loonies.

While I stood, eyes unfocused, imagining what my life would be like after he drove me to the Buffalo Asylum, I heard his sleepy voice say, "That makes for interesting reading."

I couldn't tell if he was being sarcastic.

Elvira leaped from the sofa, turned, and glared at Roger. It was as if she told him, *Don't you dare say anything derogatory about Sarah!*

I can only imagine the five or six shades of red of my face turned. "It...it's about my family," I stammered.

He sat up, rubbed his eyes. "Quite an ancestor you have."

I waited to see where he would go with this.

He glanced at the front window Fred Silbert repaired. "Plants and hoodoo," he muttered. His head tilted, one brow raised and one eye closed, he added, "You don't really think that stuff will protect you?"

Feeling like a schoolgirl who'd been called to the principal's office, I began to nod but stopped.

As if to say, *Damn right it will!* Elvira finished my nod.

"Come on Emlyn, this isn't a Harry Potter story," Roger said. "And you're not a child."

I pulled at the waistband of my pajamas (I'd been in my PJs yesterday when I ran from my house, and one thing or another, I hadn't gotten dressed since).

He reached for my hand.

I pulled back, grabbed Sarah's book, and held it to my breast.

"You're pouting?" Shaking his head, he laughed. "What am I gonna do with you?"

'Gotta love me', would have been the obvious answer. But at the moment, nothing was obvious. Even if it were, the thought of how nice it might be if he *did* love me, left me mute.

He leaned forward with his hands in his lap. His posture was supposed to convey the idea his next pronouncement would be entirely reasonable. "The only thing that'll keep you safe," he said, "is for us to catch the guy who killed Jimmy."

I finally found my voice. "I agree."

"You do?" He sounded surprised I'd given in so easily. Then, as if struck by the thought my compliance came too easily, his eyes became slits. "What's going on in your mind?"

"I said I agree with you, and I do. The only way I'll be safe is if Jimmy's killer gets caught." I held out Sarah Goode's book. "So, Woody will go about it his way, and I'll go about it mine."

He stood up to his full six foot height. His turtleneck sweater and brown slacks were creased. "Emlyn—"

"Coffee's ready," I said. "I'll get you some."

"Emlyn," he said again, drawing my name out even further.

Still holding the book, I turned on my heels, strode to the kitchen, and poured coffee into two mugs.

"You take milk and three spoons of sugar?" I stirred them into his mug.

For a minute, I stood at the sink, gazing out the window. Another overcast day. Cars crawled through the slush on River Road.

Roger came up behind me so quietly in his stocking feet, I bumped into him and nearly spilled his coffee when I turned around.

"Sit. Drink this while it's hot," I said. I'm sure I sounded far braver than I felt.

When we were both settled at the round dinette table, I said, "I don't know what information Woody's got. Whatever he knows, he's not moving fast enough. Look at what happened yesterday. If it weren't for you, I might be dead now."

"Not really," Roger said. "That Molotov cocktail was so poorly made, you would've stomped the fire out before it did real damage. Still, why give the killer another chance to get you?" He blew the steam from his coffee and sipped it.

"Yesterday I wasn't doing anything and someone tried to kill me. Who's to say the killer won't get me even if I stay locked in my house?"

I mimed throwing a Molotov cocktail through my window. "If I'm gonna get killed, I'd rather it happen while I'm doing something about it."

He peered at me while he formulated a response.

I didn't give him a chance. Pushing the leather-covered book across the dinette table, I said, "That's what Sarah would have done."

He shoved the book away, as if he might be stung by a swarm of hornets if it got too near.

"If you read it, you'll know I'm right."

He put down his mug, and raised his hands in mock surrender. "You're impossible."

I smiled at him. "That depends on your perspective, doesn't it? From where I sit, Sarah's approach seems like my best defense."

He stretched his arm over Sarah's book to take my hand. "If you insist on doing this, I'm going after the killer *my* way."

The big guy had just one-upped me. He'd told me if I used magic, he'd use a gun.

"You can't," I argued. "Woody will have your badge."

"Not if the guy can't talk when Woody finds him."

I stared at Roger. Was he serious? Had I given him an excuse to disobey his boss? My stomach began to churn.

His face broke into a smile.

I let out my breath. He was playing with me.

Making his voice sound like an old-time gangster, he said, "Okay, copper, where you gonna start?"

I stared at him with my mouth open. He *wasn't* playing. He wanted to teach me a lesson and he was right. I hadn't thought further ahead than reading more of Sarah's book to get some ideas. I didn't have time for reading today, though. With a glance at the clock nailed to the soffit over my sink, I pushed back from the table. "I'll figure out where to start later," I said. "I've got to get to Main Street Books. I have a book signing in two hours.

"You're gonna put yourself in the middle of a crowd of strangers?" He sounded shocked. "I know the store."

"You do, huh?"

"Hey, I read." Now he sounded as though I'd insulted him.

Might as well really do it. "Do tell?" I said.

"Yeah. And I even buy books. That's why I don't want you at Main Street Books. Someone hiding behind one of their stacks could pick you off at his leisure."

I hitched up my pajama bottoms. "I promised I'd do the signing."

"And you never break a promise?"

I stuck my chin out. "Never."

He sighed, and rose from the table. His square jaw set, he said, "Let's go then."

"Where?"

"I'm going with you." His tone said he'd brook no argument.

I snapped my waistband. "Think I ought to get dressed first?"

With a toothy grin, his eyes traced my body from my toes to my face. "I don't know. I've kind of gotten used to seeing you this way."

I planted a playful slap on his cheek. "Pig."

He laughed. "Nah. I'm just a guy watching a good-looking dame."

As I climbed the stairs to my bedroom, he called after me, "Might not be a bad idea, you being out there. If the guy kills you, I might catch him. Do that, Woody can't get pissed at me for working the case—I'll tell him you invited me to your book signing."

I hung onto the banister at the top of the stairs, and thought, *Great, I've set myself up to be bait.*

Chapter Twelve
Main Street Books

The book store has been on Main Street for as long as I remember. With an oval window in an old-fashioned door set between green painted pillars, the shop is in the center of a block several miles north of the carnival atmosphere summer brings to the American side of Niagara Falls. Harold Anaison used to own this shop. Everyone called him Uncle Harry. When I was a child, my mother took me to Main Street Books after church most Sundays. That's when Uncle Harry would read about Barbar the Elephant King, Eloise's exploits at the Plaza, and a large cat in a striped hat causing rainy-day mischief. When I was five years-old, those stories transported me to a world of fantasy. By age six, I decided to become a writer. Or, as my agent terms it, a professional liar.

Uncle Harry's grandson, Zack, runs the shop now. At five foot eight, he isn't much taller than I. His hair is prematurely gray, and his face is pale, long, and smooth. I imagine this is what a bookworm must look like. In fact, Bookworm Anaison is what the kids used to call Zack when we were in third grade.

Wearing jeans and a light blue thermal vest, Zack greeted me at the door with a hug (he'd long ago forgiven me for my childhood taunting). He kept up a constant line of chatter about the latest works by Nicholas Sparks, Nora Roberts, and Sue Grafton, while he led us past dusty rows of crowded shelves and tables piled so high with books, a single sneeze would surely have caused them to cascade like the Niagara River over the Falls. Next to me, Roger's head swiveled from side to side. He seemed the image of a man who'd never seen a place such as this.

Halfway between the door and the back of the store, I saw Amy Woodward browsing through discount books on one of the tables. I was surprised to find her there. Though a bright woman—she was valedictorian of her high school class—from what I'd seen of her in recent years, her reading consisted of no more than thumbing through copies of *Woman's Day* while waiting to check out at the supermarket. I smiled, waved to her.

She lifted her head. Her almond-shaped eyes glanced past me, as if looking at someone who'd just come through the door.

"Hi," I called.

At last she waved back. "I, uh…came to hear you read." She pulled a copy of my book from her bag, and held it up.

My smile broadened into a wide grin. While the detective chief's wife was a practiced hostess, she'd never struck me as particularly friendly. But she'd made a point of standing beside me at Jimmy's funeral, and now she was here. *Maybe she's finally warming up*, I thought.

Zack touched my arm. "We oughta get started," he said.

I waived again to Mrs. Woodward. "See you upstairs."

She nodded, and began to leaf through a book she picked up.

So much for her warming up, I thought.

As I came abreast of an aisle between bookshelves, I heard my name whispered. I stopped.

Again I heard a whispered, "Emlyn!"

I peered down the dim aisle to where an overhead light marked a break in the row. A head poked from behind one of the bookcases. Kevin's head. His face was paler than it had been when he sat in my living room the day before yesterday, and he sounded out of breath.

"I'm in trouble, Em. Need your help," he whispered.

"What's the holdup?" Roger said. He put a hand on my shoulder.

"Everything okay?" Zack was now on the other side of me.

"Kevin," I said, and pointed to where I'd seen him.

It took Roger only a second to scoot down the aisle. He soon returned shaking his head. "No one there."

I heard the bell on the shop door tinkle as the door opened then slammed shut. I spun around in time to see my ex's shabby gray overcoat through the window. His head low, Kevin dashed down the street.

Back at my side, Roger asked, "What did he want?"

"I don't know. He said he was in trouble."

My eyes darted from the door to the aisle where Kevin had been. Call it a moment of prescience; call it a remnant of the divination spell I had tried. Whatever the cause, I felt as though Kevin showing up at Main Street Books didn't bode well for me.

Zack's eyes flicked from me to Roger then back again, as if he were trying to figure out what just happened. He tugged at his vest, wiped his hands on the back of his jeans. "Um, folks are waiting for us upstairs," he said.

Roger hung back for a moment. I knew he was trying to decide whether to chase after my ex. Finally, he said, "Yeah, we should get this over with."

Zack gave me a knowing smile. It appeared as though he took Roger's remark as a statement from someone who didn't care much for literature, but was grudgingly here to support me.

At the rear of the shop, we passed through a doorway and climbed a flight of stairs to a meeting room that spanned the length and width of the store. In front of the large windows on the Main Street side of the room, a semi-circle of chairs surrounded a blond-wood table. Copies of my latest short story collection were stacked in two piles on the end of the table. From the doorway, I gazed around, flattered to see what looked to be more than fifty chairs filled.

These are my people, I thought, and my apprehension dwindled. For the moment I was able to shove Kevin from my mind. In fact, I was able to shove everything aside:

Jimmy's murder, the killer I'd envisioned, the attempt to burn my house.

As I strolled to the desk, I noticed Jennifer Ryan and her husband, Sean, in the fourth row. I stopped next to Jen, leaned down, and whispered, "I can't believe you came. How's your mom?"

She gave me a sad smile.

It was Sean who answered. "Marge is doing about as well as you might expect."

When I glanced at him, it struck me how much he resembled the young James Stewart in *After the Thin Man*. It was an early film from before the time Stewart drew top billing, and one of the few times he played the bad guy.

Jennifer twisted her wedding ring. "Mom didn't feel up to leaving the house yet," she said, "but she wanted me..." her eyes turned toward her husband "...uh, us to be here for you."

I noticed a bruise on her wrist. "Jen, you've hurt yourself." I thought back to the bruise I'd seen beneath her eye after her father's funeral.

She glanced at the red mark. "Oh, that—" She shrugged. "I banged it on a counter at Mom's house."

Sean stroked her hair. "That's my wife. Clumsy."

Who did Sean think he was kidding? I looked toward Roger. This wasn't the time to tell him what I suspected. I'd tell him later. I gave Jen's cheek a peck and moved on.

"Thank you all for braving the weather to be here," I said as I slid onto a seat behind the table.

I saw Roger's head turn as he scanned the room, making note of the people who had come to hear me read. I presumed he wanted to decide if anyone appeared poised to commit murder and mayhem. Apparently satisfied there wasn't a mortar or an assault rifle tucked into someone's belt, he settled on a chair near the door.

When I lifted the top book from the pile and opened it, I couldn't help but smile. *So this is what having a personal bodyguard feels like,* I thought.

I read aloud for almost forty-five minutes, pausing only to moisten my vocal chords from the bottle of water Zach had left on the table for me. I didn't close the book until I reached the point where one more word would have caused me to squawk like the Canada geese that make a rest stop in my yard on their way to and from wherever it is they roost for the winter. Then, a smile painted across my face, I began to sign my name and write a few personalized words on the front plates of books the audience carried to the table.

"Thanks for coming, Gwen," I said, handing a book back.

"What's her name?" I asked a second woman who told me her daughter was a fan.

Jennifer was next. At her side, Sean held tight to her arm, as if he were afraid she might go into a swoon if he released her.

I glanced again at Roger then wrote, *I know what he's doing to you,* in her book. Then I leaned over the table, and gave her another kiss.

When they turned to leave, I came face-to-face with a wonderful surprise. Rebecca Nurse stood next in line. Sean was so tall I hadn't seen her behind him.

As usual, my friend wore no makeup. She had on her standard uniform: a ribbed turtleneck over loose pants with a floral design, and a maroon knit sweater vest which hung to her knees. Her waist-length salt and pepper curls were pulled back in a tight braid. The design on her very large shoulder bag matched her pants.

"What are you doing here?" I said, beaming.

She leaned over the table and patted my hand. "Had to come to make sure you'd behave yourself."

I laughed. "How am I doing?"

She looked over her shoulder to where Roger stood with his hands clasped in front. "So far, so good," she said.

I was in my element. All was right with the world. I sat back, grinning, and gave myself a metaphoric pat on the head.

Then all hell broke loose.

A window to my right shattered. Splinters of glass rained onto my shoulders, the desk, the floor. Smoke billowed from a viscous blob spreading next to the desk. Something hissed. There was a spark, a flash. The black blob flared. The flame raced along the floor, under the desk. In a moment it was at my feet, on the hem of my pants. People ran for the door and got jammed in it as they shoved each other aside in a frenzy to reach the staircase. Somebody screamed—it might have been me, though I'm not sure about that.

The next thing I knew, I lay on the floor near the far wall. Roger was on top of me, his eyes flashing around the large room. Rebecca knelt next to him and slapped at my pants leg. "She's lucky," she said. "None of the glass shards cut her."

I moved my eyes from side-to-side, searching for who Rebecca referred to. I raised my head. Zack Anaison stood in the center of the room. A fire extinguisher in his hands, he sprayed foam in every direction.

My eyes turned to Roger. I truly wish I could have uttered a line a Nobel Laureate might have written, or at least a wise-ass remark such as, *We have to stop meeting this way.* But my eyes stung from the smoke and my right leg felt as though it were on fire. All I could think to say—rasp, actually—was the mundane, "What happened?"

Then the initial shock wore off. The pain in my leg flared. I cried out, broke into a whimper.

Roger gave me the briefest of hugs and rose to his knees. "You'll be okay. I'll get you the hospital."

He gazed at Rebecca who stood arms akimbo, with a stern look on her face.

"*We'll* get you to the hospital," she corrected him.

I was too stunned and in too much pain to react to the byplay between my friends. "What happened?" I asked again.

"Another firebomb," Roger said. He lifted me from the floor. "Whoever's doing this built it right this time. Nearly got you. Maybe now you'll listen to me."

Strange things run through one's mind at such a moment. Tears dripping like large raindrops down my cheeks, I said. "My book, did I sign everyone's copy?"

Roger laughed. "Yeah, every damn one of 'em."

He hefted me in his arms and hugged me to his chest. Rebecca running interference ahead of us, he carried me to his Trailblazer.

***

St. Mary's Medical Center has grown over the years. Now it's a campus consisting of brick buildings that sprawl over several acres a few miles from a bridge linking the United States to Canada.

I have no idea how we got there so quickly, though I later learned Roger drove like a maniac. I do recall, at one point he yelled at a car in front of us, "Wasn't that I'd get arrested, I'd blow you the hell off the road!"

I lay on Rebecca's lap in the back seat, still in a red world of pain. She wiped my tears with one hand, while she rubbed something on my leg with her other. All the while she whispered a chant I didn't recognize. Whatever she rubbed on the burn helped. By the time we pulled into a parking spot near the doors to the emergency room, my leg had almost stopped screaming. Bless Rebecca and her balm. If panic hadn't sapped my strength, I would have leaned forward and told Roger to never again deny the healing effect of Sarah Goode's herb mixtures and chants.

The Trailblazer slammed to a stop. Roger dropped his police tag where it could be seen through the windshield, then jumped out. He reached into the back seat, lifted me.

"I can walk," I mumbled, and tried to push his hands away.

Rebecca leaned close. "Let him do this."

"Are you a matchmaker now?" I asked.

She laughed. "No, only a friend."

As if my body weighed no more than a helium-filled balloon, Roger hoisted me in his arms and took off at a run. He seemed to glide across the icy pavement like a skater. Rebecca ran at his side, my handbag and the blackened remnant of the shoe that had been on my burned right foot in her hands. Once inside the hospital, Roger gently lowered me into a chair. While Rebecca sat next to me, holding my hand, he flashed his badge at people who were queued up to speak to the nurse behind the registry desk.

"Official business," he said as he cut to the front of the line. "Got a burn victim over there."

The nurse examined the badge, then Roger's face. She must have seen urgency in his eyes, because she dispensed with the normal questions about my medical insurance. Lifting the telephone on her desk, she called into it, "We need a gurney out here, stat!"

Seconds later, I was on a cart, headed for a swinging door.

While he trotted beside it, Roger told Rebecca, "Wait here."

She latched onto the back of the gurney. "Not a chance."

What occurred next was a blur of motion, mostly in white, green, and orange. Four hands lifted me onto a hard bed inside a curtained enclosure. A nurse slit my pants leg up to my thigh. A doctor pulled aside the curtain. Standing beside the nurse, he examined the burns on my foot and leg. I leaned up on my elbows to watch. My skin looked like crisp bacon.

"What caused this burn?" the doctor asked.

Roger answered for me. "Some kind of gel. Won't know what it is till I get it to the lab."

The doctor nodded. To me he said, "Are you in much pain?"

Strangely, I wasn't. I looked at Rebecca. Her expression was blank.

"Seems as though someone started treatment," the doctor said.

Roger turned to Rebecca.

"I rubbed her leg with oil made of sandalwood, carnation petals, and rosemary," she said.

"You had that with you?" Roger asked.

She peered through the curtains at people in green scrubs who rushed back and forth. "Never know when it might be needed."

Still on my elbows, I stared at her back. If I could see her face, I'm pretty sure there would have been a sly grin on it.

The doctor scraped some of the burned skin from my leg. "That hurt?" he asked.

I cringed.

He shook his head. I guess he thought I should have screamed in pain. He pulled a pointed instrument from his breast pocket, ran it along the sole of my foot.

The muscle contracted. I giggled.

Again the doctor shook his head. He glanced at Roger. "When did you say this occurred?"

"No more than half an hour ago."

The doctor's eyes narrowed. "You're sure? A victim doesn't always get the timeframe right."

"I was there when the fire started," Roger said. He didn't seem inclined to explain someone had tried to firebomb me twice in two days.

The doctor rubbed his chin. "Don't understand why she isn't in severe pain," he said to the nurse. "Probably shock." To me, he said, "In an hour or two the shock will abate and you might be in considerable pain."

The nurse handed him a hypodermic and a small vial. He drew the liquid in, tapped the needle. "This will help fight infection—"

"Won't be any," I heard Rebecca whisper.

"—and I'll write you a scrip for some pain meds. Meantime, we'll get that leg bandaged. Make an appointment for your primary to take a look at it in a few days."

That said, the doctor smiled at me, pulled the curtain aside, and was off to his next patient. His puzzlement over why I suffered so little pain had apparently been forgotten.

**

In less than two hours we were in Roger's car, driving to Niagara Falls at a saner rate of speed. The crutches the nurse had given me were on the floor beneath my feet. We dropped Rebecca off where her ten-year-old Saturn Ion was parked behind a couple of squad cars outside Main Street Books. When she opened the door, I tried to climb out after her.

"Where do you think you're going?" Roger asked.

"I've got to speak to Zack Anaison," I said. "I want to find out how much damage was done to his meeting room." I felt guilty about his store being hurt in an attack on me.

"You don't have to talk to him now," Roger said.

"I do," I argued. "I feel just awful about it."

He heaved a Lord-give-me-patience sigh. "Stay where you are. I'll talk to him."

He slid from the Trailblazer, said a few words to the cop standing guard at the door, and disappeared inside. Ten minutes later he returned, followed by Zack, who told me not to fret over the damage. It was minor, he said. Some sanding and stain, it would look good as new. Better even, since the room had "nary a moment's work done to it in 'bout fifty years" (Bookworm Anaison tended to talk like a character in a Zane Gray story).

"Satisfied now?" Roger said to me as he started the car.

I leaned toward the window, and glanced around. Rebecca had already left. Without saying goodbye? I hoped she wasn't angry with me. Of course, I hadn't done anything to her. But that's the way guilt affects a person. Having crept in, I felt as though I were to blame for everything since Eve handed Adam a wormy apple.

I also felt as though Roger must be angry at me, because he didn't say a word all the way from Main Street Books until he turned into my driveway. It was then I knew Rebecca, at least, wasn't angry. She had parked in a cleared spot near my garage and was leaning on the hood of her car.

I soon learned Roger wasn't angry, either. As he lifted me from the back seat, he said, "I'll take you inside, help you pack a few things. Then you'll stay at my house till we catch the bastard who's doing this to you."

I pulled my front door key from my bag.

Rebecca took the key from my hand. With a sideways glance at Roger, she said, "Emlyn can stay at home where she'll be comfortable. I'll stay with her, make sure she's all right."

I had spent so much time with Roger lately, I was able to translate the language of his sighs. This one said, *Great, now I have two of you to worry about.*

Chapter Thirteen
Reasons to Kill

Rebecca hung her coat as well as Roger's in the hall closet, and carried her ten gallon-sized floral shoulder bag into the kitchen.

Roger carried me into my living room (I have to admit I was getting happily used to this), and helped me get settled on the sofa. He tucked a couple of cushions under my leg.

"Doctor said you should keep this raised," he told me.

All the while, as if demanding, *What did you do her!* Elvira glared at him from beneath my desk.

He took the afghan from where I had folded it over the arm of my wingback chair. As he straightened the cover, he stopped and stared at the runes my grandmother sewed into it. "I saw these in that book of yours," he said. "What are they?"

Observant man, he didn't miss a thing and what he saw he remembered.

I had researched those symbols online. Though most remained a mystery I hoped to decipher someday, I did manage to find a few. "This one's for protection," I said. "And this symbolizes the wisdom to use the plants growing all around us."

"Only for good, I hope," Roger said. "I don't want to have to arrest you for poisoning someone."

I smiled at him, and pointed to the protection rune. "If I ever do, I'll use this to make sure you never find out."

He let out a booming laugh. "Wonderful, I live next door to a potential mass murderer." All at once, his face grew serious. "Best thing is to stay very close so I can keep an eye on you. Maybe we ought to—"

Before he carried the idea where he seemed to want to take it, from the kitchen, Rebecca called, "Can I get anyone something while I'm in here?"

The moment was lost.

"I'm good," I called back.

"A beer would be nice," Roger said.

He parked himself in my wingback chair next to the bookcases and beneath the railroad station clock. He began to thumb through the television section of the *Buffalo News*. After a minute, he grunted, "Daytime television." He tossed the TV section onto the coffee table. "If I had nothing to do all day but watch soap operas, I might stick a gun in my mouth."

I smiled at him. "Beer's on the bottom shelf of the fridge," I called to Rebecca. "Better get this guy one quick. He's about to go off the deep end."

In a few moments, she handed him a bottle, a glass, and a coaster.

He placed the coaster on the lamp table and the beer on top of it. Then he looked at the glass as if he had no idea what it might be for.

Rebecca solved his dilemma when she said, "That thing in your hand? The beer goes in it."

"Guys," I said, and shrugged.

Elvira shimmied from under my desk and jumped onto Roger's lap. Her head swiveling from the beer to him, she licked her lips.

"Untamed animals, both of them," Rebecca remarked.

She relieved Roger of the unwanted glass and returned to the kitchen. I heard cabinets open and close, then a couple drawers. Finally I heard the teapot whistle. In a minute she was back, carrying a mug of tea. This she handed to me.

"Don't want tea," I said.

"It's herbal. Drink it," she insisted. "It'll help the healing process."

For a moment, Roger stared at her with the same expression he had shown me when I told him about Sarah Goode. Then, with a shake of his head, he picked up the newspaper and turned to the sports section.

Perched on his lap, Elvira seemed to read along with him. My friend and my cat had apparently formed a bond.

"By the way," Rebecca said, "the message light is blinking on your phone.

"Oh?"

"Don't you want to know who it is? Might be important," Roger said without looking up from the paper.

With my mind filled by the memory of how my foot and leg had gotten burned, I wasn't much interested in who might have phoned.

"Ought to find out," Rebecca said. Without an invitation to do so, she pushed the *Message* button.

Immediately, a thin version of Marge Osborn's voice spoke from the small speaker.

"Emlyn, are you home yet?" she said. "If you are, pick up." She sounded frantic. "Jen told me what happened at the book store. Are you okay? Emmy, I'm worried about you. I hope this has nothing to do with you asking questions about my husband's death. The way you almost interrogated us the other day—who else are you questioning? Don't deny you're doing it, I know you too well. You can't help yourself. Probably want to turn it into one of your stories. Anyhow, I'd feel just awful if another person got hurt. Call me. Let me know you're okay. And promise me you'll stop snooping—I don't want you get hurt worse. Okay?"

Roger and Rebecca looked at me.

"It's not snooping," I said. "It's research."

Roger snickered. "Oh, is that what they call it these days?"

I had the good grace to blush.

124

"Well, then," Rebecca said, "go ahead, research." She held out the telephone receiver. "What's her number?"

I rolled onto my side, trying to find a position in which my leg might not sting. "Later," I said. "I don't much feel like talking right now."

We sat quietly for a while, Roger reading the sports section, Rebecca gazing through the slatted blinds on the French doors. Then, as if she realized something, her eyes scrunched.

I followed her glance to Sarah Goode's book at the edge of the coffee table. I hadn't put it away when I left the house earlier. I hadn't expected company and there was no longer a point in hiding it from Roger.

Rebecca's eyebrows crimped up as she asked a silent question.

"It's okay, he read it," I told her.

"Did he?" She peeked at Roger.

"He found it when he stayed over last night."

From the way her eyes glittered, I suspected my friend believed he had done more than just sleep on my couch. With Roger in the room, I didn't want to tell how close I'd come to letting him do *much* more. In fact, I didn't want to remind myself.

"I still don't believe in that mumbo-jumbo stuff," Roger said. He didn't raise his eyes from the *News*.

The sun had set. I looked at my watch. It was almost seven-thirty.

As if he were keeping a weather-eye on my every movement, Roger looked up and smiled.

"Sorry," I said. "Stomach's grumbling."

It was no wonder. I hadn't eaten all day. The doctor had been right when he said the shock I'd suffered would wear off in a few hours. My body had returned to normal. I was hungry. Here's the funny part, though: while my foot and leg still hurt, I didn't feel the agonizing pain the doctor had warned me to expect. Rebecca's herbal remedy actually worked. If I harbored any doubts about the effectiveness of Sarah Goode's herbal mixtures—or Rebecca's, for that matter—they were gone.

Roger broke into my thoughts when he announced, "I'm starving. How about if I order some Chinese takeout?"

"I'm in," I said.

"Me too," Rebecca said. "Order me General Tsao's Chicken."

As he tilted in the chair to pull his cell phone from his pants pocket, Roger said, "I thought all you witches were vegetarians."

"I'm not the witch," Rebecca said and smiled at him. "That's your buddy's job."

I lifted the cover to look at my bandaged leg. "Seems I'm not very good at the job yet."

Roger rolled his eyes.

***

I leaned heavily on my crutches when I hobbled to the kitchen table. Rebecca and Roger wanted me to stay off my feet, so they bickered a bit about which of them would pull out the dishes and flatware. Normally, I'm a purist where Chinese food is concerned, by which I mean I insist on using chopsticks. Not this night, though. I was so hungry, even a fork couldn't shovel the food into my mouth fast enough.

It seemed as though Elvira couldn't eat fast enough, either. Her rear end wiggled as she gulped the Cat Chow from her bowl.

While we ate, the conversation turned to Jimmy Osborn's death. As I recall, I led it there. I hoped if I learned the facts the police knew about the murder, with Rebecca's help I might put an end to the insanity before the rest of my body got fried.

"In my experience," Roger said, "the motive for most murders comes down to one thing: passion. Love, hate, a lust for money. Look behind the violence, you'll find love, hate, or greed."

"Where does Jimmy fit into that picture?" I asked.

"Ah, the Final Jeopardy question."

"Can't see behind your neighbor's Venetian blinds," I said.

Rebecca put down her fork and dabbed her napkin at her lips. "Not in the usual way." She rose from the table. "More tea, anyone?"

I lifted my cup.

Roger covered his cup with his hand. "At this point, I'd even take a hint from what your voodoo chants turn up."

"What does Woody think?" I asked. To Rebecca, I explained, "That's Harry Woodward, Roger's boss."

She nodded.

Elvira glanced up then returned to her meal.

Running a hand through his brown locks, Roger said, "I expected Woody to be all over this, a real hound dog. After all, one of his men got killed."

"He isn't?" Rebecca asked.

"Doesn't seem to be. It isn't only me he won't let work the case, it's all the guys. He says we're all too close to it." Roger rubbed his chin. "It's like he suspects one of us did it."

"Is that possible?" I asked.

"I know I didn't. The others? No matter how I try, I can't see a motive."

"Eight bullets in the chest," I said. "Someone really had it in for Jimmy."

"His wife?" Rebecca asked. I supposed she was thinking about the message Marge left on my phone, and believed it sounded like a warning. She didn't know Marge. The girl I grew up with got queasy when aliens were zapped in sci-fi movies.

Before I could disabuse her of the idea, Roger said, "Nah, I don't see it. Jimmy was crazy about her. Told me he was saving up to take a trip to Mexico. A second honeymoon, he said."

"So that leaves?" I asked.

"I'm stumped." Roger admitted. "If Woody's working the case, he's doing it alone and keeping everything very close to the vest. He got a call yesterday and went out for about an hour. That gave me a chance to sneak a peek at his file. Practically nothing in it."

Again, Elvira's head came up from her bowl. She was actually listening to us.

Surprised at the direction this had taken, I said, "You don't think Woody might have—?" I couldn't finish my sentence. From all I knew about him, Harry Woodward walked a line so straight it could be used as a yardstick. Still, sometimes yardsticks got broken.

Roger thought for a moment. "I wonder," he said at last. "He's certainly acting strange."

At the mention of strange behavior, I thought of my ex. *His* behavior was certainly stranger than usual. "How about Kevin?" I said. No need to explain to Rebecca who he was, she'd helped me damage his life. "The firebombs began just after he was here. Oh, and he was also at the book store just before—"

"I haven't forgotten," Roger said.

"And when I think about it, he used to read about the Russian revolution—that's when those Molotov cocktails were used."

"You're forgetting something," Roger said.

"What?"

"Your husband—"

"Her ex-husband," Rebecca corrected him.

"Okay, then, her ex-husband. He didn't know Jimmy. Why would he want to kill him?"

As if she wanted to participate in the conversation, Elvira jumped onto my lap. She shoved my plate aside and rested her head on her paws. With her pink eyes focused on Roger, she *meowed.*

"I agree," Rebecca said.

"With me?" Roger asked.

"No, with Elvira. Are you sure Kevin didn't know your partner?"

"That's right," I said. "He told me he was in big trouble. Oh, and he stopped by the Osborns' house looking for Jimmy. Could Jimmy have been investigating him?"

"Can't be. I'd have known if he was. My partner wasn't a cowboy. He played everything by the book."

"So that leaves us with…what?"

"Harry Woodward," Rebecca and Roger said in unison.

"I don't like it," Roger added. "No, I don't like it at all. But as Sherlock Holmes used to say, when you eliminate everything possible, whatever's left, regardless of how improbable, has to be the answer."

Elvira's head came up and she nodded.

I didn't bother to remind Roger and the cat it was Arthur Conan Doyle who put those words in his detective's mouth.

We fell silent, each of us pushing food around our plate.

While I wondered what could possibly have turned Harry Woodward's white hat black, a heavy fist rapped on my front door. After the last two days, I was so startled I nearly knocked over my chair when I jumped up.

The hazel of Roger's eyes turned dark. "Stay where you are!"

Rebecca gasped at his tone—a sound approximating air rapidly escaping a balloon.

As if he expected me to argue, he turned in my direction with his face so stiff his cheekbones might soon poke through the skin. He needn't have worried. A flash of pain shooting from my leg to my brain caused me to fall back on my chair.

Roger dropped his hand to the service pistol on his waistband as he went to the door. "Yeah?" he said in his roughest tone. "Who is it?"

I've never understood why this is: as soon as you speak about somebody, he shows up.

"Detective Frey, open the damn door!" Chief Woodward growled.

I heard the door open. A second later, a scowling Harry Woodward stomped into my kitchen.

When Roger followed him, he turned abruptly. His words clipped, he demanded, "Have I not made myself crystal clear?"

Roger's face turning crimson—from embarrassment at being scolded in front of us or from anger, I couldn't decide—he said, "About what?"

Woody pushed close to Roger's face. In a menacing tone, he said, "You know damn well, what. But in case you don't, I'll be clearer. I don't want you within twenty miles of the Osborn case."

Ready to ask in the nastiest way what Chief Woodward was doing to stop the killer from firebombing my life, I opened my mouth.

Roger must have sensed my anger. His eyes locked on his boss, he held up a hand. "What makes you think I'm working the case?"

"You were at Main Street Books this afternoon."

"Yeah, so?"

Breathing hard, Woody glared at him.

A high-pitched snarl rose from Elvira's throat.

I couldn't stand this any more than the cat could. "He was there because I had a book signing. I asked him to come."

Still glaring at Roger, Woody said, "And why would you do that?"

"First, because he's my friend. And second, because I was frightened. Someone's trying to kill me!"

"It's a good thing he was there," Rebecca added. "If he hadn't been, right now you'd be viewing her body in the morgue."

If she thought her words might deflate Chief Harry Woodward, she was wrong. The former marine colonel wasn't about to have his flame doused by the ice water in her voice.

"I've got men watching Ms. Goode," he said.

"Who? It sure as hell isn't our men."

"Never you mind, who."

"They're not doing a very good job of it," Rebecca said.

Now I jumped in. "You don't want Roger working Jimmy's murder and now you don't want him looking out for me? Obviously the two cases are connected." Tears of fear burning my eyes, I started to cry. "Dammit, Woody, whatever you're doing isn't enough!"

"If you're really doing anything," Roger said.

The detective chief's face turned as crimson as Roger's. "What's that supposed to mean?"

"No one's working the case but you and you're parked in your office most of the time. It isn't just me who's noticed. All the guys in the squad room are talking about it."

I rose unsteadily from my chair and leaned on my crutches. I hardly noticed the way the fabric of my slacks flapped where the nurse had cut the pants leg up to my thigh. My fear tempered the pain once again weakening my leg. "Kevin Reinhart was at my book signing today," I said. "So was Amy. If the place had gone up in flames, she also would've been killed. Don't you even care about your wife?"

Elvira was at our feet. She stared up as if she expected what happened next.

The chief closed his eyes, took a deep breath, and held it. Perhaps the florescent light caused an illusion, but his face seemed to go pale. "My...wife was there?"

The argument ended as quickly as it began. In two strides Woody was out of my kitchen, headed for the front door. As he opened it, he stopped and turned back. His face again red, he said, "Don't make me tell you again, Detective Frey, to stay away from this case. And as for you, Ms. Goode, I haven't figured out yet where you fit in this, but you better believe I sure as hell will!" His tone bristled like his close-cropped gray hair.

We stood in stunned silence as the door slammed, and Woody's car roared out of my driveway.

When the engine sound faded, Rebecca asked, "What just happened?" She said it so softly, she might have feared Chief Woodward would hear and return to continue bellowing at us.

Roger was rapidly blinking. "Damned if I know," he murmured.

Rebecca glanced at our food as if she had no idea what it was or how it had gotten on my dinette table.

None of us was hungry any longer.

I rubbed my hands up and down my slacks, and said, "I'll clean up."

"No, get off that leg," Rebecca said, "I'll take care of it."

Neither of us moved.

After what felt as if it were five minutes, Roger broke free from wherever his thoughts had taken him. "He's protecting Amy," he said.

"From what?" I asked.

"That's what I'm gonna find out."

I grabbed his arm. "Don't!" I said, suddenly more worried about him than about me. "Woody will bounce you off the force."

He patted my hand. The chill in his eyes said I wasn't going to dissuade him.

"Be careful. Please," I said.

Instead of assuring me he would, as he threw on his coat, he said to Rebecca, "I don't think anything else will happen tonight, but keep the door locked."

"Wait a minute," I said, and hobbled on my crutches to the living room where I pulled my keys from my purse. With a little effort, I unhooked the front door key from the others and held it out. "Take this."

For the first time since Harry Woodward broke in on us, Roger smiled. "Is this an offer to exchange keys?"

At another time I might have laughed or blushed. Right then I didn't do either.

Chapter Fourteen
Unintended Consequences

I was again stretched out on the sofa. The pain that had settled into a dull ache in my right foot and leg had flared again when Harry Woodward burst in on us. In the time since Roger left, Rebecca applied more of the sandalwood, carnation, and rosemary oil she carried in her shoulder bag. I wondered whether she always had this ointment with her, or if she might have played around with candles and chants, and learned I would need it. Whatever the answer, I was glad she had the stuff.

Magically, the pain is almost gone, I thought as the sting of my injury subsided into dull throbs.

Not so long ago, I would have said my pain was gone *as if* by magic, but not anymore. In the past few months, I'd learned there really is more in heaven and on earth than Hamlet's pal, Horatio, dreamed of in his wildest imaginings.

"Feeling better?" Rebecca asked as she settled into the wingback chair.

A sleepy smile on my face, I said, "Like my leg never got burned. That oil you concocted is better than aspirin."

A chuckle came from deep in her chest.

"You really must teach me how to make that ointment. Think it would work for a headache?"

"Don't get carried away," she said. "I have no idea what would happen if you drink it. Might turn you into a spider." She glanced at the albino cat splayed across my chest. "Or maybe turn you into one of those."

Elvira's head shot up. She glared at Rebecca.

I pushed the furry head down and assured her, "That's not an insult, cat. Nothing's wrong with the life you have."

As if to demonstrate how right I was, Elvira rubbed her face with her paws. Then, stretching, she yawned, smacked her lips, and closed her eyes.

"Being a cat's all right if you've found the person you're supposed to be with." Rebecca's eyes rolled to the left. Tilting her head in the direction of the door through which Roger had left, she added, "Speaking of which…"

"Uh-uh, don't get any ideas," I said. "The Osborns once tried to set me and Roger up. It didn't take."

"What happened?"

I shoved my body up against the cushions and lifted the hair from my neck. "Nothing. He wasn't ready. I wasn't ready."

"Looks to me like he's ready now."

"What do you mean?"

As if she wondered how I could be so dense, Rebecca sighed. "Oh, come on, Emlyn. Think about the way he fusses over you."

I sat up and looked at her through eyes not much wider than slits. "Maybe *I'm* still not ready."

A smug smile grew on her face. "In that case," she said, "you'd better not turn into a cat. So instead of drinking my oil, how about some wine?"

"Ummm. That's a much better idea." I pointed to the étagère creating a visual break where my living room became a dining area. "Bottom doors. Glasses are on the shelf above."

She stooped and pulled a bottle from the wine rack. "How about this merlot?"

When she held the bottle up, I saw the label. My eyes shot open wide and my breath caught in my throat. The relaxed, sleepy feeling that came with the abatement of pain was gone.

"Something wrong?" Rebecca asked. "Is this a special wine you're saving?"

I shook my head so hard it startled Elvira. With a screech, she toppled from my chest to the floor.

The label depicted green vines growing across a black background and had embossed gold letters. The wine came from Varney Estates, a local vineyard. The same label had been on the bottle someone chucked through my window. Probably also on the bottle that smashed into Main Street Books' meeting room, though I wasn't sure. From the shock and pain I'd suffered, I was too far out of it to notice. I didn't even know if Zack Anaison held onto the bottle and gave it to the cops when they arrived.

"Roger brought me this wine," I said, barely able to get the words out. "It was one of three Varney Estates bottles in the basket the Woodwards gave him for Christmas last year."

"You don't think he—" She couldn't get any more words out.

"I...I don't know what to think."

I knew how I *felt*, though. Betrayed. I wanted to crawl into bed and pull my quilt over my head. Jimmy was Roger's partner. If Jimmy was into something dirty, they would have been in it together. Comrades-in-arms. Best friends. But why would have Roger murdered his friend? I shuddered and thought, *Greed, of course, or jealousy—the oldest of motives. Cain killed Abel because of it.*

Yes, jealousy. Jimmy had a perfect marriage, while Roger's had fallen apart. And the way Jimmy was killed had been cold and professional. That's just how Detective Roger Frey would have done it. Then he would have come after me because I told him what I suspected while I spoke with Marge Osborn. Yet, now he was acting like my bodyguard. Why? I dropped back against the cushions. *Because he wants to find out whether I really know anything*, I thought.

My eyes now completely wet, I groaned, "It could have been Roger."

Rebecca carried the bottle to the sofa and sat beside me. "Don't be so fast in jumping to conclusions."

I looked at the front door. As if I saw my neighbor, my friend, standing there, my eyes clouded with tears.

"I can't believe Roger would do this to you," Rebecca said.

I couldn't believe it, either. Still... I sat up again. Staring at the green and black label, I rolled the bottle in my hands,

"Think this out." She took the bottle from me and placed it on the end table behind her.

I craned my neck. I couldn't peel my eyes away from the label. I couldn't yank my thoughts from what I now feared it represented. I began to shake.

Rebecca took my hands and held tight to them. "Anyone could have this wine. You said it's from a local vineyard."

Had I said that aloud or only thought it? At the moment I wasn't sure. All at once, suspicion of Rebecca overrode my suspicion of Roger. I'd bought a bottle of this merlot for her and gave it to her one day when I visited her at The Black Cat. I peered into her eyes searching for any small sign of deception, any clue I might have a murderer in my house.

That a murderer held my hands.

Rebecca could easily have done it. I'd spoken about Jimmy and Roger to her, described them in detail. Her eyes clouded over when I talked about Jimmy Osborn: handsome, brave (Roger told me in Iraq, Jim had crawled through raking gunfire to pull him from a burning Humvee), beard and hair always well groomed. Maybe Jimmy's marriage wasn't as good as everyone thought. Maybe Rebecca decided she wanted him, had an affair, then Jimmy broke it off. The glee with which she'd helped me construct the hex I threw at Kevin—yes, I was sure Rebecca could be perfectly capable of killing a man who threw her over.

I shuddered, pulled away from her, and leaned back as far as I could get. Not far enough. She had me trapped.

As if she didn't recognize it was her I now feared, the murderer who sat next to me on my sofa continued in a reasonable tone. "Where was Roger when the first bottle was thrown?"

My mind raced. I didn't dare let her read my thoughts. God knows what else she might have in her shoulder bag. "He...he was with me in his house," I said.

"And the second time?" She again took my hands.

"We were together at the book shop."

"See how much better you feel once you've thought it through?"

Yes, think it through. Think, Emlyn, think. Can't run past her, not on this bandaged leg. Can't grab the wine bottle and beat her with it, she moved it out of reach. Oh, she's smart. I glanced at Sarah Goode's book on the coffee table. *Maybe I can smack her with the book. Stun her long enough to get out the back door—*

Just as I leaned over to grab Sarah's book, my fear-frozen brain thawed. I caught my breath. "You...you were also in the room with me at Main Street Books when the second bottle crashed through the window."

My head dropped. I was too embarrassed to look at Rebecca.

She sat up straight. "You didn't think—me?"

I blinked back tears of guilt. How could I have suspected her for even a minute? She must hate me now. Having broken free of scenarios in which Rebecca's oil was actually poison, an ointment concocted to cause my certain and painful death, my imagination spun a different scene:

How could you suspect me? she would say. *I've been your friend. I've shared your secret. How dare you. I drove fifty miles on treacherous icy roads because I saw you'd need me. Would someone who wanted you dead do that? I can't believe even for a minute you'd think of me as a threat.*

138

Yes, she would surely say those words as she grabbed her bag and coat, and, not bothering to put it on, slammed out the door. I would hear her shout from outside, *Don't speak to me again! Ever!*

I would be alone then, unprotected, when Jimmy's killer came for me.

Tears dripped down my cheeks.

Rebecca stared at me. After a few seconds, she dropped my hands, leaned back into the cushion at the far end of the sofa, and laughed. In fact, holding her stomach, she laughed so hard and long, *she* now had tears in her eyes.

When she at last caught her breath, she said, "I've been accused of being a lot of things in this life—a gypsy thief, a charlatan, an adulterer—but a murderer?"

Still laughing, she yanked the cork from the bottle and poured red wine into two glasses. When she handed me one, she said, "Drink this, it'll settle your nerves."

I instantly obeyed, downing half of what was in my wineglass in a single gulp.

"You poor girl," she said, and moved to the wingback chair. "You put on a brave front, but you're terrified."

I conjured up a number of clever things I might say in response, but they all fell flat when I rehearsed them in my mind. In the end, all I could do was nod.

Elvira jumped onto the couch and snuggled under my arm.

"The cat really understands you," Rebecca said.

***

Most of the wine was gone from the bottle when we heard my front door open.

Roger stood in the doorway for a minute, his eyes swinging around my house.

"Close the door," I called, "you're letting all the warm air escape."

He glanced from me to Rebecca. "What are you two laughing about?"

He pulled off his overcoat, draped it across one of the kitchen chairs, and joined us in the living room. Smiling, he lifted my legs, dropped onto the sofa, and rested my feet on his lap. His slacks were icy cold. So were his hands. When he rubbed my legs, it sent a chill through me. At least, I *thought* the cold of his hands caused my chill.

"Pour me some of what you're drinking—if you lushes haven't finished it all."

"You're in a good mood," I said. Actually, I probably slurred the words.

"I am," he responded, but offered nothing more.

Rebecca handed him a glass with what was left of the merlot. "You gonna make us drag it out of you?"

He grinned at her. "This wine is rather good, where'd you get it?"

Harrumph. It was one thing when I teased him the way I did when Sarah Goode's book arrived. His teasing me this way was another thing altogether. I smacked his arm. "Don't be coy. You obviously learned something. What is it?"

"I'm rather good at what I do, you know?"

Again I hit him. "I could learn to hate you."

He rubbed his arm. "You've got quite a punch, lady."

"Want another one?"

Elvira sat up. The *meeeow* she gave Roger might have said, *Don't start with her, she'll bruise you.*

"Okay, okay," he said. "Don't hit me again."

"Then I suggest you start talking."

He took a swallow of his wine. "I caught up with Woody in the lot behind the precinct. He didn't know I was there—probably won't find out until the two guys watching your house report in."

I gasped. "I'm being watched?" I'd been so angry, it hadn't registered when Chief Woodward told us that. Now it finally did, and my sense of dread returned. Fearful, relaxed, fearful: my emotions bounced around on a pogo stick.

"Don't go all 'Bates Motel' on me," he said. "Yeah, there's an unmarked car just down the block."

If my eyes went any wider they would have popped from my skull, rolled along the floor, and hidden under the skirt of my wingback chair.

"Hey, don't panic. These aren't the bad guys."

"But...but Chief Woodward...he...you said he won't let anyone work the case."

"He won't," Roger said. "The guys in the car aren't ours. They're Feds—DEA most likely."

"DEA?" Rebecca and I rasped in harmony.

What was going on here? Someone emptied a clip into Jimmy Osborn's chest in a dark alley, then that someone tried to fry me like a rasher of bacon—I had no doubt the two were connected—and now the DEA thought I had a stash of drugs in my house? How did I get in the middle of this mess? All I'd done was try out a simple divination rite. *Don't fool around with anything you read in Sarah Goode's book*, Rebecca had warned me. Was that only two days ago? Her words now slammed around in my brain like Thor was in there swinging his hammer. She was right: the spell I'd played with had unintended consequences. Not the kind of socio-economic consequences Robert K. Merton wrote about in 1936 (I'd learned about him years ago while researching a story), but still rife with potential disaster.

I grabbed my head. I hoped Rebecca had a remedy in her bag for the sharp pain shooting all the way to my toes.

"Hey, take it easy," Roger said. He swiveled to Rebecca. "Get her something, would you?"

With a deep what-am-I-gonna-do-with-her sigh, she rose. Instead of going to the kitchen to grab a remedy from her shoulder bag, she pulled a bottle of Johnny Walker from the bottom cabinet of my étagère.

While she poured us both a neat glassful, Roger explained, "They're not after *you*. It's Kevin they want. They figure if he's so anxious to get money from you, he'll be back."

"How do you know?" I turned to Rebecca. "How can he know?"

"The DEA's involved?" Rebecca asked. She swallowed some scotch and poured another.

From her reaction, I wondered what else my friend carried around in her shoulder bag. Marijuana, maybe? I'd read somewhere pot helps settle a witch's mind so she can focus on her spell. If Rebecca had any illegal drugs, maybe she feared the DEA would burst in, and she would wind up dangling from a rope next to me on Gallows Hill, hanged side-by-side like our ancestors.

"That's what I'm trying to tell you," Roger said. "When I caught up with Woody, he was talking to a guy—getting bawled out by him, actually. I managed to get close enough to overhear. Apparently, the Feds have been trying to shut down a drug ring in Buffalo for more than a year."

Wine, scotch: the hot pain in my head drifted behind a cloud. My tongue felt thick. Roger's voice now sounded as though it came from my kitchen or maybe from my backyard. I forced myself to concentrate.

"Drugs? Someone's feeding drugs to buffaloes?" I asked.

Roger laughed. "You've had quite enough alcohol for one day." He took the half-filled glass from my hand and set it on the coffee table.

Elvira squiggled free of my arm and leaped onto the table. As if it were her bowl of milk, she began to lap up the scotch.

Roger shooed her away. "This cat's as bad as you two," he remarked.

Elvira grinned up at him from the floor and her tongue moved slowly across her lips. It was as though she said, *Where's that stuff been all my life?*

Leaning back against the cushions, Roger said, "All of you try to focus. From what I could make out, the Feds think a cop may be involved in the drug ring, and the guy with Woody said where there's one there's probably more."

"So Jim Osborn's death is about narcotics?" Rebecca asked.

"Seems to be," Roger said. "They think the ring's operating in Niagara Falls, too. Makes sense, now there's a casino here. They've decided Jimmy's murder is proof the drugs have crossed into the Falls."

I was shocked. Well, as shocked as I could get in my semi-inebriated condition. "Jimmy?" I said. "But you told me you would have known if he was involved in something like drugs."

Roger shrugged.

I gnawed on the idea for minute. Jimmy Osborn had been my friend. Margaret was my friend. I felt as though I would betray them if I believed for even a minute Jimmy could be part of a drug ring. I'd buried my initial suspicion by then. Now it rushed back: the Corvette in the Osborns' driveway, the expensive wedding they'd given their daughter—where had the money for such things come from?

Roger broke into the haze of my thoughts. "Anyhow, now I know why Woody won't let the guys in my squad, and especially me, work the case. With the Feds not knowing how deep it goes in the department, his hands are tied."

"And Kevin?" I asked.

With Rebecca's warning about unexpected consequences echoing in my recollection, I trembled at the idea my ex was involved. A new guilt rose like acid from my stomach and my face grew warm. I recalled the spell Rebecca and I had

143

thrown at Kevin. Our candles and herbs and chants had caused him to lose his job as an insurance agent, and go bankrupt—it happened so soon afterward, I was sure our spell was the cause. I hadn't foreseen the hex might lead him down a dark path. Now he was a hunted drug runner.

As if he read my thoughts, Roger said, "They want him to testify against the ones who are behind this."

No wonder Kevin was so panicked. I'd read in the newspaper and seen television movies about how dangerous it was to testify against drug lords. Witnesses disappeared, their bones found years later when an old building was torn down. Yes, most of such plots are made up by people like me. Knowing this didn't help, and it didn't matter that I had little love left for my ex. Damn my imagination! Half-soused and all scared, no room remained in my mind for logic.

"This is all my fault!" I blurted out.

Roger's eyes went from me to Rebecca. "What did you two do?" he demanded.

"Uh...nothing," she stammered.

"Well..." I said.

Elvira knew damn well what we had done. She'd been there. Now she was back on the coffee table, lapping at the glass of scotch. I guess she recognized the accusation in Roger's voice.

I sure did. His tone was like a hangover remedy.

Rebecca focused on her glass. My eyes wandered around the room.

Earlier, when I thought Rebecca might be the killer, I'd wondered if I could swat her with Sarah Goode's book and escape out the French doors. Now, I wondered if I could escape from Roger's stern look in such a way.

Chapter Fifteen
Something Rotten in Niagara Falls

In fits and starts, and with a lot of hemming and hawing, in tandem Rebecca and I told Roger about the candles and wine and the stuffed doll we used as the centerpiece of our vengeance ceremony. Of course, we left out some of the details—he had no need to know the name of the goddess we invoked, what we promised her, or how scantily we were clad (even thinking about the half-dressed state we were in makes me blush). When we finally finished, he shook his head and swallowed the rest of his wine.

"You can't really believe in this stuff," he said.

Rebecca had a mischievous glint in her eyes.

"The spell worked, didn't it?" I said as I wiped away tears of guilt.

Elvira's head came up so fast she nearly slid off the coffee table.

"Come on now, your chanting didn't do a thing," Roger said. "Think about it logically. Once Kevin lost his job, it wasn't a long leap for him down the rabbit hole. I didn't know him well, Emlyn, but I'd seen enough of him to lay odds he'd go looking for a fast buck in a scheme that didn't require much effort."

I wouldn't surrender my guilt so easily—my mother's ministrations left it too well embedded. Roger was just being kind. "You don't know anything of the sort," I insisted.

"I know what I saw. He was my neighbor for the three years you were married. He was happy to move here to your parents' house. In fact, I once overheard him say he was glad he glommed onto a woman with assets. And I saw the way he treated you—like a housemaid. No, I didn't like it, and I didn't like him much."

"He worked hard," I said. "All those late nights visiting clients."

I don't know why I defended Kevin. Guilt, I guess, is a rapist ripping away the clothes of one's reason.

"You think he was visiting clients?" Roger said. "I saw him a couple of nights at Flannery's, a drink in one hand and a woman in his other."

My hand flew to my mouth. A sob burst from my throat.

"Stop it!" Rebecca said. "That was mean."

Roger's brows arched. "Sorry. I shouldn't have told you."

"I always knew what Kevin is," I moaned.

He took my hand. "The bastard didn't deserve you."

I gazed into Roger's soft hazel eyes and, for a moment, forgot my hurt.

Rebecca peered over the rim of her glass. Her sly smile told me she was pleased she might have written, produced, and directed this scene. "If you lovebirds are finished cooing," she said, at last, "I'd like to remind you of something."

Without breaking eye contact with me, Roger asked—almost whispered, "What?"

"You said Kevin turned to crime after he lost his job."

"Yeah?"

"It strikes me you started in the middle. Our spell *did* work. It caused him to get fired—"

My tears erupted again. "See, I'm the cause of whatever he's done. That means Jimmy...his murder was also my fault!"

Rebecca handed me a tissue. "It wasn't just you, Emlyn. I was part of it. And what we did we can undo."

I didn't feel any less to blame.

"Magic got him fired?" Roger said. "I doubt that."

I sniffed and blew my nose. "What did it then?"

He stretched his legs onto the coffee table. His hands behind his head, he said, "There a logical answer to that, too. Shouldn't be very hard to learn what it is."

"Without your boss finding out you're asking questions?" Rebecca said.

A grin spread across Roger's face. "Yeah, there's that."

"Please, don't do anything stupid," I said. Now my bubble of guilt expanded to envelop the trouble Roger was about to get into. It would be another unexpected consequence flowing from my need for revenge.

"Sitting here, just talking about who might have done what, is stupid," Roger said. "Doing nothing about it is stupid. And I'll tell you something—I'm tired of being stupid."

"But Woody said—"

"Yeah, Woody. He's doing nothing and using the Feds as an excuse to do it. You saw what happened when you told him his wife and Kevin were both at the book signing? He couldn't get out of here fast enough. My boss, Chief Woodward, is covering for someone."

My mind flashed to the brief conversation I had with Amy Woodward at the Osborn funeral. Was it my imagination, or had she gone pale when I told her how lucky she was to have a steadfast husband? I'd also seen Kevin at the funeral. Then Amy had been at Main Street Books. For my reading and signing, she told me. But when I said hello, she seemed surprised to see me. Then, a minute later, I saw Kevin. He was in trouble, he said. He came because he knew I'd be there. After the way he'd skulked in my backyard then tried to cadge money from me, I believed him.

My imagination spun like an old $33\ ^1/_3$ rpm record on an older 78 rpm turntable (before there were tapes and CDs, there were record players—I know about record players because my parents had one). I began to construct scenarios. Had Kevin come to again beg me for money, or was he really looking for Amy?

"What's going on in that brain of yours?" Roger asked.

The thought, *Solve the crime to end the guilt*, rushed to my mind. "Huh? What makes you think—?"

"Don't give me that, Emlyn. I've watched you." He leaned over, and tapped my forehead with his finger. "When your eyes go this narrow, big cogwheels are turning in there."

"I was just thinking—"

"Uh-oh," Rebecca said.

"No, really. I just remembered something."

"Yeah?" they both said.

"Well, I could be wrong. And even if I'm not, it might not mean anything."

"Let me judge that," Roger said.

I told them what I'd seen during Jimmy's funeral, and then among the stacks of books before my reading.

"You think they planned a—what do you writers call it—a tryst?" Rebecca asked.

"A slime bucket like Kevin Reinhart with a woman like Amy Woodward?" Roger said. "Even if I caught them in bed together, I wouldn't believe it."

Rebecca considered this for a moment. "Both of them in the same place at the same time twice, it can't just be a coincidence."

"Maybe not." Deep furrows on his forehead, Roger glanced to the French doors. It was as if he thought he might see my ex slip from tree to tree in my backyard. "A guy like Kevin, desperate for money—blackmail is more likely."

"What could Amy Woodward be blackmailed over?" I asked.

"No, wait," Rebecca said. "You just told us the way she reacted at the cemetery. Maybe Kevin found out she's having an affair."

Roger rubbed the graying hair at his temple. "I don't see it. Still, the way Woody reacted this evening, maybe he thinks something like that is going on. And with the Feds hunting for Kevin—"

"Drugs. The two of them in it together. And right under your boss's nose." Rebecca nodded, as if she concluded a husband really could be so dense.

"No. It just doesn't add," Roger said. "No matter how I try, I can't put Amy in Kevin's circle.

Elvira was again on the coffee table, her lascivious pink eyes on the glass of scotch.

"Hey, that's not good for you." Roger shoved her away.

"This is all speculation," I said, though it was me who started speculating in the first place. "Besides, whether Amy Woodward and my ex are part of the drug ring or they're having an affair—"

"Or both," Rebecca offered.

"Even then, what does it have to do with Jimmy getting murdered? Eight bullets in the chest isn't a hit. What would either of them be so angry about?" I thought again about the cost of a new Corvette and the Osborn wedding. "But, if they're having an affair and Jimmy found out—could it be *he* was the blackmailer?"

"Or maybe the Osborn killing has nothing to do with Kevin and Amy Woodward," Rebecca said.

"Damned if I know," Roger said. "There are so many possibilities, I feel like I don't know anything anymore. But, all this happening in the same circle of people at the same time, it sure smells like it's tied together."

"How?" Rebecca asked.

With a grunt, Roger pulled his feet from the coffee table. "That's what I'm gonna find out."

He grabbed his coat from the back of the kitchen chair. After a glance at the front door, he crossed the living room and pulled the French doors open. Wind blowing his hair, he said, "No reason the Feds parked out front need to know

I've left." As he slipped into the night, he added, "You have my cell number. Call if anyone tries to get in."

***

The icy breeze Roger let into my house blew away the alcohol cloud in my mind, and with it, my feeling of guilt. Only anger was left. I grabbed a crutch and hobbled to the French doors. With the blind pulled aside, I peeked out. The azalea bushes slapped the glass. The branches of the naked beech tree in the center of my yard waved and hissed. The stand of trees guarding the Niagara River was a thick shadow. My calendar said this was the day of a new moon, though it was hard to tell with the sky so overcast.

After gazing around the yard to be certain my ex didn't lurk back there, I said, "Is anyone out front?"

Rebecca went to kitchen, and looked out the window. "The only thing I see is Roger's car," she said. "I thought he's going to look for his boss."

"He is. Or maybe he's trying to find Kevin."

"On foot?"

"I doubt it. He keeps a Harley under a tarp on the far side of his garage. He'll probably walk it around the curve in the road before he starts it up."

"But, to get to the city he'll still need to pass the guys who're watching your house."

"Uh-uh. Roger knows maybe fifteen ways to circle around them. I'll bet he'll start out headed toward Buffalo, turn up Ward Road, and go through North Tonawanda."

Back in the living room, Rebecca began to pick up the wine glasses.

"Leave those. We've got work to do."

A glass in each hand, she said, "What are you thinking?" She seemed afraid to look at me.

Stone sober, I'd stumbled into the middle of this swamp. I guess Rebecca figured with half a bottle of Varney

Estates and a touch of Johnny Walker sloshing through my veins, I was about to drag her into the morass.

"I need to find out if my idiot ex was fooling around with Amy Woodward."

Rebecca hooded her eyes. "You're not gonna try another divination rite."

It wasn't a question. I didn't answer.

She straightened up. "Don't you ever learn?"

I shrugged. "The killer's come after me twice. Next time he might succeed. Don't you see? I've got nothing to lose. Things can't get much worse."

It was a foolish thing to say. Tweaking the nose of fate, even a little bit, is never a bright thing to do. But recently, bright ideas hadn't been my forte.

Rebecca glanced toward the front door.

"You can leave if you're afraid the spell will boomerang," I said.

She sighed and put down the glasses. "I didn't put out the fire on your leg just to let you go up in smoke now. No, I'm staying. Someone's gotta keep you from blowing yourself up."

"I don't plan to blow either of us up," I said, and turned a complete circle. "Where's Elvira? I need her for this."

Rebecca bent low enough to see under the coffee table. The cat was curled up on the floor, snoring. Except for the broad, stupid grin on her face, the animal resembled a giant white Nerf ball. "Not much of a drinker," she said. "Come to think of it, maybe Elvira has the right idea. Let's pop another cork."

I refused to be distracted. Reaching for my other crutch, I said, "No. I've got to unravel who's after me. I won't be safe till I do."

"But the last time you tried this—"

Rebecca's objection was rather mild, I thought. With her hip flung out, she stared at the ancient book on my coffee table.

"I must have misread Sarah Goode's instructions," I said. "You'll help me figure out what I did wrong."

That Sarah's book was more a diary than a user's manual didn't register at the moment.

This time Rebecca's sigh was one of surrender. I knew then, for all her resistance, my friend wanted to see what spells Sarah wrote about, and learn if they actually worked. She couldn't try them by herself. It needed someone who had the right genes, she'd told me when we started to explore my heritage months before. It needed old Sarah's genes.

With no further argument, she lifted the book so carefully it might have been the Holy Grail. She sat in the wingback chair and opened the book to where I had slid a folded sheet from my yellow pad. She had far less trouble than I with the arcane prose. Aloud, she read:

> *"These people who knew me as a child would swear an oath they are friends. Yet to my back these friends who claim to be God-fearing, curse my name, call me filthy, mean-spirited. It is only poor I am, and in need. Mean-spirited? Aye, I have become that. I beg at doors for a crust of bread. Would I turn my townsfolk away if they, not I, were in need? Would I laugh at them and hide my children when they pass me on the street? Would I slide away from them, whispering, on the bench in church? These friends of my childhood. It is a crime, I think, to be poor in this Salem town. Ah, had my dear George Burroughs taken me as his own when my father died and left me with naught but a good name. Would that he had taken me before I wed Dan Poole whose life of debt stole*

from me even that good name. I am bitter, yes. Having seized my heart, George Burroughs fled this town against rumors he is a brother to the Devil. But he is a man of God, and is strong because of it. He knows the Lord will shield him from such accusations. So perchance it is another woman he has chosen, and he has run to her. Tonight I will know."

Rebecca looked up from the book. "There's nothing here to help."

I'd hobbled back and forth across the living room all the time she read. Thud, step, thud, step: crutches in front then swing past them. Now I stopped in front of her. "Keep reading," I said. "Sarah always rambles before she gets down to it."

Rebecca pulled her long braid over her left shoulder, and stroked it as if she were petting a cat while she scanned the next page. Her eyebrows pinched, she at last said, "What Sarah did…I don't think we have the skill to control it."

"Read," I insisted.

As if to say, *I'm sorry I got you started in this,* she rolled her eyes.

"Sarah's about to tell us how she learned if George Burroughs ran off with his soul mate," I said.

"If he did, it would make *one* of you." She peered at the French doors through which Roger had left.

"Let it go, Rebecca. I like him, but not that way."

"Yeah, right. Tell me another story." Instead of pushing further, she turned her eyes down to the open book on her lap.

"Anil is needed to dye the beeswax," she read, then stopped and looked up at me. "Makes sense—deep blue is the color of clairvoyance."

"Maybe that's why I got in trouble last time. I didn't use blue candles. What's next?"

Running a long red fingernail across the words, she again scanned the page. "A black cape."

"Black? Was Sarah planning to put a hex on George Burroughs if she saw him with another woman?"

In a flash of imagination, my distant relative became the wicked witch in the *Wizard of Oz* movie. Green face, bent nose, she cackled over her crystal ball. Had the use of magic turned the witch's skin green? I stopped in front of the mirror near my desk, leaned on a crutch, and touched my face.

Rebecca's voice put an end to my rumination over whether magic would inevitably lead to a discolored complexion. "In the old days, black wasn't considered evil," she said while she turned another page in the book. "Many practicing Wicca's don't know this anymore. Black is the absence of color. It symbolizes the night, the universe. Black is the absence of falsehood."

"Okay, I've got a black silk robe in my closet. More than one, actually."

"*Do* you? Roger will like that."

"Rebecca!"

"I'm just saying."

"And I'm not listening. What else do we need?"

"Incense. Gotta have the aroma of musk. Wait a minute." She went to the kitchen and retuned with her shoulder bag. "Yeah, I've got what we need to make it." She began to pull small jars from her bag. "Sandalwood, gum mastic, ambergris—got any nutmeg and mustard powder in the house?"

"Did you bring your whole shop with you?" I asked, wide-eyed.

"When I woke up this morning, I had a feeling you'd insist on doing this."

"A feeling, huh? Like the one that told you, you'd need a salve for my burns?"

She gave me the same arcane smile I'd seen the day I met her at The Black Cat. "A woman's gotta be prepared."

Though her tone was light, I sensed something she held back. "Prepared for what?"

She turned to the chair and fluffed the cushion. "For what we're about to do, of course."

Running in the circle of her logic left me dizzier than the alcohol I'd imbibed. A tad annoyed, I pointed to Sarah's book and said, "Then we have what we need?"

Rebecca's nod was anything but eager.

"Wake Elvira up," I said as I switched off the lamps. "Let's get started."

Chapter Sixteen
Things Better Unseen

The living room was almost as black as my robe. The only light came from three candles flickering on the end table we moved near the French doors. The candlesticks were arranged in a triangle the way Sarah Goode had instructed. The mini-blinds were raised so we would feel as though we were under the sky and could peer up to the eternity beyond. Sarah wrote she would be outside when she performed this rite. The night was far too cold for us to follow that instruction. Even if we were outside, low clouds hid the stars Sarah chanted to. It didn't matter. I intended to proceed.

Frost had crystallized in lacy patterns on the windows. Perfect jewels of frost. A stiff wind gusting from the north off Lake Ontario made me shiver, though my living room was quite warm. The constant *tap-tap-tap* of the azalea bushes on the windowpanes sounded like the knock of a spirit who wanted to be let in. I thought of it as the spirit of eternity come to participate in our ceremony.

My feet were bare. Rebecca's feet were bare. Symbolically, we stood on the earth, and were one with nature. Elvira sat beside us, watching, as if wanting to be certain we would do everything right.

On the table, a bowl of water and a bowl of salt rested on either side of the navy blue candles. I had placed a third bowl with smoldering incense at my right hand. In the white dish to my left, grated nutmeg looked like sand on a beach spread before an ocean. In my imagination, I stood on the beach and stared out over the waves to where the water became one with the sky. One with the universe.

Of course, without my crutches I couldn't stand on a beach or even on my carpeted floor. So, I leaned against the table with my right foot raised. In this position, I closed my eyes, and inhaled deeply. After our prayer to nature's deities, if the order of our service was correct and we chanted the proper words, I would *become* one with the universe. I would float in the black sky and look down at the earth, at my urban and rural piece of it. In the tapestry of city streets and farmlands, the answer to the puzzle would be spread before me.

"Fiery God," Rebecca and I intoned, "you who are the ruler of gods, master of the sun—"

She handed me the athame, my sharp, double bladed knife with runes carved in the hilt. Carefully, I drew a five-pointed star in the nutmeg then blessed the spice with the tip of my blade.

"—holding everything wild and free in your hands," we sang, "Ancient begetter of woman and man—"

I pinched grains of nutmeg from the center of the star and sprinkled the grains into the incense bowl. The aroma of musk and spice filled my nostrils. I bent down, cut three white hairs from Elvira's back. I dropped one in the flame of each candle.

"—Paramour of the Moon Goddess and shield of the Wicca, descend, we pray, with your blazing hands open wide—"

I began to feel sleepy. I didn't fight the feeling. Again I inhaled the spiced aroma of the incense...

***

Night under a moonless sky. Instead of floating in the sky, I stand at the foot of an alley which stretches beyond my sight. No snow covers the cracked concrete, tarred over in spots. On either side of the lane are the backs of wood-framed two-story dwellings, some boarded up. They look as though they had been built nearly a hundred years ago. Garages jut out, some with caved-in roofs, other roofs only sag.

I sense I've been here before. I feel as if there's no place I haven't been before.

A breeze, fragrant with musk and the promise of spring, gentles my hair. Rebecca's voice floats on this breeze...

"Glorious Goddess, you who are the mother of gods, the light in the night, the womb of everything wild and free—"

I feel dizzy, might tumble if I take a step. It's as if I've gotten drunk on the sweet air. I grasp the steel pole of a chain link fence, bend my neck. A single star glitters in the black sky. The Goddess?

"—defender of woman and man—" *Rebecca sings.*

Her voice, a whisper, becomes a shout, breaks in half. Now it is two voices arguing. "Why did you have to do it," *one says. The other voice, trembling:* "I was wrong, I know it now."

They shouldn't fight while the Goddess watches.

A patch of white flashes past me. It's Elvira. She races toward the raised voices.

I release the steel post and stagger after her.

"Bitch, it's too late for apologies." *The fury in the first voice rends the night.*

"No, no. Please, no!" *The second cries.*

"I killed once, and now you."

I drop my crutches. No pain in my foot or leg, I'm free of the need for them. Now I run toward the voices, to where Elvira sits staring into the shadows. I recognize one of the voices, though I've never heard it other than smooth, soft.

"Why? Why?" *it again cries.*

Past rattling chain fences, past sagging garages, I continue to run. I am panting. A stitch in my side. I bend over, my hands on my thighs, catch my breath. Run again.

"I have to, you see?" *The first voice is a hissed whisper. Male, female, I can't determine.* "If you tell, they'll know. You understand?"

"*I won't tell.*"

The second voice belongs to Amy Woodward. She's in danger. The other voice—whose is it? I have to find out. My safety, my life, depends on finding out.

Elvira turns her face to me, and snarls as if to ask what I'm waiting for. The answer is here, she seems to say. If I stall, it will vanish.

In panic, I run faster. Bare feet kicking pebbles. Stones, broken cement, glass. I feel the cuts. Surely the soles of my feet must be bleeding. Can't stop to tend to my feet. Have to reach Elvira at the alley's end. But the alley never ends.

"*I won't tell. Never tell.*" *Amy Woodward is pleading for her life.*

Twenty feet ahead, a figure backs out of a rickety wood barn. The wood is dry, aged, the laths no longer flush. As if the barn is a mirage, I see the sky through it.

Her hands raised, Amy turns to me. "*Help me please!*"

"*Help, help!*" *I scream.*

"Emlyn, what's wrong?" *Rebecca's voice comes from Amy's mouth.* "Emlyn, wake up!"

Wake up? I am awake. I've got to save Amy! I reach for her.

Two gunshots shatter the night. Amy Woodward falls at my feet.

I drop to my knees, cradle her head. Blood. Everywhere. So much blood. Didn't know a person had so much blood.

Elvira is beside me. She groans, rubs her face on my black silk robe. Amy is gone. I sit alone in the puddle of her blood, and gather the white cat to my breast.

To my right, light from the single star glints off the barrel of a gun. I know what kind it is: a Glock .45 caliber—I've seen pictures of this gun in a book on one of my shelves. The weapon is pointed at me. The shooter is in a black robe like mine. But it's not a robe, it's a monk's cowl. Inside the hood, his face is...he has no face. Just a shadow.

"Help us, please," I cry. "Roger!"
Crack. Crack...
Someone grabs my robe.
"Come on Emlyn, wake up!" Rebecca shouted.
"What? Where...?"
She slapped my face. "You've gotta wake up."
"Help us!" I was crying. I clearly remember I was crying.
"What's happening?" Rebecca asked, panic in her voice. The same panic as was in mine.
"Help us, help us! Roger!"
Her hands rubbed my cheeks.
At last my eyes opened. I was in my living room, kneeling at the French doors, my face pressed against a glass pane. I had Elvira cradled in my arms.
But at the same time I knelt in an alley somewhere. Kneeling in two places at the same time?
"No, no!" I raise my hand to ward off a bullet traveling in slow motion toward my heart. "Noooo!"
The bullet crashes though my hand. I scream in pain...
"Emlyn, you're scaring me. Wake up!" Rebecca shouted. She knelt beside me and stroked my hair.
Though I struggled to obey her, I couldn't break the grip of my dream.
Yet, I was awake. I was in my living room, my face against the cold glass of the French doors.
And outside the window, a black-caped ancient crone now stands. Stringy white hair partly tied in back. She points a gnarled finger, moves toward me. She leaves no footprints in the snow.
"Who...who are you?" I ask.
Elvira whines, paws at the glass.
Her head shaking as if she pities me, the old hag croons, "Seek ye after truth in the heart? The heart betrays."
"Emmy!" Rebecca called into my waking dream.

160

The wind swirls. Snow swirls. My backyard is a mass of blinding white. From inside the curtain of snow, I hear the crone moan, "Remember this: betrayal."

My hand is on the glass, next to Elvira's paw. My fingers scratch at the panes. I have to claw my way out of the white hole I'm falling into...

***

The next thing I knew, I was laid out on my sofa, a cold compress on my forehead.

"You're awake," Rebecca said. She sounded relieved.

"What happened?" I asked.

"You tell us," Roger said. He emerged from the kitchen carrying a pot of coffee.

"You're here," I stated the obvious.

I pulled the cloth from my forehead, then dropped it and grabbed my other hand. It felt as though the bones were broken. As though a bullet had smashed through my hand. When I tried to sit up the pain shot up my arm. The room spun.

Roger sat next to me, laid the cloth again across my forehead.

"I called him," Rebecca said. "Didn't know what else to do. I was so frightened."

"Did you see her?"

"Who?" Roger asked.

Even turning my eyes to him hurt. "The old woman." Moving as little as possible, I extended my arm, and pointed to the French doors. "Out there. She's caught in the blizzard. I've got to let her in before she freezes."

His eyes followed my finger. "It's not snowing," he said. "Hasn't even been a flurry all day."

"See what I mean?" Rebecca said. "I can't get her back."

Roger stood up. "We're taking her to the hospital," he told Rebecca. "Get her coat."

I shook my head and groaned when a bolt of lightning shot through it. "Not going anywhere."

Rebecca was by the table we'd set up near the window, her face as gray as her salt and pepper hair. Now she was as white as the snow on the ground; now, as translucent as an ice sculpture. "I've got something in my bag that'll clear her head," she said.

"Why didn't you give her that before?"

She seemed about to cry. "I couldn't wake her up to give it to her."

Roger glared at her. "I told you not to let her fool around with your witch nonsense—didn't I tell you that?" His glance fell from Rebecca's face to the end table by the doors, and to the dish of grated nutmeg and the remains of the incense. "That stuff probably got her stoned."

Assaulted by his tone, Rebecca took a step backward. "Did you ever try to stop a freight train?"

"I'm not stoned," I said.

He looked down at me and his face softened. "Emlyn's a freight train?" He smiled. "Yeah, I know what you mean."

The ice sculpture that was my friend, Rebecca, went into the kitchen. In a few seconds she returned with a narrow vial. She shooed Roger aside and dropped beside me on the sofa.

At the movement of the cushions, another sharp pain shot through my body. "*Aaaah,*" I groaned.

Gently, she lifted my head. "Drink this down."

"You're sure this stuff will work?" Roger asked. He hovered over us like an anxious husband.

"It should. I brewed it myself."

"Not very comforting," he said. "Won't kill her, will it?"

Rebecca smiled. "Hasn't killed anyone yet."

"How many times have you tried it?"

She flipped her long braid over her shoulder, and raised her chin to him. "Let me see. Um, this'll be the first."

He snorted. "Great. On her tombstone we'll write *An Experiment that Failed.*"

"Hush," she said. "This is my grandmother's recipe and she lived to a hundred."

I knew what their by-play was about: when you visit a sick friend, you make jokes to raise her spirits. Right then, I didn't want my spirits raised. I wanted my friends to let the old woman into my house.

Rebecca pushed the vial against my lips. "Swallow!"

The elixir tasted like— I have no idea what it tasted like. I'd never had anything like it. My lips curled. My stomach tightened.

"What a face," Roger said.

I sat up, spitting. "That stuff is awful," I gasped when my dry-heaves finally stopped.

"See? It's working. She's back," Rebecca said.

I reached out and cried, "Water!"

"No water!" Her command stopped Roger who had started toward the kitchen. "Don't want to dilute the mixture."

I've got to find out what she mixed together so I can feed that stuff to someone I don't like, I thought, though I did feel a trifle better. Still, something bothered me. Something I had to remember. Damn, what was it?

I looked to the altar, still set up in front of the French doors. The blue tapers had burned almost halfway down. How long had I been out? I turned my eyes to the railroad station clock screwed onto the wall near my bookcases. It was well past midnight. I'd been gone for hours. I must have done something, seen something, or learned something. What was it? I only remembered the old woman in the snow, pointing at me. The heart betrays, she had said.

I rolled onto my side and saw Elvira at the French doors, peering outside. *Looking for the gray-haired crone?*

"What?" Rebecca asked.

"Huh?" I said.

"You seem puzzled."

"No. Uh-uh. I'm...fine."

Roger's pinched lips said he doubted I was fine.

"Really, I am," I insisted.

"If you're sure—"

"She will be," Rebecca said. "Just needs a few minutes to gather herself."

What can't I remember? I thought. *Something about an alley and why I ran through it.*

Still sounding uncertain, Roger said, "I'll go home then, grab some sleep. Tomorrow I wanna catch up with Woody before he has a chance to lock himself in his office."

An alley? I thought. *Woody. Amy—* At last what I had seen rushed back. Though my head hurt when I moved, and though my hand ached where the bullet in my dream had shattered the bones, I reached out to him. "No! Not tomorrow, tonight. Amy Woodward—we have to help her. She's been shot."

"What?" Roger said.

"She was shot. So much blood. She's dying. I saw it happen."

Rebecca's jaw dropped. "You saw—? The divination spell worked? Tell me. I have to write it in the *Book of Shadows*."

This wasn't the time to make notes about what we'd accomplished. I pushed her hand away, and sat up. "Amy Woodward's in trouble!"

Roger sat heavily in my wingback chair. "How did you...when...?"

"No questions. Please." I had to get him to move. "You need to trust me, Roger. This once, trust me."

"Do what she says," Rebecca said.

"Do what she says? I have no idea what she's saying."

I took a breath deep enough to loosen the knot in my throat. Then, in a very few words I told them about the alley and the argument I heard.

"You just described the back lane off Nineteenth Street," Roger said. "That's where they found Jimmy." He looked at Rebecca. "She must have read about the alley in the *Gazette*."

Yes, I had read about the alley in the newspaper, but my seeing it in a trance wasn't a drug-induced delusion. Explaining that, though, would have wasted valuable time.

"We have to help Amy!" I shouted, and tried to rise. As if the pain in my head had a hand, it shoved me back on the arm of the sofa.

For a nonbeliever, Roger reacted rather quickly. He grabbed his coat and car keys. "*We're* not going anywhere," he said. "You two stay here. I'll find out if something happened." At the door, he stopped, turned back. "And no more candles and incense, please. Not tonight, at least."

I held my head to keep it from toppling off my shoulders while I gave him half a nod—half a nod was as much as I could manage.

Apparently, he didn't believe I would stay put. He returned to the living room and snatched the athame from our altar. "Just to make sure," he said as he slipped the knife into his coat pocket. Then he was out my front door.

"Guess he's not overly concerned about the Feds outside warning Chief Woodward he's on the prowl," Rebecca remarked.

Roger was right not to take me at my word. Although, I hadn't really promised—I mean, a half-nod could have meant anything. As soon as I heard the engine of his SUV roar, I said, "Turn off the lights. We still have time before the candles burn out."

Rebecca didn't move.

165

"Hey, come on. Help me get up. I've got another knife we can use."

She sat like a rock next to me on the sofa. "Uh-uh. If I let you do anymore tonight, Roger will wind up in jail."

"What are you talking about?"

"He'll get arrested for killing me if I let you do anything but lay there."

I stumbled to my feet without her help. "Who are you more afraid of, me or him?"

"*He's* got a gun," she answered.

I refused to be put off. "Rebecca, I have to get back there—into the trance. The old woman I saw? I think she's Sarah Goode. She tried to tell me something."

Instead of giving me her hand, she went to the altar and pinched out the candles.

"How many times do I have to warn you about unintended consequences?" she said. "Sure, the woman might have been Sarah. But it could just as easily have been a dark spirit who wants to lead you to a place I won't be able to bring you back from. I know witches that's happened to."

"They never came back?"

"Never. Not their minds. They just sit, babbling nonsense. Do you wanna wind up that way? Thought not. So knock it off. You've done enough tonight. Let's wait to see if Amy Woodward really is hurt."

It was only a couple of hours before we found out.

Chapter Seventeen
What Detective Frey Found

The phone call from Roger was short and terse. Amy Woodward was dead, he said. He was with her husband at the precinct. They'd probably be there the rest of the night. We didn't hear what happened until the next afternoon.

Still dressed in the black robes we wore when Roger left, Rebecca and I just sat down to lunch—grilled cheese and tomato bisque, my favorite winter meal—when I heard the latch click, and my front door opened.

I jumped from my seat.

"Everyone decent?" Roger called from the hall.

With all that happened last night, I'd forgotten I gave him my key.

Rebecca grabbed my hand and eased me back down. "About as decent as you might expect," she said. "We've been up all night."

Roger leaned through the kitchen door. "Sorry, I shouldn't have phoned so late."

"If you hadn't," I said, "I'd have hit you with a spell to make your hair fall out."

"Yeah, huh?" I pictured him patting his head to be sure his brown curls were still there.

"Or else I would have made you drink some of that elixir Rebecca fed me." My lips curled and I shivered when I recalled the taste.

"She's not kidding," my friend said. "After last night, you ought to realize Emlyn's not a woman to mess with."

The hall closet opened. Hangers rattled. A moment later, Roger was in the kitchen doorway. His face was drawn. Lines and dark circles around his eyes made him look far older than his forty-two years. Instead of the sweatshirt and jeans he had on when he left my house, he wore a fresh green shirt and pressed brown slacks. I smelled the Royal Copenhagen aftershave he always used. Clearly, he'd stopped at home before coming over.

"So, tell us," I said.

He pulled out a chair, sat next to me, and leaned over to sniff my soup. "Got any more of this? I'm famished."

"What do you think?" I said to Rebecca. "Should we feed him?"

"That depends on whether he's gonna tell us what happened."

"Very nice. I sneak out of an interrogation so I can let you know you were right—nearly get my head chewed off for doing it—and this is how you treat me?"

I dipped a spoon into my soup, blew on it, and put it in my mouth. "This is rather good. What did you put in it?"

"A little of this, a little of that," Rebecca said.

Roger took the spoon from my hand. "Let me taste it."

I pushed the bowl to the other side of the table. "I don't hear anything about last night. Do you, Rebecca?"

"Nope, not a word. Oh, and try your sandwich. Three different cheeses in it."

Roger shoved his lower lip out in a sulk. "You're just cruel, both of you."

"What do you expect?" I said. "I'm a witch."

He sat back and sighed. "After last night, I'm almost ready to believe you are."

If a mirror were nearby, I would have gazed into it to see if my skin had turned green yet.

"So, if you don't want to spend the rest of your life saying *riiibit*," Rebecca said, "tell us."

"The soup's awfully good," I added.

My mother always says a man's stomach is the shortest distance to his heart. In this instance, it proved to be the quickest route to his vocal cords. While Rebecca grilled him a sandwich and ladled soup into a bowl, Roger began by telling us what he'd done the first time he left my house.

***

Roger slipped out the French doors. So he wouldn't be noticed if one of the DEA agents had camped in my yard, he hugged the wall of the house, squeezed through my azalea bushes, and scaled the fence dividing our property. He entered his house through the back door, put on heavy denim jeans, several layers of shirts, and his black hooded sweatshirt with the Niagara Falls Police Department logo. He zipped his blue quilted jacket over the sweatshirt. Prepared now for the cold night, he brushed more than a foot of snow from the tarp covering his motorcycle. Steadying the bike, he walked it through two neighboring yards to a point where the curve in River Road made him invisible to the men parked outside my house.

As I expected he'd do, he took an indirect route to the Falls. Even bundled up, he was colder than he could ever recall being (colder than a witch's tit, is how he described it, and then he leered at me). Through the twenty minutes from his house to where the Woodwards lived, he shivered, and cussed at himself for being so stupid as to be out on a night such as this. Still, he wouldn't quit and return home before he caught pneumonia. Not Detective Roger Frey. Not once he'd made up his mind he had to find out what his boss was hiding (and he says *I'm* the most obstinate, pigheaded person he's ever met).

The house Harry and Amy Woodward owned was off Hyde Park Road, a few blocks from what used to be the Amtrak station. One of the many pre-war wood-frame homes along the tree-lined streets in Niagara Falls, it was painted white with blue shutters and trim, and had a covered front porch. In summer, the house was a welcoming sight. Not so on a late March evening when the headlight of Roger's Harley lit snow drifts blown high against the clapboards, and icicles hanging from the eaves. When he steered into the driveway, the house was dark.

He climbed the three wood stairs to the porch, opened the storm door, and knocked.

Not a sound from inside.

He walked along the porch. Hand above his brow, he peered through one window, then another. A single light cast a yellow glow through the door from the kitchen to the dining room.

He rapped on the window, and called, "Woody, Amy, you home?"

The hiss of the wind and rustling of tree branches was the only response.

Again on his motorcycle, Roger rode down Hyde Park Road to the police station. As if he'd run the entire way, he was out of breath when he arrived. Woody's Buick Skylark wasn't in the lot.

His helmet under his arm, he entered the precinct. "Seen Chief Woodward tonight?" he asked.

The desk sergeant, tall and gawky, raised one eye from the crossword puzzle in the newspaper folded on his desk. He yawned into his uniform jacket, licked the point of his pencil, and filled in a six letter word. After inspecting the puzzle grid, he said, "The Chief was here. Left about twenty minutes ago."

Frustrated, Roger slapped the desk. As he turned to leave, the sergeant called to him, "The man smelled like he had a snootful and he looked pissed."

Back in the lot behind the precinct, Roger climbed onto his bike, revved the engine, and roared down Pine Avenue to where it fed into Niagara Falls Boulevard. Racing along the almost deserted street, he headed for the Royal Apartments—the low-rent complex my ex moved into after our divorce. Having seen the way Harry Woodward reacted when I told him his wife and Kevin had both been at Main Street Books, Roger feared his boss had leapt to the conclusion they were having an affair. Earlier in the evening, I had wondered the same thing. So Roger figured Chief Woodward might go to Kevin's place, expecting to catch them in *flagrante delicto*. More anxious each time a red light halted his progress, Roger muttered to himself. He wanted to get to Kevin before Chief Woodward made a mistake he could never undo.

He sped up the boulevard, onto Military Road, then down a side street. Overhead, a low-flying military transport dipped its wings and circled for a landing at the airbase near the apartment complex.

When he arrived, Roger skidded in a circle in front of Kevin's unit. He saw no sign of Harry Woodward's Skylark. No lights were on in the apartment.

Roger straddled his Harley and pounded the handlebars.

This is when Rebecca caused his cell phone to sing. He heard the worry in her voice and returned to my house, where I told him of the vision I'd had. Though he refused to believe I *witnessed* Amy's murder, his recollection of the single light in the Woodward house on a frigid weekday night worried him. Had Chief Woodward killed his wife in a jealous rage then fled? Fed by my fear, he didn't stop to consider whether Woody might be at a late meeting with the DEA, and Amy might have left the light on for him when she went to bed.

Now in his Trailblazer, and much the warmer for the exchange of vehicles, he sped back to the white and blue clapboard house.

When he pulled up, he saw his boss's Buick in the driveway. The house was now lit. The front door was open.

Breathing a sigh of relief, Roger climbed from his car and started up the steps. As he reached to open the storm door, he heard a loud moan and a sobbed, "Amy! Why?"

Dreading his worst fear had been realized, he rushed inside.

"Why, Amy? Why?" Harry Woodward cried.

171

Roger nearly tripped on the dining room area rug as he rounded the corner and burst into the Woodwards' kitchen. What he saw brought him to a skidding stop.

Harry Woodward sat on the tile floor, his back against the dishwasher. He was covered in blood. Amy's head in his lap, one arm draped across her shoulders, he rocked back and forth. A red pool spread beneath his wife's body.

"Why? Why?" Chief Woodward groaned.

Roger gasped. "Woody, what happened?"

"Why?" the Chief said again, as if he didn't realize anyone else was there.

His eyes quickly scanning the scene, Roger noticed a sink full of soapy water. There were red splatters on the backboard and a broken plate on the floor. It appeared as though Amy had been washing dishes when a shot hit her in the back.

Two pots had fallen from the stove. Amy must have knocked them over when she fell.

A pane of glass just above the kitchen doorknob was shattered. Wooden dinette chairs were overturned. A purse lay on the floor, its contents scattered. Drawers were open. Knives, forks, and spoons were also strewn about.

Had this been the work of an intruder who entered through the back door, intending to rob the house? If so, why was Amy Woodward's back turned? Surely she would have turned to the door when the glass pane broke. Surely she would have run from the kitchen. Roger concluded Amy knew the person who shot her and the signs of a break-in were a red herring.

He glanced down. A Glock .45 was loosely held in his boss's hand. Same caliber as the pistol that killed Jim Osborn—he'd seen the ballistic report in Chief Woodward's sparse file.

"Woody, what have you done?" he whispered.

The detective chief lifted his head. "It's my fault," he groaned and dropped his gaze to the pistol. Now his eyes turned up to Roger. "Tell Amy I'm sorry."

"I'll take the gun," Roger said. He knelt. Gently, careful to touch only the trigger guard, he pulled the pistol from Woody's fingers. He slipped it into his jacket pocket where it clinked against my athame. Exhausted, he sank down next to his boss and pulled out his cell phone.

"Sarge? Detective Frey," he said when the desk sergeant answered. "I need a bus and a squad car at Chief Woodward's house." He glanced at Woody, who still sat unmoving. "Call the crime scene techs and the medical examiner. Oh, and you'd better wake up the deputy chief. Tell him we've got a problem."

Within fifteen minutes, sirens whooped down Hyde Park Road.

Roger spent the rest of the night in a precinct interrogation room, where Chief Woodard sat, eyes clouded, while Deputy Chief Reynolds questioned him. Woody answered each question with a blank stare and a moan. It was as if his mind had fled to some warm, distant land.

At last, as the sun began to peek through low clouds, Chief Woodward was led to a holding cell.

***

"I can't believe Woody would murder anyone, much less his wife," Roger told us. He dropped his half-eaten cheese sandwich on his plate.

Stunned by the detailed description of the murder scene, Rebecca and I were as silent as Woody must have been during his interrogation.

"I just can't believe it," Roger said again. He pushed away the bowl of soup that had gone cold while he spoke. "I've known the man ever since I got my gold badge. Ten years. It isn't in him to do something like this."

He glanced at Rebecca, then at me. His eyes glistened with tears.

Elvira poked her head from under the table and looked up at Roger. She mewed, sprang onto his lap, and curled up.

I started to reach out to him, but stopped. I sat on my hands to keep them from doing what my heart wanted them to.

Rebecca peered at me and snorted.

I was about to tell her to mind her own business, when Roger groaned. Stroking the cat's soft white fur, he muttered, "It can't be."

"If not Woody, who?" I asked. My eyes shifted to Elvira. I was certain she'd give us the answer.

The cat stood. Her paws on Roger's chest, she stared at him.

He sniffed and drew his shirtsleeve across his eyes. "I'll tell you something," he said. "Jimmie's death and Amy Woodward's are tied together. And I'll tell you something else. If *I* don't find out how, no one will."

"Is there, uh…something we can do to help?" Rebecca said. She glanced at me. "Maybe go to the library, do some research?"

She clearly didn't want to come face-to-face with a killer, but knew I was too angry to stay out of it. The library would be a place both of us would be safe—well, safer than chasing someone who had killed twice.

"I've got to do more than look through books and old newspapers," I said.

Elvira mewed and crawled onto Roger's shoulder. From that vantage, she seemed to look past the counter and posts separating my kitchen from my dining and living areas. Her eyes were fixed on the table we'd set up near the French doors.

Roger turned in his seat. When he saw the table, he said, "Not that I believe in the hoodoo you guys are doing, but…Emlyn, you didn't happen to see the face of whoever shot Amy Woodward?

I shook my head.

"Recognize the voice?"

"Uh-uh."

His eyes dropped to his cold soup and sandwich. "Could've been Woody, then."

"No, it couldn't be," I said.

Rebecca and Roger snapped their attention to me.

"I just remembered. Woody's six-six or so. The person I saw wearing the hoody—both times—was too short to be him."

"Both times?" Roger asked.

I told him about the first divination spell I tried—the one where I saw the person put a pistol in a wall safe. The one in which Jimmy Osborn's killer recognized me, and started the chain of events which led to my leg being sautéed like a chicken breast. "The face was hidden by shadows the first time, too," I said. "But whoever it was, the killer's only an inch or two taller than me."

Roger thought for a minute. "About the same height as Kevin Reinhart?"

I caught my breath. I'd pulled Chief Woodward away from a speeding bus, only to shove my ex under it.

"At least we're sure the two killings are somehow connected," Rebecca said. "That's a start."

"Maybe also connected to the drug ring," Roger added. "If it is, I'm willing to bet your ex-husband's the connection."

Elvira jumped from his shoulder, landed at his feet and growled, as if to say, *What are you waiting for? Get the slimy bastard before he kills us all!*

Yes, I admit I put my thought into the cat's mouth.

Roger said, "Kevin's the key." He took a bite of his cheese sandwich. "He's not at his apartment. Where else would he hole up?"

I closed my eyes and tried to think. "His parents used to own a place on Saunders Settlement Road. It's a stone house on the north side, just before you get to the high school."

"Could he be there?"

I rested my elbows on the table and my head in my hands. I disliked my ex to the point at which just the thought of him turned my stomach—you don't throw a hex at someone you care about. But I'd gotten to know him in the three years we lived together. Kevin was sleazy, yes, and underhanded. But he was also a coward, afraid of guns. The first thing he did when he moved into my house was get rid of my father's hunting rifles. So, while it didn't strain my imagination to believe he might be peddling drugs, or that he'd try to blackmail Amy Woodward—though I had no idea for what—no matter how hard I tried, I couldn't picture him killing her.

Looking at Roger, I said, "It's an old house, been around a century and a half. I once went inside. Most of what I remember is the dust and cobwebs." I shuddered. "Broken walls, sagging floors. I used it as the setting for one of my stories."

"Sounds like the perfect place for a man to hide out," Rebecca said. She rose and began to clear the table.

"Maybe. But Kevin?" I shook my head. "When I went in to explore the stone house, get details for my story, he insisted on waiting outside. Said it creeped him out."

"I'll check the place," Roger said. "Never know. Being afraid for his life might've given Reinhart the guts to crawl in there."

I pushed myself up from the table and reached for my crutches. "All right, let's do it."

Elvira sat up at my feet, eager to come with us.

"Where are you going?" Roger asked.

"With you. It'll make it easier on Kevin if I'm there."

"Uh-uh. This is police business."

I felt my spine stiffen. Stubbornness does that to me. I raised my arm and pointed a crutch at Roger. "Federal police business. You're not supposed to get involved, either. Or have you forgotten that?"

I'd finally found someone whose back could get as stiff as mine. "Doesn't matter," he said. "I'm making it my case. And the last thing I need is to worry about whether you're gonna fall through a hole in the floor."

"I can't sit here and do nothing," I argued.

Elvira mewed. Obviously she agreed with me.

I glanced at the end table and the remnants of our divination rite. My lips bent into a small grin. "Maybe there *is* something I can do."

"Oh, no! Uh-uh," Roger said. "The last thing I need is to have your brain go haywire again."

My grin widened enough to show the result of orthodontic work my parents paid a fortune for when I was fourteen. "You just said the last thing you need is for me to fall into a hole. How many last things do you have?"

He ignored my remark.

I hobbled to the closet for my coat.

"Stay!" he said, as if he were talking to Elvira.

While I stood, fuming, he snatched my coat and exchanged it for his.

The crutches under my arms, from inside the glass storm door I watched him stride down my driveway to the unmarked car. He knocked on the driver's window and leaned down. A minute later he was in his Trailblazer. As he passed the DEA agents, they made a U-turn and followed him down River Road.

Now at my side, Rebecca said, "Well, that's that." She seemed relieved.

"I don't think so."

"But Roger said—"

"Yeah, I heard him. He doesn't want us at the stone house. He didn't say anything about looking for Kevin elsewhere."

Elvira looked up at me.

Rebecca didn't move. Her eyes flicked from my sofa to the door, and her lips turned down. "This isn't a good idea."

I leaned my crutches against the wall. Standing on my one good leg, I took my coat from the closet. "Where'd you put my bag?" I said. "I need my car keys."

"How are you gonna drive, you can hardly walk?"

"You can ride along with me or not. Either way, I'm going." I opened the storm door.

Rebecca rolled her eyes and muttered, "Did I say something about standing in the way of a freight train?"

She took a deep breath while trying to figure a way, I thought, to stop me from going after a man who wouldn't hesitate to kill us both. After half a minute, she released her breath. It seemed as though she decided she couldn't stop me. She grabbed her coat from the closet, and said, "I'm driving."

While I swung my crutches down the front steps, I called back to her, "Take Elvira. She's got a better handle on this than we do."

Chapter Eighteen
What Kevin Was Up To

We passed beneath a sign announcing we had entered Little Italy. Set on concrete replicas of Roman pillars, and adorned with green and red iron grapes, the sign spanned Pine Avenue. This was the business district in downtown Niagara Falls. Up and down the street, strands of plastic holly and Christmas wreaths still hung from lampposts. In New York's Snow Belt, we cling to the warmth of the holiday season and keep the remnants of it around as long as possible.

Rebecca was behind the wheel of my second-hand, brown Plymouth Valiant.

Elvira stood on my lap and gazed out the window. Her head swiveled from side-to-side. At times, she climbed up my chest and leaned over my shoulder with her neck stretched.

"You're a real tourist," I said to her.

She bent down and stared into my eyes, as if to say, *One of us has to pay attention to what's going on.*

We passed restaurants, small clothing stores, and a furniture repair shop. When we neared Flannery's Bar, the cat scampered onto Rebecca's lap and pressed her face against the driver's side window.

I grabbed her. "Hey, you're gonna get us into an accident."

She twisted in my arms and opened her mouth.

I understood what she wanted to say. A man with a scarf wrapped around his face had just come out of Flannery's door. I took a close look at him. In a minute, I settled back in the passenger seat, and shook my head. "Looks a little like Kevin—the right height, but that's not the way he walks." My ex shuffled his feet when he walked, as if he were weary from a long and laborious day.

Just before the Baptist church, we pulled to the curb in front of a building of Mediterranean design. It had ivory stucco walls, brown beams, and arched orange shingles on the overhangs and roof. The ground floor housed a bakery and an Italian deli. Between them was a small courtyard with a staircase on either side. Above the courtyard was an exposed walkway, along which were the heavy oak doors of a law firm and a political office. Where the walkway bent back toward the street, raised black letters on weathered wood marked the office of IRA SMITH, INSURANCE BROKER. It was there my ex used to work. It was there we were headed.

The crutches clutched in my right hand, I leaned heavily on the rail as I climbed the stairs. Rebecca followed me, carrying the cat.

I hesitated in front of the Insurance Broker sign, unsure whether I really wanted to go in. My uncertainty might have lasted more than a few seconds, if I hadn't felt Elvira's paw push on my back.

A tinny bell sounded when I opened the door. Without looking up from the folder on her desk, the blond receptionist asked, "May I help you?"

The walls were papered in black and white zebra stripes. The outer office was only large enough to hold one chair, a small two-seat sofa with silver metal arms and black Naugahyde upholstery, and a table on which a few issues of *National Geographic* and *Sports Illustrated* were scattered. Looking at the stained covers, I thought those same magazines might have been on the table when I was last here seven years ago. The same blond secretary was at the desk.

"Is Ira Smith in?" I asked.

She glanced up. "Oh, Mrs. Reinhart." Her face turned bright red.

She should have been embarrassed. This was the woman my ex had slept with—the straw that broke the back of my marriage.

"Not Mrs. Reinhart, Mary Beth," I said. "I haven't been that for a long time, as you well know."

She shuffled some pages in her file.

There was already one cat in the reception area—a large albino cat. It would be over-kill if I were to behave like one. To put a leash on the remark I wanted to make, I took a breath. "I'm no longer angry about you and Kevin," I said. "I've realized he wasn't much to lose."

Under her breath, Mary Beth muttered, "You can say that again."

I fought a smile. Apparently, my revenge spell had swept up this blond bimbo in its wake. "So, is Ira in?"

She pushed a button on her phone. "Mr. Smith, Mrs. Rein…uh, Emlyn…" She lifted her eyes to me.

I leaned over her desk. "Ira, it's Emlyn Goode. Got a minute?"

In far less than a minute, one of the two inner doors opened.

"Emlyn, great to see you!" Ira Smith said even before he stepped out. The epitome of a salesman, an effervescent personality was his stock-in-trade. He sounded as though he *was* glad I stopped by. He was as slimy as Kevin and had made several passes at me while I was still Mrs. Reinhart. Maybe he thought I'd come to take him up on his offer.

He came through the door with his arms open and a wide smile plastered across his face. In his brown suit with wide white strips, he reminded me of a carnival barker. "How've you been?" Just short of embracing me, he stopped and stared at my crutches. "Good Lord, what happened?"

"You don't want to know," I said.

He glanced past me to where Rebecca was bent over the table, thumbing through a worn issue of *National Geographic*. Her long salt and pepper braid almost touched the floor.

"This is my friend—"

She stood up and turned to him.

"—Rebecca Nurse."

The smarmy smile froze on his face.

"I know Ira." She held out her hand. "He came to my shop a few times for tarot card readings last year."

I wondered whether tarot readings were how this man handled risk management.

Ira glanced at his secretary through the corner of eyes almost as dark as the reception area's decor. It appeared as though he didn't want Mary Beth to know he believed in such things.

The blond buried her face in the file on her desk.

"Yes, I recall," he said. "Uh, please come in."

I felt a bit uneasy, learning of a connection, albeit indirect, between Rebecca and my ex. I shot her a look.

Focused on Ira instead of me, she held out the cat. "This is Elvira."

Immediately, Ira's eyes began to water. He stepped back, rubbing them. "Uh, Mary Beth, could you watch the cat for a few minutes?"

"Not a good idea," I said. "Elvira doesn't do well with strangers."

The secretary didn't look up from her file.

Ira considered the cat for a moment, before he waved us into his office and to the two chairs in front of his Ikea faux mahogany desk. When he followed us in, he edged along the wall so as to remain as far from Elvira as the close space permitted.

Behind the desk was a display of framed photographs of Ira standing alongside men in the uniforms of our local football, baseball, and hockey teams. In others, he shook hands with a former mayor and some town councilmen.

After hanging his suit jacket on the back of his leather executive chair, he asked, "What can I do for you?" He glanced at my crutches. "We ought to start by reviewing your coverage."

In his early forties, Ira Smith had thick red hair and sideburns crawling down his long, narrow face.

"That's not why I came by," I said.

Elvira jumped from Rebecca's arms and slithered under the desk.

Ira sneezed. He pulled a tissue from a drawer. "Sorry." He sniffed. "I'm allergic to cats."

Elvira crawled next to his chair and pawed his jacket pocket.

"Stop it! You're not being nice," Rebecca said to her. As she bent over to pick up the cat, she glanced at the pocket.

"We won't stay long," I said. "I'm trying to find Kevin. Do you know where he might be?"

Ira swiveled in his chair to face the window. "What's he done now?"

Rebecca's brows crept up and she sucked in her lower lip.

"Nothing as far as I know," I said. "I just need to speak with him." This wasn't really a lie. I didn't *know* my ex had blackmailed or murdered anyone.

Ira blew his nose and glanced accusingly at Elvira. "Haven't seen him in a couple of months," was his curt reply. "Not since—" He averted his eyes.

I opened my bag, pushed my house keys to the side, and pushed my wallet to the other side. There wasn't anything I needed in my purse. I pushed things around so my next question would sound casual.

"I always wondered what happened between you and Kevin, why you, um—" I took out my compact, checked my lipstick. "Why you fired him."

Ira and Kevin had been high school friends. They'd run together on the relay team that went to the state finals in their senior year. They were still passing the baton back and forth, at least metaphorically, the last time I saw them together. It seemed to me whatever Kevin was involved in, Ira was probably right there with him.

He swiveled back to his desk. "I really shouldn't say."

"Come on, Ira, I lived with the man. Nothing you tell me would be a shock."

He wiped his nose and tossed the tissue into the trash. "No, I really shouldn't. Possible liability, my lawyer says."

This was something of an answer, but not as much of one as I wanted.

Before I had a chance to press him further, Rebecca handed me the cat and leaned across the desk. In a stage whisper, she said, "That question you asked me the last time you came for a reading? I know the answer."

His face turned so red, I could barely tell where his forehead ended and his hair began. He turned his head from Rebecca to me. "No, that's okay. I found out what I wanted to know."

She sat back with a satisfied smile.

I knew my friend had sent him a message. To double-team him, I now leaned forward. "Oh, Ira," I crooned. "It's just me. Who am I going to tell?"

His eyes went blank. He shook his head. His longish red hair didn't move (did he use hairspray?).

"You're good," he finally said. "Okay, then, I let him go because he was selling cocaine to our clients. I didn't find out about it until a cop showed up here."

Ira slouched in his chair, watching, I supposed, for shock to spread across my face.

Instead of saying, *Right, like you weren't in that together,* I remarked, "Yeah, I figured it might be something of the kind. Or maybe blackmail?"

He tried to hide the flush again rising to his cheeks by blowing his nose. "Not that I ever heard about." His eyes turned up and to the left. A classic "tell." I knew he lied.

"Who was he bleeding, Ira?"

His lips tight, he gripped the arms of his chair.

I realized Ira Smith wouldn't tell me, no matter how much I flirted with him. I figured he held his silence because he still bled people he and Kevin sold the white powder to. I had researched the psychological effects of cocaine for a story I wrote. Like heroin, it's an insidious drug with talons digging into your soul. But at the same time, you'll do almost anything—pay almost anything—to keep from being labeled a junkie. Could Amy Woodward have been one of the people they blackmailed? Jimmy Osborn? They both had a lot to lose if anyone found out they snorted cocaine.

I dropped the compact into my purse. With a frown, I said. "That's my ex-husband. Always looking for an easy buck. Well, thanks for your time, Ira. If you see Kevin, tell him I want to talk to him."

Rebecca handed me my crutches and I hobbled down the stairs to my car. As she turned the key in the ignition, I latched onto her hand. I still had a bone to pick with her.

"You know Ira Smith?" I said. "Why didn't you tell me?"

I'd trusted her, thought she was a friend. Had she betrayed me? My mind flashed back to my earlier suspicion: could Rebecca be part of the killings and the drugs? Had she insinuated herself into my life to protect her secret? The crone in black I'd seen outside my French doors—I was certain she had been my ancestor—had come to warn me about a betrayal. Was it Rebecca Sarah's gnarled finger pointed to?

"You didn't say we were coming to see him," she responded.

"But you knew he and Kevin worked together."

"Actually, I didn't. Ira never mentioned it during our sessions, and you didn't tell me when we worked the vengeance spell."

I closed my eyes.

She touched my shoulder. "Emlyn, I *am* your friend. I'd never lie to you."

"If that's true, tell me what question Ira Smith wanted answered."

"Not now," she said. "He's watching us."

I turned my face up to the second floor and saw Ira at his window, looking down.

As we pulled from the curb, she said, "You know he had coke in his jacket pocket."

Did she think this would distract me? Learning of the line from Rebecca to Ira Smith, and through him to Kevin and the two murders, made her a mystery inside an enigma. I felt as though my survival depended on unravelling this tangled thread. Immediately.

***

I told Rebecca to make a right at the corner. Two blocks up, I had her make another right then pull over halfway down the block. If she told me what she knew about Ira Smith—if I could believe her—I might begin to understand what was going on: why Jimmy Osborn and Amy Woodward had been killed; why the killer intended to do the same to me. I especially wanted to know why she suddenly appeared at Main Street Books. I didn't dare wait until we got back to my house.

"Okay, Ira's not watching now," I said as soon as she parked.

She slid the bench seat back, unfastened her seatbelt, and turned to me. "The last time he came for a reading, he seemed rather nervous. A friend of his had dragged him into something, he said, and now unsavory people had gotten involved. He was afraid of those people, wanted the cards to tell him how to get free of them. He wouldn't tell me who the friend was or what he was doing."

"What did the cards say?"

"Tarot cards only read the future of the path you're on. You know that. They don't tell you how to get off that path."

"But, you told Ira you had an answer. In his office, you said so."

She stroked her braid. "We needed a lie. If he didn't think I knew something, he wouldn't have told us the little he did."

"And the rest of it—the part about his being involved with dangerous people?—didn't you think it was important to tell Roger about that? Shouldn't you have told me? Those dangerous people could be the ones who've tried to kill me." Was Rebecca one of those dangerous people? Tears sprang up in my eyes.

She took Elvira from my arms. "I didn't see the connection before."

My stomach quivered. She still held something back. "When you used the oil you brewed on my leg, you said you brought it because you thought it would be needed."

Staring out the window, she stroked Elvira.

"Rebecca, why did you have it with you?"

She sighed. "Yesterday morning when I did a reading for myself, I saw..." her voice faded into the hum of the car's engine.

"What?" The quivering climbed from my stomach to my chest.

She seemed ready to cry. "The cards told me I might lose a friend."

"Lose?" Now the quivering was in my voice.

"I saw a...a funeral."

I gasped. "Mine?"

She took my hand, held it tight. "We can change the future. We have to. That's why I came to your book signing."

Elvira mewed. It was as if she said my friend spoke the truth.

Panicked now, I shouted, "We have to tell Roger!" I didn't stop to wonder why I equated him with safety.

"You're right." She handed me the cat and slid the Valiant into gear.

As we swung from the curb, Elvira jumped onto Rebecca's lap and clawed the window.

Not for the first time that day, I said to her, "Hey, you're gonna get us killed."

She growled and continued to scratch the glass.

"What is it?" Rebecca asked.

Elvira hissed and smacked the window with her paw. She seemed to be saying, *It isn't me who's gonna get us killed!*

I leaned over to see what she tried to attack.

Behind the ramshackle house on the other side of the street I noticed a narrow lane. In the center of the lane I saw a weathered wooden barn with shrunken slats through which I could almost see the buildings beyond. The barn appeared to be so old it might have stood there since before the city became a city, since the long ago time when Niagara County was nothing but woods and farmland. In all the years I'd lived in the area, all the times I'd spent in Niagara Falls, walked along these streets, I'd never noticed it. Now as I did, I felt something unsettling about the sight. The barn and the boarded up houses surrounding it looked familiar.

"What?" Rebecca asked.

"I...this...it...it looks like..." Had I been able to finish the sentence, I would have told her this might be the place

Amy Woodward was killed in my vision. At last I was able to get a few more words out. "Circle the block. I have to see this alley from its end."

Elvira's head seemed to twist nearly a hundred and eighty degrees. She looked at me with wild eyes.

I ignored her.

Following my directions through the maze of one-way streets, Rebecca brought us to alley's entrance. When we got there, I rolled down my window and leaned out.

As my eyes panned along the row of run-down houses, a black SUV, its windows tinted almost the same black, backed out of the barn. Half-hidden behind a chain link fence and scant leafless trees, a figure dressed in black with what appeared to be a ski mask over his face, climbed from the passenger seat. He reached back inside and pulled out what appeared to be a rifle of some kind, maybe an Uzi. Another figure, similarly clad, came around the front of the SUV. He stopped by the first man and leaned close as if speaking to him. Then they both turned in our direction. One pointed at us, the other leaned on the fence.

Weeraaaah! Elvira screeched.

A third man emerged from the barn. He joined the other two near the SUV. The first man raised his rifle, rested it on the fence, bent, and peered through the sight.

"We have to get out of here!" I shouted.

I didn't need to tell Rebecca twice. She gunned the engine and we shot down the street.

Chapter Nineteen
Home but Not Safe

We were being followed. I'd seen the three men jump into the black vehicle as we sped down the street. Fear crept up my spine on tarantula legs. I felt the damn spider bite my neck. Felt its venom seep into the marrow of my bones.

"Go, go, go!" I hollered.

Rebecca spun the steering wheel to the left, to the right then left again. My brown Valiant squealed around corners. If my right foot and leg were once again on fire, I wouldn't have noticed. Fear is the greatest anesthetic. I twisted my body to look out the rear window. My eyes flicked as I searched for the SUV with tinted windows I was certain would soon nip at our tailpipe. I was also certain an Uzi would be aimed at us from one of the SUV's windows.

A car pulled out of a driveway, slammed on its brakes. We barreled past doing far more than the thirty-mile-an-hour legal speed limit on the city streets. The driver opened his door and leaned out. His middle finger raised, he yelled at us.

"Turn here!" I shouted.

We swerved around another corner.

Her claws out, Elvira clung to my coat.

We were on Independence Avenue, a wide street with one lane in each direction separated by a raised median. Hyde Park Road loomed ten blocks ahead. A long time ago, boats sailing the Niagara River had been unloaded, and the goods carted overland to Lake Ontario along what was then called the Salt Road. The endless Ontario wasn't our goal. We needed to avoid being blasted into an endless sleep. Once on Hyde Park Road, we'd make a right turn and my car would be pointed at the police precinct, at safety.

Just ahead, a large black vehicle ran the stop sign. It shot across the intersection.

I pointed. Rebecca turned right, then right again. We were headed back where we'd come from. The alley off Nineteenth Street was the last place we wanted to be.

"Turn here!"

Halfway through the intersection, my Valiant fishtailed. The tires scraped against the curb, bounced off. Steering into the skid, Rebecca knocked over two garbage cans. Trash flew across the street behind us. The tires gripped the road just before we sideswiped a parked Cadillac. A woman jumped from the driver's door, and shook her fist at us. We weren't making any friends today.

I unsnapped my seatbelt and climbed onto my knees so I could peer through the rear window. A black SUV turned onto the street. Maybe it was dark gray. Maybe it wasn't the one we'd seen outside the barn. I had no desire to find out.

"Faster!" I yelled, as I dropped back down and refastened my seatbelt.

Rebecca hit the gas. The rear tires spun on a patch of black ice. The SUV drew closer. Now it was only a half block behind. Yes, the SUV was black.

Traction at last. We barreled toward the red light on Pine Avenue.

"Run it!"

Rebecca shook her head and tapped the brakes.

"What are you doing?"

"I don't wanna get a ticket."

I glared at her. "Would you rather get dead?"

She glanced over her shoulder. The SUV had gained on us. "I see your point," she said.

We picked up speed.

"Hold on!"

Elvira screeched.

We raced past the Italian deli and bounced into the intersection. My car thudded as the shock absorbers pushed back against gravity. We shot through.

Brakes screamed on vehicles coming from both directions. Thank goodness not everyone in Niagara Falls was moving as fast as my car. Although, I did hear a thud behind us, but no police sirens. There's never a cop when you need one. Even a cop waving a ticket book would have been welcome.

I looked back. The SUV had stopped at the light. This didn't mean those weren't the guys from the barn.

I directed Rebecca though another series of turns. Down a dead end street, through a backyard where a stunned older man was pouring seed into a bird feeder, then onto a road near the casino. After another mile, we drove onto the entrance ramp of a parkway Robert Moses had laid out. The parkway merged into the LaSalle Highway. At eighty-miles-an-hour, we reached the highway's end. The black SUV wasn't behind us. I exhaled. Two more turns and we were on River Road. Home.

Rebecca pulled toward my driveway, my car still moving fast. I didn't lean over to check the speedometer.

"Where's the garage door opener?" she asked.

Her foot wasn't on the brake.

"Don't have one."

From the way she blinked, I thought my friend intended to crash through the garage door.

"Damn!" she muttered.

My body lurched forward when she slammed her foot on the brakes. Elvira bounced against the dashboard.

Rebecca jumped from the car. In a few seconds she had the garage door open. Back in the car, she drove inside. She jammed the driver's-side door against the wall as she leaped out to close the garage.

My hand shaking, I leaned over and turned off the ignition. We'd escaped the guys who chased us. No reason to let carbon monoxide do the job they hadn't.

Rebecca climbed back into the car and sat, panting, behind the wheel. Equally out of breath, I clutched Elvira to my chest.

We sat there, our eyes dead ahead, staring at the tire hanging on the back wall, at the garden hose dangling like a snake from a hook screwed into a stud. At the hood of my Valiant that was no more than a millimeter from the tire and the hose.

Five minutes passed. Ten minutes. Our breathing slowed.

Elvira squiggled out of my arms. Her hind legs on the floor, her front legs on my lap, she looked up at me with an expression that asked, *Are we gonna sit here the rest of our lives?*

"We should get into the house," I whispered.

Rebecca's knuckles were white on the steering wheel. "Speak for yourself."

Another minute passed.

I shivered. "I'm cold."

"Me too," she said.

Neither of us moved.

"We should go in," I said a minute later.

She shook her head. "Those men may be out there."

I glanced at the side door my father had built into the garage. Beyond the garage, a brick path led to the side door that opened into my kitchen.

"If we duck, stay below the top of the fence," I said, "chances are no one will see us."

"But they might."

I shrugged. "Either we risk being seen, or catch pneumonia."

The crutches poked under my arm, I opened the door. Rebecca slid across the bench seat and followed me out of the garage. Elvira slunk along next to us.

Inside, I slammed the kitchen door and double-locked it. Rebecca drew the shades. We didn't dare turn on any lights.

Now on my sofa, huddled together under the knitted cover, we began to giggle. Then laugh hysterically with tears in our eyes. We couldn't stop.

That is, until my cell phone rang.

***

Before I had a chance to say hello, Roger hollered at me.

"What the hell have you been up to?"

As if the bad guys were parked outside, waiting for the slightest sound to tell them we were here, I whispered, "Uh, what do you mean?"

"The desk sergeant just got a report about two maniacs barreling though Niagara Falls like Thelma and Louise on the lam. A brown Plymouth—the description sounded like *your* car."

"There…are lots of cars like mine."

"With your license plate hitched to them?"

"Oh," I said.

"I told you to stay put!"

"You told me nothing of the sort!" I yelled back. "And don't you dare holler at me."

At the sound of my raised voice, Elvira scampered to her hiding place under the skirt of my wingback chair.

Rebecca's face fell. "*Shhh,*" she said, "they'll hear us."

Angry, my fear fled as quickly as the cat. "No one's out there." I tossed off the cover, stumbled from the sofa, and stood on tiptoe to peek through a window in the front door. What I saw probably turned my face as white as the walls.

A black SUV pulled up in front of my mailbox. The passenger door opened. A figure in black leaned out, and peered up and down the road.

I gasped.

"What's going on there?" Roger asked. "Another bottle of wine?"

I dropped to my knees, cringing against the door. Shielding the phone and my mouth with a hand, I whispered, "They're outside."

"Who's outside? Emlyn, what's going on?" Roger no longer sounded angry, not even annoyed. "Talk to me."

I found my voice. "The men."

"What men?"

"From the barn."

"The— What?"

Rebecca was now crouched at the door. She leaned on me, her ear against the phone.

"Emlyn, you're not making sense," Roger said.

"Help us, Roger!" I said.

He didn't hesitate. "I'll be there in fifteen minutes."

"Tell him we haven't got that long!"

"Rebecca?" Roger said.

"They know we're here."

"Who?"

"I don't know," I said.

"Okay, stay calm. Go down the basement. Now! I'll get a squad car over there."

Rebecca grabbed my shoulders and yanked me to my feet. Bent low so we would remain below the white Formica counter separating the hall from the kitchen, we moved—almost crawled—the eight feet along the wooden hallway floor to the basement door. When she opened the door, I latched onto the jamb.

"Elvira! Where's Elvira?" I said.

"Don't worry about her. She'll be all right."

Glass shattered behind me. My eyes shot open wide. I clasped a hand across my mouth to hold in a scream.

Rebecca all but lifted me from the floor. She turned me around and pushed me toward the basement steps. The door squeaked when she closed it behind us.

I don't know how long we remained in the dark, huddled on the cement floor against the cinderblocks in a corner of the frigid basement. I don't recall taking the hammer from the tool bench beside me. The next thing I remember, I heard heavy footsteps in the hall above. The footsteps stopped at the basement door.

Rebecca clutched my blouse.

The door creaked open.

I leaned back to get a bit of purchase. Then, with all my might, I heaved the hammer at legs descending the stairs.

"Ouch!" Roger howled. He dropped heavily onto a wooden step and rubbed his shin. Peering at us through the darkness, he said, "You could've killed me."

Relieved it was him instead of the men in ski masks, I laughed. "I only need one crutch. Here, you can have the other."

I guess I didn't sound sufficiently repentant. His cheeks pinched in as though he had sucked on a lemon. For a minute, I thought he might grab the crutch I offered and beat me with it.

***

For the second time in three days, I had a shattered window in my living room. At least the guys who chased us hadn't burned my carpet—the condition my leg was in, I couldn't have gotten on my knees to scrub it clean.

When he could walk again, Roger hobbled to his house and returned with a sheet of plywood. Rebecca and I resumed our places on the sofa. Elvira crawled from under the chair and stretched out across our laps. Roger nailed the plywood over the window then began to carefully caulk the edges. While he worked, he questioned us about our afternoon.

Who were the men in the SUV? Why were they after us?

We didn't know who they were, we told him. We saw them back out of the broken-down barn in the alley off a street north of Pine Avenue. We didn't know why they aimed a rifle at us then chased us through the Falls.

"I thought we lost them," I said. "How'd they learn where I live?"

Roger stepped off the dinette chair he'd set near the window and turned to us. His face was drawn. He didn't have to answer. It was clear he thought those men had a connection in the police department, someone who could access the Department of Motor Vehicle's database.

"I don't understand," I said. "Why'd they come after us?"

He stared at me.

It was a foolish question. While we tried to learn if my ex was connected to the drug ring the DEA believed was active in the area, and how that connection might have led to the murders of a Niagara Falls detective and the wife of the detective chief, we'd accidentally stubbed a toe on the place from which the ring operated.

Nervously bouncing words off each other, Rebecca and I described the barn and what we'd seen in the lane off Nineteenth Street.

"It was the alley from my vision," I said. "The place where I saw Amy Woodward killed. Except it wasn't exactly like it."

Rebecca jumped in. "But it was close enough, so we had to see. Visions aren't always precise. Sometimes they're more metaphoric—"

"And while I tried to figure out where—"

Like a traffic cop, Roger held up his hand. When we stopped jabbering, he pulled his cell phone from his pants pocket. In a few terse words, he told about the barn, the SUV, and the men in black ski masks.

As soon as he snapped the lid of his phone closed, I asked, "They're letting you work the case?"

It was another rhetorical question.

He came to the sofa and tucked the afghan tight around me and Rebecca. "With Woody locked up while we investigate his wife's homicide," he said, "the Feds decided to let me work with them. Deputy Chief Reynolds vouched for me."

He picked up the caulking gun and returned to the window.

Rebecca glanced at me. "Kevin?" she whispered.

After fearing for my life while we were chased, and the utter relief when it turned out the legs on my basement step were attached to Roger's body, I'd completely lost sight of the reason Rebecca and I left my house in the first place.

"Roger, was Kevin at the stone house?" I asked.

He shook his head. "Your ex was there sometime in the past few days, though. Seems like he camped out in one of the bedrooms. We found a sleeping bag and fast food wrappers on the floor."

Rebecca and I exchanged glances.

"There's something I need to tell you," she said.

Without hesitation, she spoke about the tarot readings she'd done for Ira Smith, how nervous he'd been at their last session, and what he told her about Kevin getting him involved with dangerous people. "Only he didn't mention Kevin Reinhart's name. That's why I didn't know Ira was connected to all this."

Roger was again on the chair, sealing the upper edge of the window. When Rebecca got to the part about her own reading and the funeral the cards showed her, a long line of clay spurted from the caulking gun. His back to me, I saw

198

the muscles twitch in his shoulders and tense in his neck. I was glad I couldn't see his face when, in words almost hissed, he said, "That won't happen on my watch."

He climbed from the chair, carefully laid the caulking gun on the old sheet he'd spread across the carpet and turned to us. "In ten minutes there'll be a squad car in front of your house. A cop will check your backyard regularly. No way those guys are gonna get another chance at you—" he glanced at Rebecca "—at either of you. You know why?"

I figured he didn't expect an answer. I knew I was right when he strode to the sofa, loomed over us, and answered his own question in a staccato monotone.

"Because you are both going to stay put, is why."

The way Roger's forehead creased and his eyes flared, he was more frightening than the man in a black ski mask who'd aimed a rifle at my car.

Rebecca latched onto my blouse and meekly nodded.

Elvira buried her head between us.

"But—" I got no further.

"Am I being perfectly clear this time?"

My mouth snapped shut.

I guess he thought my compliance came too easy, because he glanced around and said, "Where are your car keys?"

My lips tight, I dropped my eyes to my lap.

Her face still buried and her body shaking, Elvira whined in a way that said, *Don't ask me, sir. I'm just a cat. I don't drive.*

Rebecca pulled her hand from under the cover. She pointed at her floral shoulder bag on the coffee table.

I glared at her.

"Your keys in there, too?" Roger said.

She nodded.

"Are you going to let him get away with this?" I said.

Again Rebecca nodded.

This time Elvira's whine told me to shut up, Roger was already angry enough.

After dropping our keys in his pocket, he said, "I suppose I won't have to worry about you pushing your car back to the Falls?"

I hadn't been scolded this way since Mrs. Keller made me stand in the corner for hours when I was in the third grade. Or maybe it was Mrs. Edelman, my seventh grade gym teacher. Regardless, it had been a long time. My face grew hot. My temper was about to flare.

Roger must have sensed this. He slowly turned back to us with a tight-lipped grin. "Of course, I could lock you both in a cell for reckless driving if you prefer. I hear the traffic squad would like to have a few words with the maniacs who ran a light and caused an accident on Pine Avenue this afternoon."

I had to hand it to him, he played quite a good trump card. It shut me up.

For the moment.

Chapter Twenty
Sarah's Goode Advice

Before he left for the Hyde Park Road precinct, Roger checked the windows and the locks on the French doors and the kitchen door.

"These stay closed," he instructed. "Don't let anyone in."

"But my window," I said. "I have to call Fred Silbert, have him come over and fix it."

Roger dropped his hands to his hips. "You aren't deaf. I know you heard me. No one gets in here. Not Fred, not even one of the cops from the patrol car. No one."

I gazed at the plywood sheet nailed over my front window. I dropped my eyes to the burn marks on my living room carpet. In my mind, my house had begun to look like the ramshackle hovels I saw in my vision. Soon, it would look like the falling-apart barn those masked men came out of. This wasn't a hovel. It was my home, my sanctuary. No way would I let it stay a rundown mess.

Roger must have seen my eyes roam around the room, because he muttered, "You are such a pain."

He lifted the skirt of his camelhair coat and reached into his back pocket. When his hand emerged, a pair of handcuffs dangled from his fingers. He took a step toward me, and held them out. "Let's go."

The man was serious.

I grabbed the armrest of the sofa and shook my head. Hard.

"Let's *go*," he said more firmly. "I don't need to be distracted by worrying about you."

I pulled the afghan up to my chin. The movement shook Elvira to the floor. She rolled over and sat for a moment with a stunned expression.

"Coming?" Roger said.

If I didn't know better, I would swear the cat stuck out her front paws for him to cuff (what was it I said about my strange imagination?).

I leaned as far from Roger as I could. "Okay." I said.

A satisfied smile crossed his lips. "Okay, what?"

"Okay, we'll stay put."

"And no one gets in?"

I sighed. "I won't let anyone in."

A writer, I try to use words precisely.

Roger had known me long enough to sense what was on my mind. He held the handcuffs out to Rebecca, "*You* won't let anyone in, either. Right?"

She raised her hand, three fingers up as if giving the Girl Scout oath.

"Good, now we understand each other," he said, and headed for the front door. As he opened it, he called over his shoulder, "Elvira, you're the only one here with any sense. Make sure they keep their promise."

I looked down. The big white suck-up wore a smug expression.

***

As soon as I heard Roger's Trailblazer pull out of my driveway, I turned to Rebecca. "Now what do we do?"

"We do what we promised," she said. "We stay put."

"I can't do that. I won't be a sitting target when people are trying to kill me."

"Trying to kill *us*," she said with a pout.

"Okay, us. You don't want to make it easy for them, do you?"

She shoved the knit cover from her lap. "I swear to you, Emlyn Goode, if the cards had shown you'd get me into this kind of trouble, I…I would have let that stupid Molotov cocktail burn you to a cinder."

She jumped from the sofa, sidled around the coffee table, and stormed past the wingback chair and into the kitchen. Water hissed in the sink. Metal clanked, a cabinet opened. How could she make tea at a time like this?

I heard her mutter, "I can't believe the way I drove today. I never do anything like that. Never even drive as fast as the speed limit."

My eyes turned down to Elvira. "You'll help me, won't you?"

She gave a long *meeeeow*.

I had really gotten to understand her. She'd just told me, *Uh-uh. I don't want to land in jail. That's where Sarah Goode wound up, and you know what happened to her*.

"Traitor," I muttered, then called aloud, "You hear me, Rebecca Nurse? You're both traitors!"

My friend came from the kitchen carrying two steaming mugs. On her face she had what I took as a wistful smile. "You know," she said, "it was actually fun, sort of, being bad today."

"We weren't bad. We were trying to stay alive."

"Still—" she handed me a mug. "Here, drink this."

"What's in it, sleeping pills?"

"No, rosemary and lavender. This will calm you."

"I don't need to be calm," I shouted. "I need to do something!"

"I know," she said. "But we won't be able to figure out what with our minds beating a tattoo because of the excitement. So, we drink this tea and relax."

"Then what? We take a nap?"

"No. Then we sit quietly and listen. The earth and wind will tell us what to do."

I took a few breaths—what my yoga instructor called calming breaths. In a few moments I had calmed enough to realize Rebecca was right. It seemed as though she always was—well, at least most of the time. I raised my mug. "Here's to the earth and the wind."

As we sipped the rosemary and lavender brew, the windows on the French doors rattled. Apparently the wind agreed with my friend.

We sat with our backs straight against the cushions, me on the sofa, Rebecca in the wingback chair below the railroad station clock. Through deep and relaxing breaths, I visualized the wind and how it swept across the earth. How it caressed the branches of trees. How it swirled upward to the heavens. The wind was free, moved with its own will.

My eyes fell on Sarah Goode's *Book of Shadows*. When I lifted it, the book fell open. I scanned the page. It seemed as though my ancient relative spoke to me from the distant past.

4 March, in the year of our Lord, 1692.

It has happened. Those foolish children, Elizabeth Parris and Abigail Williams, have denounced me as a witch, a Devil worshiper. Why? I did naught but seek them comfort from the brain fever that causes them to twitch and moan, and run among the wheat stalks unclad. So today I have a roof above me, and I sleep on cold straw. Bars on the door keep me from bringing low other weak-minded children with my potion that is naught but lavender and rosemary.

The black slave, Tituba, lies here also, for the crime of obeying her superstitious mistress's demand for a devil cake. And though fed to those children the cake cured their brain fever, Magistrates Hathorne and Corwin say it was the Evil One's work.

Is there no end to this madness?

And, oh, the shame! Two days ago the Magistrates entered my cell, tore from me my blouse, and examined my bare breasts, seeking, they said, for a mark to show I have suckled the

Devil's familiars. And my youngest daughter, my Dorothy, only four, is held in custody until she swears an oath against me, and says the Devil's milk nourished her at my breast.

I must flee this place. I must do as some in this Salem town now swear they have seen me do, and soar on the wind across the night sky. This is a real and true gift, even if it is only in my mind. Without my herbs and spices I can do this. The good God has seen fit to give me this gift by which, with breaths and concentration, I might fly from here to confront those who would do me evil...

I shut the book and looked over at the wingback chair. Rebecca's eyes were closed. Her breaths came at an easy, steady rate. Elvira was curled on her lap, snoring.

I placed the book gently on the table. I tiptoed to the basement door. Strange, I didn't think to take my crutches. Yet I didn't limp. I felt no pain in my foot and leg.

The door didn't squeak when I opened it.

Roger must have oiled the door when he fixed my window, I thought. I glanced at the window. No plywood covered it now. When was Fred Silbert here? I didn't dwell on the question. The sun had set. An east wind whipped though the birch branches. The trees danced to a manic rhythm.

Elizabeth Parris and Abigail Williams must have behaved like those tree limbs, hands flashing this way and that as if they were bewitched.

In the basement, I opened the door to the closet in which I stored my candles, athame, and other tools of my new craft. In a corner was a besom, an old fashioned broom made of twigs. The kind Sarah Goode would have used. Where had it come from? I had no time to consider that.

I clutched the broom in my arms and climbed the stairs, then another flight to the second floor of my cottage. In the upper hall, I yanked the string to drop the trap door. I pulled down the ladder-like steps and climbed to the attic. Even with insulation tacked between the joists, the beating of the wind on the roof sounded like thunder. I didn't feel the bitter cold, though. I knew why: the wind could not touch me while my complete concentration rested on the flight I was about to take.

Carefully, I stepped from beam to beam until I reached the round portal at the far end of the house. The back end. If I flew out this way, the officers in the patrol car parked out front wouldn't see me leave. They wouldn't call Roger and tell him to come over and pull me back.

With my shoulder, I shoved the round window open. The chill wind blew through my hair and caressed my face. I felt as though I were one with the wind, one with the air. I could do this. I knew I could.

I took a step back. The broom between my legs, I bent over and launched myself into the dark universe.

In moments, I soared over Niagara Falls and hovered above the Hyde Park Road precinct. Looking down, I saw Roger's Trailblazer parked in the lot. He stood beside it, earnestly speaking with two men. I tilted my body like a plane dipping its wings and veered toward the Woodwards' house. Again I looked down—

Pounding. Where did that pounding come from? Was it the wind beating against my ear drums?

"Emlyn."

The wind shook me.

"Emlyn!"

Now it called my name.

"Wake up, Emlyn."

I began to twist, like in a whirlwind. No, like in a whirl*pool.* A gust of wind must have blown me over the

Niagara River just before it flows into Lake Ontario. I tilted downward, drawn toward the eddying frigid water—

"C'mon, wake up."

"Huh?" My eyes shot open. "What…what happened?"

"You fell asleep."

My head sprung forward. My mouth as wide as my eyes, I looked down. My grandmother's knitted afghan was spread across my lap. Sarah's book was open in my hands.

I heard more pounding. This wasn't the wind. I shifted left, right.

The raps grew louder, more insistent.

Rebecca had a death-grip on my arm. Her face taught, her nails dug into my flesh. "Someone's at the French doors."

"Who?"

"How would I know?" she said. "Probably those men. They came back! They're trying to break in. We have to call Roger."

"There's no time for a phone call. Quick. Outside. The cops watching the house—get them!"

While I sat, stunned by my abrupt awakening, Rebecca ran for the front door. She threw it open. Within minutes I heard running in my backyard and frantic voices.

"Stop! Now!"

"Over there! He's there by the tree."

"I see him."

"He's climbing. Gonna swing over the fence."

"Got his leg. Help me!"

I heard a thud and the sound of a struggle.

The *wawawa* of a siren broke the silence on River Road.

"Got him!" someone shouted.

Another voice said, "Stop fighting, dammit!"

My storm door flew open. Roger ran in. In a few long strides, he crossed the living room and unlatched the French doors. He dashed out.

207

Rebecca came in from the front. She closed, locked the door and stood in the hallway, her arms crossed, slapping her shoulders. "*Brrr.*"

I threw off the cover and hobbled to her. "What's happening?"

"I don't know," she said. Her ribbed turtleneck was so stiff it might have frozen when she ran from my door to the patrol car.

Holding tight to each other's hands, using my friend as a crutch, in half-steps we approached the French doors. We leaned out.

To the left of the azalea bushes, beneath the birch tree a pile of heavy blue uniforms rolled in the snow. It looked as though it were a gang of children at play. Roger stood over them. With his pistol drawn, he leaned down.

"Knock it off," he said. "Or would you rather get a bullet in that pea-sized thing you call your brain."

The struggle ended. One cop put his knee on the spine of the man he'd tackled, the other cop pulled out his handcuffs. Looking very much the way I imagine Wyatt Earp appeared on the streets of Dodge City, Roger tossed back the skirt of his overcoat and holstered his weapon. Only then did the man beneath the pile sit up.

It was Kevin.

"What the hell is wrong with you?" Roger said. "Do you have a death wish? Get inside!"

Two rather large officers, one young and dark, the other blond and considerably older than Roger, pushed the much shorter Kevin through the French doors. Their coats were matted with snow.

Roger followed them in. "Park yourself," he told Kevin.

One of the officers roughly turned my ex around and shoved him down on one of the wooden stools at the kitchen counter.

"Sorry 'bout the snow and mud on your carpet, ma'am," the other cop said.

I stared at their tracks, then at where the carpet had been burned. With a sigh, I said, "It needs to be replaced anyway."

Rebecca took the policemen's coats. "Come with me," she told them, "I'll make you some hot tea."

For a moment, I wondered what my friend might mix into the tea, and whether the men would turn green and come hopping out of the kitchen. Silly thought, I know. But the sudden eruption of activity, the fear, then the relief when I saw my ex finally captured, had cooked my brain well past the point of done.

Roger hovered over Kevin. "You led us on quite a chase."

"Sorry," he mumbled. His hands cuffed behind his back, he dropped his head.

Kevin's blond hair seemed stringier, dirtier than it had been when he cowered on my sofa a few days before. He had a three- or four-day growth on his round face. Though his face was pale, his cheeks were florid. His gray coat was torn at the elbows. Red lines radiated from his pupils, which told me it had been a while since he slept.

"Not sorry enough," Roger said. "Do you know what you've put this woman through?" He pointed at me, as if there were several women in my living room to choose from.

Balanced now on my crutches with my right leg raised behind, I glared at Kevin. "How could you do this—" I pointed to my bandaged leg "—try to kill me?"

He let out a low groan. His eyes misting, he said, "It wasn't me, I swear it. I'd never hurt you, Emmy."

Roger's face set, his eyes on fire, he asked, "Who is it, then? Who's trying to hurt her?"

"I…I don't know."

"You know, dammit!" Roger took a half-step back and flipped his coat. With a hand on his holster, in a low, menacing tone, he said. "Tell me who, or I swear something to you, you little shit—I'll put a bullet in your forehead, and say you were trying to escape—"

"Roger!" I shouted.

Chairs clattered. The two uniformed officers ran from the kitchen.

His eyes locked on Kevin, Roger raised his left hand as though he were directing traffic. "It's okay, Matt, Ed." He moved his hand from his gun. "The perp and I were just having a quiet conversation."

My ex glanced from the cops, to Roger, to me, with a wide-eyed look of terror on his face. "I never...I couldn't... Tell 'em, Em!"

I shook my head in disgust. "He might be a lot of nasty things, but he hasn't got the gumption to kill. He nearly cried when I made him destroy a nest of wasps in the backyard."

Roger dropped his face close to his prisoner. "Maybe, maybe not. Cowards do all kinds of things we never thought they could. Like blackmail?" He let the accusation hang.

Kevin averted his eyes.

"You were trying to blackmail Amy Woodward," Roger said.

Kevin clamped his jaw.

"I'll take that as an admission. Then what? She wouldn't pay or couldn't pay, so you killed her and ransacked her house?"

"Why would I do that?"

"Same reason you tried to get money out of Emlyn—to get out of town before the DEA caught up with you."

My breath caught in my throat. "Kevin didn't kill Amy," I whispered.

Roger's head swung in my direction.

I pointed with my crutch. "I know it wasn't him."

"How?"

210

I couldn't tell Roger that while I flew in an out-of-body state above Niagara Falls, I'd seen a car drive up to the Woodwards' house, seen the person who got out of the car and knocked on the back door. No, I couldn't tell Roger without sounding like an escapee from an asylum. I especially couldn't let the two cops in my house hear about my flight (at the moment I would have argued with anyone who told me I'd dreamt the episode).

With an impatient, "Uh-huh," Roger dismissed what I said. Again he focused on Kevin. "And Detective Osborn—did you kill him, too? Were you trying to blackmail him?"

The two officers closed in. With Roger, they formed a tight circle around the prisoner. Jimmy had been one of their own.

The older cop elbowed Kevin in the ribs. "Did you?"

"Might as well give it up, Reinhart," Roger said. "An hour ago the Feds raided the barn your playmates used as a drugstore. They reeled three of 'em in. Quite a crew you're running with. Right now they're probably singing the score from a Broadway musical, and guess who they're gonna claim wrote lyrics?"

His head spinning from one accuser to the other, Kevin whined, "You...you've got it all wrong. I wasn't blackmailing Osborn. He was bleeding me."

Kevin's words rang in my ears. My mind rotated like an out-of-control carousel. Ira Smith had told us a detective came to his office. Looking for Kevin, he said. Was the detective Jimmy Osborn? If it was, had Jimmy known it was both Ira and Kevin who supplied drugs to their clients? Was he the dangerous character Ira had suggested to Rebecca? Again, I thought of the Corvette in the Osborns' driveway. Was blackmail how Jimmy got the money to buy it? Then there was the car I saw pull to the curb across the street from the Woodwards' house—

It didn't matter that I'd dreamed my flight; my mind struggled to make connections. Patches of a crazy quilt began to slide into place. They formed a pattern. I could almost see how everything on it would fit together. But, the quilt had a few patches missing. Critical patches. Like a motive for killing Jimmy then Amy. A motive for coming after me. Could it be there was a real motive for just one of the murders? Agatha Christie wrote a story about a man who slew three people to keep anyone from noticing the motive for the one murder he wanted to commit. Was that what happened here?

While I leaned on my crutches wondering what to do next and trying hard to conjure how I might find those last critical pieces of the pattern, Kevin leaned back and said, "Is…is there a deal here someplace?"

A slight smile danced on Roger's lips. "What have you got to trade?"

Before my ex could answer, someone pounded on my front door.

Chapter Twenty-One
The Short Drop

Since the Molotov cocktail crashed through the window at Main Street Books and lit my leg like a Roman candle, a sudden noise had made me jump so far I might have qualified for the Olympics. This time I didn't jump or even flinch. Elvira did. I was so lost in visions of patches sliding over my imaginary quilt, which when finished would reveal the entire picture of drugs, blackmail, and murder in my small city, I hardly heard knuckles beat a tattoo on my door.

Kevin heard the pounding, though. As if he guessed who was outside, he whined like a child about to be spanked.

"I'll see who it is," Rebecca said.

"No. Please!" Kevin cried.

Clearly annoyed at the interruption, Roger grumbled.

"Stay where you are," the younger, dark uniform instructed. "I'll get it."

His service revolver held at his side, the officer moved to the door and opened it the length of the chain.

"Is Detective Frey in there?" a harsh voice demanded from outside. The words were so loud, the entire neighborhood could have heard.

The officer at the door glanced over his shoulder.

Still hunched threateningly over Kevin, Roger shook his head.

"No, he ain't here," the dark officer said.

"Don't give me that crap," the voice shouted. "Open the damn door!"

Again the uniform looked over his shoulder.

Roger snapped his tongue. Then he gave an almost imperceptible nod.

The officer closed the door and slid off the chain. When he opened the door again, two men burst in, tracking more snow and mud across my floor. They pushed past the officer, past Rebecca, past me.

Elvira swished her tail out of the way a nanosecond before one of the men stomped on it. With a screech, she leaped onto the kitchen counter and ducked behind a group of canisters where she became almost invisible in my white kitchen.

The man who had growled like a hungry wolf at my door, moved tight against Roger's side, and so close to me I smelled stale smoke from the pipe shoved into the breast pocket of his overcoat. The man reached for Kevin's lapel. "This him?" he said.

Both invaders of my home were similarly clad in dark gray coats, with trousers of the same color. On their feet were the same highly polished heavy black brogans. The five o'clock stubble on their faces gave the appearance they'd recently dug through a trash bin. The only difference between the two was that the man who clearly was in charge had very short black hair, while his colleague's military cut was light brown.

Roger's face turned bright red. He appeared too angry to speak.

As if he might hide, Kevin twisted on the stool and ducked his head toward the kitchen counter.

The cat poked her face from behind a canister and hissed. Elvira had no affection for my ex. I couldn't blame her.

For more than a minute, everyone stared at Kevin.

At last, the man with the pipe in his pocket said, "This the way you cooperate on cases in Niagara Falls?" His eyebrows almost formed a *V*. He sounded as annoyed as he looked.

"What do you want from me, Agent Parker?" Roger said. "I got the call and came over here. Should I have waited for you while Reinhart took off again?"

It might have been a good bluff, if the cop who opened the door didn't at first deny Roger was here, and if both cops didn't look away when they heard what Roger said.

Elvira scampered across the counter. She stopped near Agent Parker. When the DEA Agent turned to her, she glared at him, as if she might freeze the man with her pink eyes then bend him to her will (that's what she'd done to me months earlier when I refused to read about the Salem witches). Or maybe she thought she could make him disappear altogether. The only effect her stare had was to deepen the man's frown.

"What's with this damn cat?" Agent Parker said.

With one hand on a crutch, I scooped Elvira up in my arm and held her away.

Snorting at Elvira, at me, at Roger, or maybe at what he saw as our conspiracy to keep my ex out of his hands, Parker commanded, "We'll take our prisoner now."

I intended to inform him Kevin was our prisoner, not his, but Roger laid a hand on my wrist.

One of the federal agents grabbed Kevin by the handcuffs. The other latched onto his overcoat. With his shoulders hunched, my former mate looked as though he'd shrunken into himself.

"This will wrap up the drug ring in a nice tidy package," Parker said.

I pushed Roger's hand away. "What about Detective Osborn and Amy Woodward?" I said. "Doesn't the DEA care they were murdered?"

Halfway out the door, the second agent replied, "We'll let you know if we get anything out of Reinhart."

"I want a lawyer," Kevin whined.

Rebecca slammed the door behind the agents and leaned against it. She seemed to be out of breath. Her braid had begun to come apart, long tendrils sticking out here and there. Over the past hour her hair had gone from tight curls to frizz. The damp air wasn't the only cause. My friend got nervous around this many policemen. I knew why: in her teenage years she'd learned the art of reading cards and palms from women in a family that moved down from Canada. Eastern European—Romanian, she thought. The family had darker skin than others in the small mid-western town Rebecca came from. After 9/11, people became xenophobic, wary of accents. Germanic, Slavic, Arabic—to the simple folk she'd grown up among, they were the same. Neighbors were suspicious of her new friends. So were the police. If a car backfired in the town, someone would call the sheriff's office and shout about a bomber on the loose. Next thing, her new friends would be hauled in for questioning, harassed on general principles. Rebecca would be hauled in, too, since the townsfolk thought she'd been brainwashed by the damn foreigners.

Still leaning against the door minutes after the DEA agents left, she said, "What do we do now?"

"Get some sleep," Roger said. "With Reinhart and the gang from the barn corralled, you won't be bothered any longer." His tone told me he was far from satisfied with the way his case ended.

I knew Roger wouldn't sleep. He hated loose ends. In this, he and I are alike—I'm not done with a story until every subplot has been resolved.

"Aren't you going to follow Agent Parker?" I asked. "*You* caught Kevin. Parker's got to let you help question him."

"What for?" Roger said. "We got the whole drug gang."

"Because I'm sure he knows something that'll point us toward the killer."

"Still don't believe Reinhart's the one who pulled the trigger?"

I stooped and put Elvira on the floor. "Do you still believe Chief Woodward didn't kill his wife?"

"Yes. I think your ex-husband did it."

"Well then, if you want to get Woody off the hook," I said, "you ought to force your way in while they question Kevin."

"She's right, you know," Rebecca said.

The cat rolled over, then sat at Roger's feet. Craning her neck to him, she let out a long *meeeow*.

Roger bent at the waist. With hands on his hips, he spoke directly to Elvira. "Of course, I want to do that."

The cat cocked her head.

"Because the Feds won't let me," he said. "You saw how pissed they were when they left."

I was surprised. When had Roger learned to speak cat?

"Keep arguing with us, and they'll have Kevin halfway back to Washington," I said. "Then you'll never find out what he knows."

Rebecca added, "And Chief Woodward will spend his life in jail for a murder you're sure he didn't commit."

"Can you live with that?" I said.

Elvira's *purrrr* echoed my sentiment.

His back to us, Roger muttered, "You're a royal pain in my ass, all three of you."

This was his way of admitting without having to say it, we were right. Men! But at least he stopped arguing.

No need to grab his overcoat before he stomped out my front door—he hadn't taken it off since he arrived—without another word, Roger was in his Trailblazer and gone. I guess he found it easier to do what we asked, than to keep trading words with a stubborn cat…um, Elvira, I mean, not me or Rebecca.

***

Rebecca let out a long breath. "I thought he'd never leave."

"I just hope the DEA lets Roger question Kevin," I said. "But, even if they don't—"

"You think you know who did it, don't you?"

I shrugged. "Maybe."

During the past two days, my friend had shown little inclination to chase after the killer. From the time she appeared at Main Street Books, it seemed she sought only to keep me from becoming the third victim. Though I knew I would have been in rather bad shape if she hadn't shown up, I'd grown a bit annoyed at her reluctance. Now, her posture was relaxed, her face calm.

"Good. Let's get the bastard," she said, at last ready to fight back.

"Don't you want to know who I think it is?"

Her jaw slid from side to side and she shook her head. "I'll find out soon enough. Where do we go from here?"

I looked around and saw Elvira on the coffee table, pawing at Sarah Goode's book.

"The cat's right," I said. "What Sarah wrote has pointed us in the right direction from the start." I scratched the white fur on the cat's neck then picked up the book. "Where do I look?" I asked.

Her head tilted, Elvira gave me a quizzical look.

"*She* might not know what to do," Rebecca said as she dropped onto the wingback chair. "But she knows Sarah does."

I settled on my sofa and flipped the book open. Pages turned. There was nothing supernatural about this. It was the principle of friction or something such as that. What do I know?—in twelfth grade, my science teacher gave me a passing grade only because I helped his daughter with the essay for her college application.

I began to read from where the pages came to rest: "Third of July, by the grace of…I cannot call Him God."

I glanced over at Rebecca. "Sarah can't say God? Do you think a demon got into her?"

"This isn't the time to worry about a demon eating your ancestor's soul," she said. "Keep reading."

"Don't worry about it? We're practicing what she did. What if we're following her down the dark road to hell? Maybe my leg got burned as a warning about where I'm headed."

Elvira jumped on my lap and pawed the page.

"Your white fur's going to get full of soot in hell," I told her.

"Read," Rebecca instructed.

This was a reverse of our roles the day before. Yesterday my friend had been loath to walk in Sarah Goode's footprints. Today, I was the one who felt hellfire lick my back. Still, I knew Rebecca was right: if I were ever to put an end to the madness around me, we'd have to follow where Sarah led.

"Okay," I said. "This is what she wrote:

"*I am betrayed by all I have known, by all I have trusted. I have trusted my life to Him, and by Him, too, have I been betrayed. I have been tried and convicted by the words of simple children, who chew the wheat in the field instead of working it as they must. And when caught in their idleness, they twitch and rant, and swear they are bewitched. Swear before Him they are bewitched. Swear before the magistrates, it is I who bewitched them. It was not bewitching I did when I gave them an herbal tea to ease their brain fever. It was the work of Him who showed me I might cure the fever by such means. And now, oh, I am betrayed.*

"*At ordeal three days past, my young daughter, my Dorothy, testified I forced her also to partake of this tea. The Devil's tea, Magistrate Corwin insisted she say. And my husband, William, swore, too, it was a Devil's brew. He needed no prodding by Corwin or Hathorne to swear it is so. Why? In this dark cell I have asked*

God why. And God tells me it is an answer I know. He is wise.

"Though I sought to hide it among my candles beneath straw in the loft, William has found this book, and read in it my yearning after dear George Burroughs. Jealousy brought from him the lies by which I am condemned to a short drop on Gallows Hill. William brought this book to me in my cell this morning and told me I have soiled his spirit with so great a treachery only God's wrath against me will cleanse it. He said then he would swear an oath also against George, if Heaven permits. In this manner has God shown me it is by my own words, writ by moonlight, that I am condemned.

"I fear God's retribution. Is there yet a way I may postpone His wrath and live to atone? Aye, there may be. Now must I use my herbs to save myself instead of others. I will write on these pages those plants I require for an amulet of truth. When my eldest, Emlyn, comes to me tomorrow, I will give her my book for safekeeping, and tell her how to tie those herbs in white linen. White is the color of truth. The herbs when combined will draw forth in public from the husband I have betrayed, the reason behind his lie."

I stopped and looked up at Rebecca.

"Keep reading," she said. "What herbs do we need?"

I turned to the next page, turned back. "I don't know."

She leaned from her chair. "What do you mean, you don't know?"

"What I said." I wiped sweat from my forehead. "Did you turn the heat up?"

"Forget the heat, what's the mixture for the amulet?"

I pointed to the book. "It's not here!"

Rebecca's eyes went wide. I could almost see smoke waft from her nose. It was as if she'd been engrossed in a mystery and someone tore the last page from her book—which, when I think about it, is what happened.

"Gimme that!"

She grabbed Sarah's book from my hands and dropped it on the coffee table. With manic motions, she turned page after page. Then, as if she'd spent every bit of her energy, she slumped back in her chair.

"Now what do we do?" she said.

"Damn," I muttered and looked to Elvira. "Any ideas?"

The cat looked back, her eyes hooded, as if she searched for one. Then she opened her eyes and her mouth.

As crazy as it sounds, I believe Rebecca and I both expected Elvira would verbalize an answer in clear, grammatically correct English. She didn't get the chance. Just then my cell phone played the chorus of *The Cats in the Cradle*.

Chapter Twenty-Two
Arresting Developments

When I flipped up the lid of my phone, Roger said, "Turns out you were right—"

The *honk-honk* of horns crowded out the rest of his sentence.

As if it were me who couldn't be heard above the racket, I shouted, "Talk louder!"

"Damn!" he said.

I heard a quick *wroo-wroo* of a police siren. Obviously, Roger was in his car. Just as obviously, he was caught in traffic.

"Get the hell outta my way!" he hollered. "Can't you see this is official business?"

"What's going on?"

"Don't have to shout at me. I hear you," he said.

"Okay, okay." In a quieter voice, I repeated, "What's going on?"

"Kevin *was* holding something back," Roger told me. "A big something. Blew this case wide open when he finally started to sing."

I felt such instant relief, my leg stopped hurting. "How'd you get it out of him?" I asked.

"What?" Rebecca said.

I repeated Roger's words.

"How'd they do it?" she asked.

"*Shh.*" I flapped my wrist to stop her from talking. "He's about to tell me." Into the phone, I said, "You're going to tell me, right?"

"Yeah, I'll tell you." Though Roger clearly felt pressure to get somewhere, he had less tension in his voice than there had been since a bottle bomb smashed the window of my house. "Agent Parker also thought Reinhart knew more, though it wasn't the murders Parker wanted to know about.

That federal lummox was only after a pretty ribbon to tie around his drug case. Soon as he offered your ex witness protection, Parker got what he needed to round up the big kahunas in Buffalo."

"Who'd Kevin give up?"

Rebecca poked me. "What? What?"

"*Shh!*" I pushed the button to put his voice on the phone's small speaker. "Happy now? Okay, Roger, go on. We're listening."

"It's Jimmy's son-in-law, Sean Ryan, who's behind everything going on in Niagara Falls."

My jaw dropped. Sean's face hadn't been on one of the patches of my quilt. Could I have been wrong about how all the patches fit together? My eyes shot around my living room, as if to search for what I'd missed.

"Sean?" I said.

"According to your ex it's him."

This can't be right, I thought. "Can we believe Kevin?"

"I'm about to find out."

Rebecca nearly jumped out of her seat. "C'mon, c'mon, what did Kevin say?"

Roger explained Sean Ryan had been chasing a story for the *Buffalo News* about the drug ring operating on the south end, and he got chummy with some guys who brought the drugs in from downstate. Sean allegedly convinced those guys there was big money to be had peddling the powder to high rollers at the Niagara Falls casino. Kevin saw Ryan pass the stuff out one night, and sold him on the idea of selling the coke to clients of Ira Smith's insurance agency. When Smith found out what Kevin was up to, he wanted in, too.

"I'm told Smith bawled like a baby when he opened his door and saw Deputy Chief Reynolds and a couple of squad cars outside his house," Roger said. "The DEA decided he's small potatoes. Since they don't need Smith to make their main case, they're gonna let us prosecute him locally. That made Reynolds happy."

What Roger said made sense. It tied in nicely to what Ira had hinted to Rebecca and what he'd told us. As for Sean Ryan, I remembered the way he hadn't let Jennifer out of his sight when I visited Marge Osborn. Then there was the way he held tight to her arm when he saw Roger with me at the book signing. So Jennifer probably knew what Sean was up to. Still, I had a nagging sensation a piece was missing. What was it? Stuck in the back of my mind was something I'd seen when I dropped by the Osborn house after the funeral. Or could it have been something that wasn't there? I knew whatever it was would tell me what questions I hadn't thought to ask. What I'd missed was right there, just beyond my grasp. Figuratively, I stretched out my hand until I almost had it—

"Wait a minute," Rebecca said. "Where does Detective Osborn come into this? Did he belong to the gang?"

Her question knocked my hand from what I almost had in my grasp. As if it were a butterfly, the recollection fluttered away.

"Uh-uh," Roger said. "Jimmy learned about the operation. Stupid kid, how'd Sean think he could keep it a secret from his wife? Jennifer got suspicious one night when she was at the casino and saw him skulking in a corner with Reinhart. She phoned Jimmy. Jimmy went to Smith's office looking for Kevin. Figured he'd implicate Sean. Smith told Reinhart about the visit, then Reinhart blabbed to Sean. Family." Roger sighed. "I guess that's why Jimmy didn't tell me what he found out." He sounded relieved his partner, his friend, hadn't been dirty.

Kevin's version of what happened didn't convince me. I couldn't let go of the new Corvette in the Osborns' driveway. Where had Jimmy gotten the money to buy it? Marge said they'd scrimped for every penny— Damn, what was it I couldn't remember?

"So the Ryan kid killed Detective Osborn?" Rebecca asked.

"That's what Reinhart thinks."

"But, did Kevin *see* him do it?" I said.

"No."

"Did Sean *tell* Kevin he did it?"

"Hey, what's with you?" Roger said. "I thought you'd be glad, knowing it's over."

I looked at Rebecca with doubt in my eyes. We both passed a doubtful expression to Elvira. On the floor at our feet, the cat craned her neck and looked through the French doors to where I'd imagined seeing Sarah in the snow. Instead of my ancestor out there now, I imagined the butterfly I mentally chased. The winged bug floated closer.

"It's not over, Roger," I said. "Even if Sean killed Jimmy to keep from being arrested, why did he kill Amy Woodward?"

"Who knows what goes through the guy's mind?" The lightness was gone from Roger's voice. He sounded distracted. "Maybe she bought drugs from him and couldn't pay. Maybe she threatened to tell Woody."

"Amy Woodward was a cokehead? Oh, come on." I never would have written her character that way. I glanced at the wall across from me. On it, hung above my computer desk, was a framed page from my first published story.

In my mind, I saw Roger shrug. "Maybe the two murders aren't connected. Have you considered that?"

"They are. They have to be," Rebecca insisted. "If they're not, why's someone trying to kill Emlyn?"

I smiled at her. Good girl, she had spoken my thought.

"And your theory still leaves your boss on the hook for his wife's murder," I added.

My smile faded. If I were wrong, and the Osborn and the Woodward murders weren't committed by the same person— "If the two aren't connected, it means someone is still after me, Roger. Why? What did I do to make someone want to—?"

"Maybe it's that creepy Fred Silbert. Maybe he broke your window so you'd call him and he could get close to you, give you comfort."

"Comfort from a firebomb?" I shouted into the phone. "If it was Freddy and he just wanted my attention, why'd he try to kill me by burning down Main Street Books?"

For a long moment all we heard were honks of car horns and engines revving. At last Roger said, "Yeah, I hadn't thought of that. Well, you and Rebecca stay tucked in at your house. I'll be by later and we'll figure it out. Meantime, I'm just getting to the *Buffalo News* with an arrest warrant made out in Sean Ryan's name. I called Marge Osborn an hour ago and she told me he said he was coming here. Don't wanna give him a chance to slip away."

***

I grumbled. "Stay tucked in until he gets back? Not gonna happen."

"Just what I was thinking," Rebecca said. "You seem to have an idea about what's really going on. What do we do?"

Again my mind flashed to the old crone I'd envisioned in the snow in my backyard. "We go where Sarah pointed," I said.

Rebecca's brow creased.

"She told us what we need to know."

My friend stared, as if I'd winked at her with the third eye Roger sometimes saw in the center of my forehead. "What did Sarah tell us? The herbs we need for an amulet of truth aren't written in her book."

"We don't need to know them. Think about what Sarah said."

Rebecca's lips moved when she silently repeated my words.

"Betrayal," I said.

Elvira rubbed against my leg. When she lifted her head, I think I saw pride in her eyes.

"I don't get it," Rebecca said. "From what we've heard, this has been about illegal drugs."

"Yes and no."

She gave me another look of incomprehension.

"Sure, cocaine is at the bottom of it," I said, "and that might explain why Jimmy Osborn was killed. But it doesn't tell us why Amy Woodward died, or why someone's come after me. Roger's content with the idea Amy's murder isn't connected, that happening when it did is just a coincidence."

"It might be."

"It might," I agreed. "But if it isn't—" I thought for a minute then said firmly, "No, it's not."

Rebecca gave a short laugh. "Chasing after your spinning mind exhausts me."

"No, no, listen," I said. "Presume for a second Sarah wasn't being metaphorical when she wrote about betrayal. What if the murders were really about—?"

I stopped in mid-sentence, recalling the way Marge glared at Sean when I brought the casserole the day of Jimmy's funeral. The message she wanted to send me finally got delivered. But there was one other thing. I closed my eyes and sighed. The butterfly I'd been trying to grasp at last flitted close enough to snatch. What I saw on its wings was such a small thing. The killer hadn't thought it would be a give-away, but it was. Now the final patch for the crazy quilt fell into place. As if I finally saw the true meaning beneath one of my story-lines, the complete scenario spread out before me in all its lovely complexity— lovely, being a relative term for the ruptured protagonist I envisioned. My hands folded across my stomach, I closed my eyes and smiled. What I pictured explained everything:

the drugs, the Corvette, Jimmy's death, Amy's, the bottles thrown through windows—

There was one tiny detail that refused to fit into the pattern.

As if out of breath from running to catch up with me, Rebecca panted, "Yes, betrayal. Sean Ryan betrayed his father-in-law. Kevin Reinhart betrayed you and Sean Ryan and the guys from the barn."

"No. Sarah wrote of a deeper, more hurtful betrayal."

"I really can't follow you." Rebecca bit the corner of her lip.

That one tiny detail nagged at me, as if it were a flaw in one of my stories. I turned to the French doors, hoping I'd see Sarah Goode outside and she'd provide the final answer. I saw only a white blanket spread across my yard. I sat up straight. At this point the missing detail didn't matter, I decided. Everything else fit so perfectly.

I knew what I had to do.

"Is there any undyed linen in your shoulder bag?" I asked Rebecca.

She rapidly blinked, trying, I supposed, to conjure up a path through the maze into which I'd led her.

"And some dry herbs."

"What herbs? Sarah didn't tell us—"

"Doesn't matter. We can grab a couple from my spice closet. And silk thread. Red. I have a spool in my sewing kit."

"I don't get it," Rebecca said. "Without the right ingredients and a ceremony to purify them, the amulet you're gonna make won't do anything."

"Oh, but it will," I said.

The creases in her forehead grew so deep I thought her eyeballs might roll into the crevices.

"While those gypsy women were teaching you to read tarot cards," I said, "my father taught me to play with a poker deck. 'Daughter,' he'd say to me while he systematically won back my allowance, 'it doesn't matter what cards you're holding if you know how to bluff.'"

Rebecca laughed out loud.

"What?"

"I think the student has become the teacher," she said.

"We'll soon find out." I rose from the sofa and grabbed my crutches and coat. "I'll put the amulet together in the car."

She didn't move.

"Come on!" I said.

"Uh, have you forgotten something?"

With my hand on the doorknob, I counted my supplies. "Linen, dried oregano, dried thyme, dried rosemary, silk thread—nope, I've got it all."

Again she laughed. "What about car keys? Roger confiscated both yours and mine after our little romp through town. Remember?"

"Is that all?" I said.

I hobbled to the kitchen and opened what I call my utility drawer. In it were three spare sets of keys. As I pulled one out, I said, "When I'm writing, time isn't the only thing I lose track of." I handed her the keys. "It's easier to have lots of these than to try and remember where I left them."

Still laughing, she scooped up Elvira and followed me out.

Chapter Twenty-Three
The Elusive Butterfly

Snow again fell. An inch or so of fresh white powder covered my driveway. In the southern part of the United States, half this amount could bring a city to a standstill. Not in Western New York. On almost every block, plows were at work. Between the plows, salt-spreaders, and heat from the friction of rubber tires on the pavement as cars sped past, the streets from my house to Niagara Falls were reasonably clear. In a quarter of an hour, we turned the corner onto Twenty-Third Street, then right onto Independence Avenue.

The brick ranch stood about a quarter of the way down the block. Instead of the Corvette, a green Chevy Malibu was parked in the driveway. It looked to be the car I saw across the street from the Woodwards' house while I floated above Niagara Falls on a besom. Of course, I knew I hadn't really ridden a broom across the night sky and into the day before. That was a dream I had when I fell asleep while meditating. The experience seemed real enough, though, to have been the kind of out-of-body flight Sarah Goode suggested in her *Book of Shadows*. Maybe, as Roger told me when this whole mess began, I actually had seen or heard something that remained just beyond the edge of my awareness. Maybe what I saw or heard was why, in a dream state, I placed the Malibu at the Woodwards' house the night Amy was murdered. This was certainly a more logical answer—one Roger would leap for if I told him of my broom ride. Regardless of why, I recognized the car then and I recognized it now. It was the '67 Malibu Sean Ryan had restored.

Rebecca saw a smile crease my lips. "What?" she said.

I pointed at the green car. "If Sean came here instead of heading for Buffalo, we can write an end to this story right now."

At the moment, it didn't occur to me if Roger's solution was correct, Sean would have the gun that had already killed two people, and desperate, he wouldn't hesitate to use it again. I didn't think of it because I was distracted when Elvira began to scratch at the window of my Valiant.

Clutching the amulet I'd put together while we drove, I opened my car door.

Elvira leaped out and made a beeline for the Osborns' house.

"Let's go," I said.

Rebecca seemed as anxious as I. She slid from behind the steering wheel, and we chased after the cat—well, to be exact, she chased, I hobbled.

Marge's front door stood open. Elvira now clawed the storm door. As we climbed the two front steps, I heard crying inside. Rebecca nudged the cat away from the door. I opened it a crack. Elvira shoved it the rest of the way and scooted in.

When we followed, I saw Marge Osborn on her couch in front of the oriel window. Her arms were wrapped around her daughter. I glanced at them, then turned and peered past the formal dining room and through the door to the dark kitchen.

"Sean, are you back there?" I called.

Jennifer let out a long wail.

"Is he here?" Rebecca said.

Except for Jennifer's moans, nothing stirred in the house.

"Doesn't seem so," I said.

"Why did you come here?" Marge's shrill voice bled into what sounded like two sirens somewhere on her block.

She wore the same floral housecoat she had on the last time I'd been at her house. Her face was strained, her eyes red. Jennifer was in a flannel bath robe. She had rubber boots over her bare legs. It was as if she'd fled from her apartment without taking time to dress. I didn't need a degree in psychology to understand why she would have fled. Her cheek and left eye were bruised. I was sure her husband had beaten her.

Before I could ask if my assumption was correct, the storm door flew open.

My head snapped around.

Roger's broad body filled the doorway. He had his pistol out. "Where's Ryan?" he demanded.

Jennifer's moan became a loud cry.

In a few long strides, he was near the kitchen. His gun held out in both hands, he slid along the wall, then rushed through the door.

"Ryan's not out here," a male voice called from the side of the house.

"Clear on this side," another voice called.

Roger's shoulders relaxed. He holstered his gun.

Marge hissed, "That dirty bastard. Sean's to blame for everything!"

Roger returned to the living room. He glanced at me then at Rebecca. "I should have known you two wouldn't stay put," he muttered. He reached into the pocket of his camelhair coat, pulled out two sets of car keys—Rebecca's and mine—and looked questioningly at them.

Rebecca smiled. I shrugged. Elvira rubbed her back against his legs (I was sure if I looked closely, I'd see the cat's nose was brown).

"I should run the two of you in for interfering with an investigation." Roger didn't sound amused.

"Your investigation was in Buffalo," I said. "Rebecca and I came here to comfort my friend."

He glared at me and gave a long-suffering sigh. "You and I are gonna have a long conversation later."

Satisfied I'd been sufficiently chastised for the moment, Roger brushed me aside and leaned over the couch. It seemed as though he wanted to leave no room for the two women on it to escape into a lie. Again he demanded, "Where's Ryan?"

"Gone," Jennifer groaned.

"Where?"

"Leave her alone!" Marge growled. "Don't you see what that monster's done to my baby?"

Her reaction to the bruises on Jennifer's face, Sean Ryan's car at the Woodwards' house: the elusive last patch settled into place on the crazy quilt my imagination had stitched together. I knew how the last scene was intended to play out. I wouldn't let it. I'd already written the story's end my way.

I elbowed Roger aside and dropped down on the couch. Gently, I touched the mouse under Jennifer's eye. "He did this to you?"

She nodded, and sniffed.

"When?" Roger's voice was still harsh.

I shot a warning glance at him. "You're not helping."

He huffed. For a second I thought he might lift me from the couch and toss me out the door. Thank goodness he didn't act on such an impulse. Grumbling, he backed away.

I smiled a thank you. Then, stroking Jennifer's cheek, I asked, "He hits you all the time, doesn't he?"

I felt all her muscles tense.

Marge shoved me. "Stop it. Stop this right now!"

I refused to be moved. "We need to stop Sean so he never hits you again."

"It's my fault!" burst from Jennifer.

Tears ran down Marge's cheeks. She rubbed her daughter's arm. "It's not your fault."

Jen leaned away from her mother. Her face in her hands, still crying, she said, "It is. They work him so hard at that newspaper. They insist he has to stay at it night and day if he wants to keep his job. Then he comes home, and just wants to rest up. But I won't let him. I'm tired of being in the house all day, I tell him. I want to go out to dinner or…or to a movie…" Her voice quivered into another sob.

"He told you they work him hard?" Roger said. "I just came from the *News*. His editor told me Ryan was fired a couple of weeks ago because he stopped showing up."

"It's…it's not true. It can't be."

I had no idea whether Roger had told her the truth. But, to draw out the admission we needed I knew I had to swear it was so.

"The paper let him go," I said. "Half Niagara Falls knows it. Now you also have to let him go."

Jennifer buried her face in Marge's ample bosom.

I turned to Rebecca. "Is there any more of that balm you used on my leg?"

She dug into her shoulder bag and pulled out a vial. Then she reached for Jennifer's hand. "Come with me, hon," she said. "This will help ease your pain."

I knew Rebecca and the brews she concocted. The pain her balm would ease was both the physical and the emotional kind. I pointed to the hall running next to the kitchen. Rebecca led the still crying Jennifer to a bedroom.

Roger dropped onto an armchair close to the sofa and leaned forward. Adopting my approach, he took Marge's hand. In an intimate tone, he said, "I know what you and your daughter have had to put up with. Let me help you put an end to it. Tell me where Sean is."

She shook her head. "I don't know."

"Does Jen?" I asked.

"She only knows he burst into their apartment and then left again."

While she wrung a tissue, Marge told us Sean had gotten to his apartment nearly two hours ago. Without a word, he threw clothes into a suitcase. When Jennifer asked where he was going, he smacked her. He didn't have time for her stupid questions, he said. A friend waited for him downstairs. He told Jen if anyone asked, she was to say she didn't know anything, hadn't seen him in days. If she didn't, he said, he would come back and kill her and Marge, too. Ryan said he'd killed before, Marge told us, and would do it again. Just to be certain Jennifer understood, he punched her three times and left her crumpled on their bedroom floor.

"For all Jen knows," Marge said, "he's across the border in Canada by now. He has family in Toronto." She let out a wail. "Jimmy! That bastard killed my Jimmy." She closed her eyes and fell against the arm of the couch.

Roger sat back in his chair. "I doubt Ryan's gotten over the river yet," he said. "There's a Homeland Security alert at the border crossings. All the bridges to Canada are backed up for hours.

He stood, pulled out his cell phone, moved to the dining area, and leaned against the china cabinet. With his back to us, he made a call. In a few minutes, he returned to his chair.

"Sean won't get far if Canada's where he's headed," Roger said.

The hope such news would ease Marge's concern was misplaced. She sat up and again twisted the tissue. If I were right about all that had happened, I knew why: she didn't want Sean to be caught.

I held out the amulet I'd had in my hand since we arrived. "Mom taught me to make these things," I said. "It's supposed to help you feel better."

She stared at it.

Roger's eyes narrowed. It was as if he asked what I was up to.

I held the amulet out. "I don't know why," I said, "but these things Mom made always helped me."

Marge sighed. "Your mother's always been a little strange."

I nodded and laughed. "Don't I know it?"

Now was the time to find out if my theory proved right.

Elvira scampered onto the fireplace mantel and brushed a paw on one of the photos. While Marge concentrated on the amulet, turning it over in her hands, I examined the family pictures: Marge and Jennifer, Jennifer and Sean. I had remembered correctly. There wasn't a single picture of Jimmy in the room. It was as if Marge had tried to erase the memory of her husband.

Betrayal, Sarah Goode had written. She hadn't been thinking of the way teenage girls in Salem had betrayed her. No, it was a true betrayal of the heart, and in the end she'd accepted the blame for her betrayal of the marriage vows she had made to William Goode. When William learned she had given her heart to George Burroughs, longed only to be with him, and would run to him if she were able, he swore the oath that figuratively shoved her off a tree limb to dangle on Gallows Hill.

I turned back to Marge. "The police will have Sean soon. When they get him, they'll turn him over to the DEA. He'll spend a lot of years in jail. But you don't want that, do you?"

Jennifer and Rebecca came back into the room. Rebecca took the chair next to Roger. Jen sat on the couch on the other side of her mother. The bruises on her face had lightened a bit. This wasn't the time, though, to wonder how Rebecca's potion accomplished that.

"I was just saying," I told Jennifer, "the police will have Sean soon. You'll never have to worry about him hitting you again."

Her smile was small and sad. It's strange how a woman who's so badly mistreated, could still love the man who hurt her. The story I'd begun to write just before I learned of my heritage—the one about a maltreated woman who flees into a northern swamp? At last I understood what the story was truly about. But again, this wasn't the time to consider how my fictional plot would play out. At the moment I had to write the end to a different, real life drama.

"Sean's a miserable human being," I told Jennifer, "and you're better off without him."

I looked into Marge's eyes. "Yes, he's a poor excuse for a man—a drug dealer, a wife beater. But like Kevin Reinhart, he hasn't got the stomach for murder."

Her hand tightened on the amulet.

I shifted on the couch to look at Roger. "You see, everything *is* connected."

"I know it is," he said. "Sean Ryan—"

I stopped him. "Yes, Sean was in the middle of it all. But he wasn't the beginning or the end. This story actually started with Jimmy. I'm right, aren't I, Marge?"

She looked out the window.

"Roger, I'm afraid your friend and partner wasn't the good guy you wanted him to be. Maybe he was when you served in the army together, maybe he still was those first years on the Falls police force. But, at the end—" I touched his wrist. "I'm sorry."

Marge Osborn tried to rise from her couch. I held onto her arm. "You and Jimmy weren't close anymore. He was having an affair. That's what started it. He wanted to be with another woman, to run off with her and leave you behind." To Roger, I said, "The Mexican vacation Jimmy told you he was planning? It wasn't Marge he wanted to take with him. When he found out about Sean and the drugs, he realized he had an opportunity to grab some quick money, and use it to disappear with his new love."

"Mother?" Jennifer said.

"No!" Marge shouted. "How dare you say such a thing."

237

Her angry reaction was exactly what I waited for. It told me I was right about the rest of what I suspected.

"I said it because it's true. After you'd given Jimmy your life, made your desires secondary to his happiness, he was about to leave you with nothing. Marge, Jimmy betrayed you."

"He didn't! Not ever!"

"Careful, Marge," I said. "The amulet you're holding—in it is a mixture of herbs that require total truthfulness. It'll crumble under the weight of lies."

Elvira jumped from the mantel. With her rear legs on the floor, she stretched up onto Marge's lap, and fixed pink eyes on her.

"You were afraid to be seen driving the Corvette," I continued, "and everyone would know who was in the rattle-trap Jimmy drove to work. So you borrowed Sean's car the night you went to the Woodwards' house. You figured if anyone saw it there, Sean would get blamed—just the way you want him blamed for killing Jimmy." I glanced at Jennifer. "Your mother knew what Sean has been doing to you. You'd be safe if he was framed for the murders."

Marge's hand clenched into a fist. The thin thread binding the amulet tore loose and the dried herbs poured out.

"Mom, what have you done?" Jennifer cried.

***

The next afternoon we were at my house. Roger relaxed on the sofa. I reclaimed my overstuffed wingback chair next to the bookcases. Contentedly snuggled on my lap, Elvira snored. The mini-blinds on the French doors were raised, and I looked out over my backyard to the trees lining the Niagara River. The foul weather broke when a gentle breeze from the south nudged the cloud cover northward. The sun brought the first buds to the azaleas around my patio. It felt as though spring, that coy mistress, had at last decided to unpack her bags and stay awhile.

After rattling around in my kitchen, Rebecca carried three mugs of tea into the living room. Roger laughed when she handed one to him.

"Should I be afraid of what you put in this?" he asked.

I considered the woman who in just a few months had become my very dear friend. "Should he?"

Her face took on the most innocent expression I have ever seen. "Why, my dears," she said, "whatever do you mean?"

We all laughed and sipped our tea.

After a few minutes, Roger yawned and rested his head on the back of the sofa. Careful not to jostle the ancient book in which Sarah Goode had written both her mystical recipes and secret thoughts, he rested his size fourteen feet, crossed at the ankles, on the coffee table.

"Marge made a full confession," he said. "She claimed she lost control of her emotions when Jimmy showed up with the Corvette. She'd suspected something was up for months. Then, when he came home with the car—to get the cash to buy it, he had to be into something dirty. When she realized that, she knew his next steps would be out the door. It drove her nuts, she said."

"Good description," Rebecca said.

Again Roger yawned. "Yeah, I figure she'll go with an insanity plea. But how crazy could she be if she planned it all out so Ryan would take the blame? And you were right, Emlyn—she didn't want him caught. In fact, she phoned him right after I called to tell her I was looking for him. Put the wind up his skirt—that's why the bastard took off for Canada."

A sad smile flitted across my lips. "Still, I understand how Marge felt. Giving your whole being over to a man is certainly not a sane thing to do."

Roger raised his head. "Do you really believe that?"

I shrugged.

Rebecca stared into her mug of tea. "Of course, the way you feel might change."

I glared at her then looked suspiciously at the liquid in my mug.

"Yet," Roger said, "when Reinhart started fooling around with other women, you didn't grab a gun and go after him."

I sighed and carefully laid my mug on the side table. "I didn't have to shoot Kevin. The way he was, sooner or later he was bound to shoot himself. Which, when you think about it, is exactly what he did." I looked at Sarah's book, wondering whether the hex I'd thrown at my ex actually caused his downfall—Roger would certainly insist he'd fallen without anyone having to shove him.

"Where will witness protection send Kevin?" I asked. "The outback of Alaska, I hope."

Rebecca looked at the altar still set up on the end table near the French doors. "I know a way we can make sure he winds up there."

Roger shook his head with vehemence. "Thank you, no. We've had enough hoodoo around here for a while." He also turned his eyes to the altar. "Still, I'd like to know how you figured out Marge was the killer—and please, don't tell me you did it with magic."

"But, Roger, it was," I said, and raised three fingers as a sign of the truth.

He groaned.

I laughed. "Okay, it was only partly the magic. The rest—" I picked up Sarah's book. "My great, great, great, great—"

"Yeah, yeah. I know who she was," he said and took a sip of his tea. "You gonna tell me she whispered the answer to you while you slept?"

I smiled back at him. "Well, in a way she did."

For a second, I thought about telling him I'd seen Sarah in the snow outside my window, and she warned me about betrayal. I thought better of it.

"The answer was in this book," I said. "Once I read what Sarah wrote about how her husband believed her betrayal could only be avenged by the death of both Sarah and her lover, everything fell into place."

All at once, I knew what Agatha Christie's Jane Marple felt when she explained how she knew who murdered whom and why. Except, of course, Miss Marple knitted while she dissected the clues. I never learned to knit. I glanced at my grandmother's afghan and the designs she sewed into it. *Someday I'll figure out what Grandma wanted those runes to tell me,* I thought.

Roger pulled my mind back when he asked, "What fell into place?"

"Excuse me?" I had been drifting a bit lately. I would have to watch that.

"He asked what fell into place," Rebecca said.

"Oh, yes. And by the way, Roger, you were right."

"How so?"

"A lot of the patches on this quilt pictured things I'd seen but didn't think anything of at the time. For example, at the Woodwards' backyard barbeques Jimmy always rushed to help Amy carry plates from the kitchen. And once or twice I saw him look at her the way that—"

"The way Roger looks at you?" Rebecca said.

I felt a blush rise so high, it must have been impossible to distinguish my face from my red hair. "Hey, we're neighbors and friends. That's all," I insisted

Elvira's head came up. Her pink eyes stared at me.

I shoved her head down. "Don't you start with me, too," I told her. I turned to Roger. "And you—say something!"

"Uh-uh, I'm not getting into a debate with a woman who might turn me into something unnatural."

I snorted.

"So, you saw Jimmy flirt with Amy Woodward?"

Smart man. He also wanted to keep the conversation away from him and me.

"Yeah," I said. "Then, after the funeral, I saw there were no pictures of Jimmy at his house." During my divination spell, I saw Marge put his off-duty pistol into a wall safe in their second bedroom. But I wasn't about to mention that, either. "I think Marge noticed how I studied those pictures and worried I might suspect something."

"So that's why she tried to kill you with those firebombs," Rebecca said.

I shook my head. "If she really wanted to kill me, she would have used the gun. She could have done it any time. She's my childhood friend, so I would have let her get close enough. No, I think she just wanted to frighten me so I'd stop snooping. Marge isn't a sociopath. She's just a woman who's been badly hurt."

"And the drugs?" Roger said.

He obviously knew the answer, but wanted me to have this moment.

"The drugs were what started everything. When Jen told her father what she suspected, he didn't go out to investigate Sean. He decided it would be a source of quick and easy money—the money he needed to disappear to Mexico with Amy."

"How did you tumble to the fact that Amy would leave Woody for Jimmy?" Roger asked.

"Something she said to me at the funeral made me think she no longer loved her husband. And then the way she cried like she, not Marge, was the new widow—"

"What about the drug operation out of the barn in the alley?" Rebecca asked. It seemed that piece of our adventure fascinated my friend more than the Osborn/Woodward love story.

"Yeah. Of everything, the drug connection was truly a coincidence. We stumbled on the barn by accident. But if you think about it, the tapestry of lies and deceit wouldn't have unraveled if those guys hadn't thought we were watching them." *Or if I hadn't had a vision of Marge shooting Amy in that alley,* I thought.

Roger sat back and smiled.

I picked up my mug. Watching him over the brim, I brought it to my lips. With each sip, the idea of Detective Frey becoming more than a friend didn't seem like such a bad idea—

I stopped in the middle of the thought and stared into the mug. I really needed to find out what Rebecca put in this tea.

Afterward

I've spoken of my abhorrence of things left dangling at the end of a story. Such unfinished business bothers me to the point at which I can't sleep at night. Because I can't write when I'm overtired, and since writing is a need, not a choice, these dangling ends have to be properly braided.

Amy Woodward's funeral took place the week after Marge Osborn was arrested. Again, most of the Niagara Falls Police Force was in attendance. Roger and I had dinner with Woody afterward. He took us to the Red Coach Inn, a rather fancy restaurant overlooking Goat Island and the falls. He was grateful, he said, that Roger hadn't obeyed his order to stay out of the Osborn case.

"If you'd listened to me for once, *I* would have been on trial instead of Marge," he told us over desert.

Roger didn't mention the role I played in finding the real killer. I'm glad he didn't. I suspect my life will be a good deal quieter if my part remains a secret only Rebecca, he and I share. Of course, Elvira also knows about it, but I'm sure she won't tell anyone.

While we walked to our cars after dinner, Woody told us, "I meant what I said."

"What's that?" Roger asked.

"When you found me with Amy's body, I told you it's my fault she's dead. Well, it is."

"How can you say such a thing?" I said. "You were great to her, gave her anything she could have wanted."

He shook his head. "I only gave her things. What she wanted was my time, my attention." He opened the door to his car and leaned on the roof. "First the marines, then the department—I didn't leave much time for her."

"I know what you mean, Woody," Roger said. "Judy left me for the same reason. But I'll tell you something—"

he glanced at me "—I won't make that mistake a second time."

I decided not to ask what was on his mind.

Woody sighed. "I don't see how you can avoid it. But listen to me, you've gotta try. That's what I'm gonna do."

"What are you going to do?" I asked.

He graced me with a smile. "After all the trouble these past weeks—and mostly after losing my wife—I need some time away from the job. Gotta see something of life before it's over and I've got nothing to show for it."

"You're not hanging it up, Woody?" Roger sounded distraught over the possibility.

"Nah, nothing as final as that. But I want to get away from here for awhile, get my bearings again. That'll make Pete Reynolds Acting Chief for the next couple of months. Think you can work with him?"

"I'd rather be working for you," Roger said. "But, sure, no problem, I'll work for Pete.

"Good." Woody held out his hand and shook Roger's. "In that case, congratulations Acting Deputy Chief of Detectives."

I don't know how to describe the stunned expression that spread across my friend's face.

***

As to the rest, as Roger predicted, Sean Ryan was stopped at the border, and turned over to the DEA. His trial is scheduled to begin in September. I spoke with Jennifer a few weeks ago. She told me she'll be front and center in the court to support him. "Sean's changed since he's been in jail," she said.

What is it people say about love's eyesight?

I'm glad my vision is clearer.

I don't know where Witness Protection sent Kevin, and have no desire to find out. Roger believes I'll hear from him sooner or later. I might ask Rebecca whether I will, perhaps have her do a tarot reading for me—

No. On second thought, I'd rather be surprised by where my path might lead.

About the author

Formerly a Manhattan entertainment attorney and a contributing editor to the quarterly art magazine SunStorm Fine Arts, Susan Lynn Solomon now lives in Niagara Falls, New York, where she is in charge of legal and financial affairs for a management consulting firm.

After moving to Niagara Falls she became a member of the Just Buffalo Literary Center's Writers Critique Group, and turned her attention to writing fiction. Since 2009, a number of her short stories have appeared in literary journals, including, *Abigail Bender* (awarded an Honorable Mention in a Writer's Journal short romance competition), *Witches Gumbo*, *Ginger Man*, *The Memory Tree*, *Elvira*, *Second Hand*, *Sabbath* (nominated for *2013 Best of the Net* by the editor of *Prick of the Spindle*), and *Kaddish*.

Her latest short stories are, *Yesterday's Wings*, about a woman searching for the courage of her past, which appears in the October 2015 edition of, *Imitation Fruit*; and *Captive Soul*, which is included in Solstice Publishing's Halloween anthology, *Now I Lay Me Down To Sleep*.

The Magic of Murder is Susan Lynn Solomon's first published novel.

Acknowledgements:

It has often been said that writing is a lonely profession. I have found this not always to be the case. My writing has been enlivened by a wonderful and talented group of people. In this regard, I wish to acknowledge Solstice Publishing's Mel Massey, my Editor-in Chief, who believed in this story, and the marvelous editor, Fred Crook, who found and graciously corrected so many mistakes. I also need to acknowledge those who helped shape my writing: the Edgar Award winning author, Gary Earl Ross, moderator of the Just Buffalo Literary Center's Writer's Critique Group, who challenged me to write a murder mystery, then helped edit the story (and pounded into my head that a rifle is not merely referred to as a gun). I must also acknowledge the talented writers who are members of this group, and its former moderator, Jerome Gentes, all of whom helped shape my sense of metaphor and make my stories cohesive. Finally, I acknowledge Victor Forbes, editor of SunStorm Fine Arts, who allowed me the freedom to write creatively.

Made in the USA
Middletown, DE
19 February 2024